CRYSTAL FORCE

JOE DUCIE

HOT
KEY
BOOKS

First published in Great Britain in 2015 by Hot Key Books
Northburgh House, 10 Northburgh Street, London EC1V 0AT

A CIP catalogue record for this book is available from the British Library.

ISBN: 978-1-4714-0455-9

1

This book is typeset in 10.5 Berling LT Std using Atomik ePublisher

Printed and bound by Clays Ltd, St Ives Plc

www.hotkeybooks.com

Hot Key Books is part of the Bonnier Publishing Group
www.bonnierpublishing.com

ALSO BY JOE DUCIE

The Rig

For Lil Beth
Stop growing up so fast, kid.

Two weeks after
the events in
The Rig . . .

Chapter One

Droning On and On

Irene Finlay eased herself down onto the cold ground and held her hands to the orb of fire. A biting wind rustled the leaves in the canopy overhead and shook penny-sized drops of rain loose from the trees. The water sizzled as it struck the crystal-blue glow of the flames.

'I haven't slept in three days,' Will Drake said, sitting on her left, his breath a warm mist against the cold. 'I don't even feel tired – just *wired*, you know? Like I could tear these trees out of the ground or . . . or *fly*, or something.' He rubbed at his eyelids, and his body shook. Irene thought for a moment he was crying, but no, it was laughter. 'It's messing with my head, Irene. What if this is how it starts? Did Grey not sleep? Did Anderson?' His voice dropped to a whisper. 'Is this what drove them mad?'

Irene shuffled her cold feet, encased in a pair of sodden, muddy Rig-issue sneakers, closer to the warm blue blaze emanating from the sphere of fire Drake had hung in the air with his crystal power. In the two weeks since their escape from the Rig, it had only stopped raining for all of five minutes, and then only for a brief snowfall. Even now, rain drizzled through the canopy of the mighty white pine trees. Moisture clung to the air in a cool mist.

Irene looked back on her time on the Rig in varying degrees of disbelief, terror, and wonder. Wonder for the powers and abilities she and Drake had gained there, terror at what the Alliance had been doing, and disbelief that they had managed to escape at all. When Will Drake had first come to the Rig, his exploits were already legend. He had broken out of three other Alliance prisons. Irene had met him for the first time in the Rig's infirmary, after he had been injured. They had discovered the dark experiments using the Crystal-X mineral beneath the Rig together, looking for a way to escape.

Facing off against Warden Storm and his mad guard, Marcus Brand, Irene had nearly died half a dozen times. Drake and Michael Tristan had saved her life, as she had saved them. In the end, Drake had absorbed more Crystal-X than anyone, and he had used that power to help them escape.

'I think the fact that you're worrying about going mad means you're OK,' Irene said. *For now.* She smiled and rubbed Drake's right hand between her own. His left was stuffed deep into his pocket for warmth. The afternoon was cold, perhaps even cold enough to snow again. *What are we going to do tonight?* Last night had been freezing, but they had spent most of it huddled in the small, dilapidated hunter's shack. 'Yeah?'

Drake shrugged and glared at the blue-glowing orb, radiating faint but consistent warmth into their small glen. His glare seemed to enrage the flames, which spun within the orb from soft blue to hot white. The forests along the coast and south of St. John's – the capital city of Newfoundland and Labrador, the easternmost province of Canada – had provided meagre shelter but had kept them hidden from prying eyes. Irene felt at home, back on Canadian soil and off the twisted steel of the Rig.

'Oh, I'm worried.' Drake glanced up at the sky through the trees, but Irene kept her eyes on his, watching for more strange light. 'Going to snow, isn't it? Late in the year for that.'

'Not really.' The heat of the orb pierced the sheet of ice that had settled on Irene's bones. She sighed. 'Canada can get snow as late as May, some years.'

'We need to be inside tonight, somewhere warm. Warmer than that leaky hut,' Drake said, seemingly putting aside his worry for now. Irene was worried enough for both of them, but she was trying to maintain a brave face for his sake. After all, he had saved her life more than once on the Rig. And she owed him her freedom. 'I can't guarantee I'll be able to make another of these fire things. I'm just guessing, when it comes to the crystal power. We need some new clothes, get out of these Rig jumpsuits, and we need some proper food.'

'I've got that covered,' Michael Tristan said as he stepped into the glen, carrying a backpack and a paper bag full of burgers, fries and hopefully apple pies, from a solo mission into the outer suburbs of St. John's. He'd been gone for an hour, a worrisome hour, and was drenched.

3

The scent of greasy food wafted over to Irene, and her mouth watered. Without another word, the three of them divided up the mess and ate in silence. The meal was soon devoured.

'And that's the last of the cash,' Tristan said, licking the salt from his fingers. 'We're going to have to find some more.'

Drake grunted, and Irene knew he was bothered by what they'd done to acquire even the pitiful funds that had kept them fed for the past two weeks. Halfway down the rocky beach from the docks and helipad where Warden Storm had landed their escape chopper, they had come across a small beachfront tourist shop – locked and dark, given the early hour of the morning. Drake had simply *melted* the lock on the door with a blazing palm. The cash register proved even less of a safeguard, and he'd stolen about fifty dollars in coins and loaded the backpack Tristan now carried with snacks and drinks.

Irene's stomach tied itself in knots at the thought of what else was hidden in the bottom of the pack – a sleek silver revolver, fully loaded with six shots in the cylinder. Drake had stolen the gun from Warden Storm during their escape. She hated that he had kept it.

'Did anyone recognise you?' Drake asked Tristan.

Tristan pushed his glasses up the bridge of his nose and shrugged. The lens over his right eye was cracked, and dirty tape held the rims together. 'Can't know for sure, but I was in and out quickly. The shirt helps, I guess.'

Another item stolen from the beachfront store during their hasty getaway – a white shirt that read *St. John's Bay*. Worn over his green jumpsuit, the shirt still looked a bit odd, but it was better than just prison overalls.

'There was one thing.' Tristan said carefully, not quite meeting Drake's eyes. 'A news report on the TV while I was waiting for the order.'

Drake didn't say anything, so Irene asked, 'About us?'

'Not us,' Tristan said. 'Just Will . . . and they were calling you a terrorist, mate. The terrorist William Drake, wanted for murder and sabotage of the Rig.'

Irene gasped.

Drake merely chuckled. 'Alliance News Network? Bet I've been the top story since the escape.'

'Well, yeah.'

He rolled his eyes. 'Figures. Who did I murder?'

Tristan grimaced. 'Look, Will, I don't think you –'

Drake's stony gaze made Irene shiver. *He's not going mad. He's fine. His eyes haven't even flashed red or blue today.*

'You're wanted for the murder of Brand,' Tristan said. 'As well as Alan Grey and . . . and Carl Anderson. They flashed a list of names on the screen, and I was trying not to look too interested, you know.' Tristan kicked at the dirt around the orb with the heel of his sneaker. 'Elias was on there, and so was . . . Will, I'm sorry. So was Doctor Lambros.'

Irene had studied in the Infirmary under Elias, before she had been subjected to the dark experiments with Crystal-X going on under the Rig. Elias had exposed her fellow inmates to the mineral, used them as lab rats, and was responsible for more than one death – or, worse in Irene's opinion, driven them mad. Drake had knocked him out and left him for dead, as the underwater facility was torn apart by one of his test subjects. Irene didn't feel too bad about that. Doctor Lambros, however,

5

had been almost a friend to Drake. And he blamed himself for her death, for sharing his concerns about the Rig. Marcus Brand, the scariest man Irene had ever known, had killed her.

Doctor Lambros's name brought a scowl to Drake's face, and Irene patted his shoulder. He shrugged her hand away and hunched against the cold. 'Brand and Storm killed her, not me.'

'We know,' Tristan said quickly. 'It's just the Alliance, making you out to be some sort of . . .'

Monster, Irene thought, hating that the word had popped into her head. She knew Drake – she *knew* him, had spent weeks with him on the Rig – and trusted him. After all, she had a touch of magic from the Crystal-X, too. Not nearly as powerful, of course, but she could heal, among other talents.

'This may actually be a good thing,' Drake said, tapping his stubbly chin. 'If the Alliance are only broadcasting that I escaped, it means you two may be able to move about relatively easily.'

'Yeah, I thought that, too,' Tristan said. 'I watched the whole report, and it only talked about you, Will. Why wouldn't they mention us?'

Drake shrugged. 'Perhaps they're trying to avoid the embarrassment. I've escaped before and tarnished their *sterling* reputation, but now I've escaped with one of their secrets: the Crystal-X. I'm proof of the experiments on the Rig, of the kids they tortured and killed. They'll want me dead far more than they'll want to keep my latest escape under wraps.' He clenched his fist and glared at the fiery orb. 'As far as they know, Irene didn't take to the crystal, and you were never tested. You're not as, well, important to them.'

Irene tilted her head and looked at Drake askance. 'But we're important to you, aren't we?'

Drake gave an honest laugh. 'You, Irene – you are sunshine on a rainy day to me. You are chocolate milk over regular. A fresh jar of blackberry jam. Starlight on a moonless night. Oh, Irene Finlay, you are the marshmallows in my cereal, the cherry on top of my ice cream –'

'And the sprinkles,' Tristan chimed in.

'– and the sprinkles, too. You're more important than . . . than . . .' Drake snapped his fingers and cursed.

'Than thick socks and warm cider by the fire in winter?' Irene offered, then snorted. 'Boys,' she muttered fondly. 'My boys.'

Tristan cocked his head. 'Can you hear that?'

'Hear what?' Irene asked.

'That,' Tristan said, and Irene *could* hear something, almost below hearing. A subtle whine, like the hum of an idling car engine. 'It almost sounds like –'

Something sleek and silver burst through the trees, and the noise intensified in the glen.

Drake was on his feet in the same moment, and Irene watched, frightened, as his eyes flared crimson and he moved in a blur. A bolt of sizzling energy arced from his outstretched fingers and struck the tree canopy.

He moved so fast!

The noise stopped abruptly, and amidst a rain of singed leaves and cracked branches, a silver sphere about the size of a grapefruit fell from the sky and struck the ground hard with a dull mechanical *thunk*. Tendrils of smoke rose from the grapefruit, and Irene shuffled away as it rolled towards her.

'Bloody hell,' Tristan said. 'That was cool.'

Drake quickly buried his clenched fists back in his pockets. His eyes were wild, and he closed them, breathing hard. After a moment, he released a heavy breath and shook his head.

'What is it?' Irene asked.

'An Alliance search drone,' Drake said grimly.

No, what is it with you, *Will?*

Tristan blinked at him in surprise. 'Yeah, that's right. These are pretty high-tech. How do you know about them?'

'One of these things tripped me up after I escaped Harronway. That's how the Alliance caught me and sent me to the Rig. The damn thing followed me for hours until the Alliance goons could swoop in.'

'Well, I think you killed it.' Tristan knelt down and picked up the drone. The white smoke rising from the device caught the wind and was swept away into the forest. 'If it's not too damaged . . .'

'What?' Irene asked.

Tristan shrugged. 'If it's not too damaged, I could reprogram it, download my own operating platform from the global cloud – something I made before I landed on the Rig.'

'What can it do?' Drake asked.

Tristan stood with the drone in his hands. He fiddled with the panels and tossed it up and down a few times, as if he were trying to shake it awake. 'Well, that's the thing. This drone is pretty advanced. It's worth a few hundred thousand dollars. We could link it to a phone or a tablet screen and access the internet, emails, even social media sites.'

Drake chuckled. 'You want to use it to send a tweet?' He shook his head and grinned. 'You're too good with all this tech stuff. First getting the trackers off on the Rig, now you're saying I can catch up on all the funny cat videos I've missed while locked up?'

Tristan bit his lip and considered for a long moment. 'If we can get it working for us, we could plan our route a little better, if we figure out where we're going. Set it to scout the area ahead or float on guard when we're asleep, even book tickets for a bus or a train over the internet or . . . make secure, encrypted phone calls.'

Drake squeezed Tristan's shoulder. 'I could call home?'

Tristan nodded absently and worked his fingers under one of the panels Drake had damaged with his blast. The panel came away easily, and Tristan gazed into the device. 'There's the power source . . .'

'We should probably think about moving,' Irene said. She felt exposed – if the Alliance had one of those things, there would be more, and close. 'Won't the Alliance know that it went down? And is that a camera lens on the bottom there? What if whoever was piloting the drone saw us?'

'I'm just removing its battery,' Tristan said. 'So we can bring it with us. But yeah, you're right. We need to move.'

Drake unzipped the backpack, which still held three candy bars and a litre of bottled water – all the food they had in the world. Tristan placed the device in the bag as carefully as if it were a newborn baby. Irene thought he looked almost giddy. He picked up a short cylinder, about the size and width of a lipstick case, and slipped it into his pocket.

'So which way are we heading?' Tristan asked.

'Nothing for it,' Drake said. 'We need to head into town.'

'Is that wise?' Irene kept her hands stretched out near the fire, but the orb had begun to flicker and die.

'We're on the run from the largest, most powerful corporation on the planet,' Drake said wryly. 'A corporation with its own private army, surveillance drones and who knows how many Crystal-X-enhanced soldiers! A corporation we bloodied and pissed off not two weeks ago. Nothing we do is going to be wise for very long.'

Chapter Two

Savings Account

'So where do you want to spend the night?' Drake asked as they skirted the edge of the forest that ran along the outer districts south of St. John's. The city stood across a small river, grey and windswept against tall cathedrals of storm clouds. 'An abandoned building would be just wonderful . . . we're not going to find many huts this close to town. Maybe a shed or a barn in someone's back yard, if we can swing it.'

Irene stared at him, wondering just how serious he was. 'You want to spend the night in a barn?'

Drake grinned. Despite the rings around his eyes and the lines creasing his forehead, his eyes were wild and alive – awake. Irene felt a rush of something wonderful – excitement and anticipation. *He's going to get us through this. We might just be OK.* She tried not to think about the fact that, even if they did get away that day, there was the one after that, and the next one, and so on . . . *Where does this all end? I'm a fugitive.*

'We can't exactly check into a hotel,' Tristan said.

11

Drake skipped a step and looked contemplative for a moment. 'No,' he said. 'That would be silly.' He chuckled and pointed at St. John's across the water. 'But if we could swing it, that's exactly what we *should* do. Go to ground somewhere fancy, somewhere they won't expect, and then find a train or something out of here. We just need money, and new clothes.'

'No, you're not understanding,' Tristan said. 'The Alliance has cameras everywhere – and analytics software that can pick your face out of a crowd of thousands.' He wiped rainwater from his forehead and shuddered. 'I mean, hell, one of their drones already collared us. If we go anywhere populated – *anywhere* – at the very least we need hats and sunglasses. I'd say even boots with thick heels to change our height, as well.'

'What? Really?' Irene felt the fatigue and strain of the last few weeks like a noose around her neck. She was tired, tense, and Tristan's paranoia made the trapdoor beneath her feet creak. Any moment now she was half convinced the ground would be swept from under her feet. 'Are the cameras really that good?'

'Not *good*,' Tristan said. 'Smart. Clever. The software running on these camera networks was developed for use in complex environments under time-restricted conditions, like airports. Mass population centres and places with heavy crowd traffic. It's actually replaced a lot of security guards in the major ports. It can catch people not only by face recognition but by how they carry themselves. The damn things not only recognise your face and height but can tell if you're trying to hide or acting suspicious.'

Drake cursed. 'So we not only have to disguise our faces, but act like we're not being hunted by the Alliance at all.' He grimaced. 'This . . . won't be easy.'

'I'd say impossible.' Tristan looked at Drake sideways. 'But then I would've said escaping the Rig was impossible, too.'

'That ATM is Alliance-owned,' Drake said. 'I don't feel guilty about robbing them, do you?'

Irene shuffled from foot to foot behind a hedge across from the bank, realised she was looking guilty, and forced herself to stop. The traffic on the road was sparse, but they were no longer in the forest, and if what Tristan had said about the cameras was true . . .

'What about the cameras?' she asked.

Drake shrugged. 'We'll be out of here before anyone arrives, and I don't think the Alliance are really going to want to show the general population what I'm about to do.'

'And what's that?' Tristan asked, but the look on his face suggested he already knew.

Drake raised his right hand, keeping his left tucked in his pocket, and stared at his fingers. He concentrated, frowning, until a subtle glow began to flow under his skin, through his veins, as if his hand had been tattooed with currents of electric blue ink.

'Make a withdrawal,' Drake said. 'I reckon we're owed back pay for all that work we did on the Rig, eh?'

A steady stream of customers entered and exited the bank. They were going to have to be quick and out of the area in minutes, if they were going to have any hope of escaping the Alliance.

We have to do this, Irene opened her mouth to say.

'Yes, we do,' Drake muttered.

Irene blinked. 'Sorry?'

'You said we have to do this. And you're right, we do.'

Drake shouldered the backpack and stepped out from behind the hedge and onto the sidewalk. His palm ablaze with blue light, he strolled across the road with his head held tall, as if he robbed a bank every day before lunch.

Tristan gave Irene a significant look, a mixed canvas of worry and fear. 'Did he just . . .'

'He either read my mind,' she whispered, rubbing her throat, 'or he knew what I was going to say before I said it.'

'What's happening to him, do you think?'

Irene could only shake her head. 'He didn't realise, did he? He thought I said it aloud. I was about to say it . . .'

Tristan slipped his hand into Irene's and squeezed her fingers. 'He absorbed a lot of that stuff. Way more than you or . . . or anyone, from what we understand. Hell, he should be raving in a cage or dead. God only knows what it's doing to him.'

Irene wasn't so sure even God knew. 'Look, he's at the cash machine.'

In the two weeks he'd been on the run with his friends, hiding in the forest and sending Tristan for food, Drake had tried to figure out just what he could do with his crystal talent. It was slow, nervous work. Some days he could click his fingers, light up the clearing, and create a buffer against the cold. Other days he had burnt his jumpsuit and scorched the earth. Using his power had also made Irene and Tristan uncomfortable, so he'd limited his experiments. It also made Drake slightly nervous he was losing his mind, like Alan Grey and Carl Anderson. But through trial and error, he'd managed a rough sort of control. If he thought hard enough about what he wanted, the power would flow.

He had managed some truly remarkable things. Arrows of hard crystal which he had hurled into trees, spheres of hot fire (which he hadn't been certain wouldn't explode, but given the choice between warmth and freezing to death, he'd taken the chance), and even buffers of air that provided protection from the wind. Shields of energy that had taken the bite out of the freezing nights.

Drake stood in front of the ATM and stared at the screen for a long moment, his right palm glowing with ethereal light and his left hand shoved deep into his pocket. A tiny pinhole camera stared back at him, and he wondered if his face was lighting up security screens and pinging off Alliance satellites already.

'Nothing for it.' Drake clenched his glowing hand and drove it into the machine. The moulded plastic and keypad simply melted around his fist. He removed his other hand from his pocket and grasped the edge of the machine, where it met the bricks. With a grunt that was more frustration than effort, he *ripped* the console from the wall in a shower of dust, debris, and drops of hot plastic.

As light as a feather, he thought, marvelling at the impossible strength in his arms. The melted plastic ran down his hand, but the light glowing within his skin protected him from harm. He couldn't even feel the scalding heat.

The crowd within the bank gaped at him like goldfish in a bowl. Drake offered them a wink and then tore the cash machine in half, right down the middle. Wires, machinery, and a whirlwind of red and green Canadian bank notes exploded from the guts of the cash beast.

A siren wailed from within the bank, echoing down the street, and tyres squealed against the road. Drake tossed what was left of the machine aside and shook his hands, as if trying to dry them. The ethereal blue light faded, and the skin on his right hand was unblemished, whole and healthy. Pinpricks of light still danced slowly within the fingers on his left, the hand he'd been keeping in his pocket and out of sight.

'That's a worry,' Drake muttered, glaring at his limb. 'But not at the top of the list just yet.'

The bank staff and customers had backed away from the glass window as the wail of the internal alarm echoed along the street. Drake unzipped his backpack and began to stuff cash down into its depths. He worked quickly, grabbing wads of notes from the ground. A lot of the smooth notes were melting from the heat, burning with blue flame, and giving off an acrid stink.

He zipped up the backpack and took to his heels, dashing back across the street and weaving in and out of idling cars that had come to a stop on the road.

Irene and Tristan stared at him solemnly when he ducked back behind the hedge.

He gave them both a grin. 'Right. That was dumb but necessary. Clothes and then somewhere to hide, yeah?'

Chapter Three

Shelter from the Storm

'I think it's safe to say the Alliance won't be making that footage available to the public,' Drake said, as he paused for breath a few blocks over from the bank. The pack dug into his shoulders, weighted down with cash and the drone, but he had barely broken a sweat. *The Crystal-X is increasing my endurance . . . or just not letting me feel how knackered I really am.*

Irene had kept pace with him well, but Tristan was gasping for air. 'You . . . you were quick back there,' he panted. 'But I think a few of the people in the bank recorded you on their phones.'

Drake hadn't considered that. 'Well, then I guess the Alliance may have some explaining to do.'

Tristan shrugged. 'The Alliance controls most of the global wireless networks and the phone carriers. If they act quickly – and they will – then anyone trying to upload video is going to find themselves suddenly disconnected.' He glanced up at the sky. 'In fact, I bet we're already under a dark spot.'

'Dark spot?' Irene asked.

'They'll have pulled the plug, basically,' Tristan said. 'Over this whole area. That's what happens when one company owns everything, all the networks, the hard lines . . . the politicians and the banks.'

Shut down the phone service, Drake thought. *And the wireless. Scary clever.*

'No phones, no wireless, for a good few miles.' Tristan glanced at Drake. 'It's what I'd do, to stop something getting out. May actually work in our favour, if we get out of here quickly. Every phone has a camera, and don't think for a moment the Alliance can't tap into them. But with the network blacked out, we're technically off the radar – for now.'

Drake saw a man across the road glaring down at a small device in his hand. He held it up above his head, as if trying to coax a signal from the air. 'Blimey, looks like they've done just that. Cheeky buggers being scary.'

'Not as scary as footage of you pulling apart a building with your bare hands would be if it leaked,' Tristan pointed out.

'Just a small piece of a building,' Irene offered.

Drake laughed. 'Barely part of the building at all. Come on, let's duck into that op shop.'

'That what shop?' Tristan asked.

Drake gestured down the road. 'There. You know, donated clothes and whatnot. Get ourselves some new threads.'

'Oh.' Tristan pushed his glasses up the bridge of his nose.

Drake fell back, putting himself between Irene and Tristan and hunching his shoulders. He glanced through the shopfront and saw a young girl idling behind the counter, looking bored and flipping through the pages of a magazine. 'Right. They're not hunting you two, remember, so go in first. I'll stay behind you and head into the changing rooms. Just bring me whatever clothes you think will fit.'

A tiny bell chimed over the door when they entered, and the girl at the counter glanced up, smiled briefly, and looked back down at her magazine.

Drake ducked behind a rack of suit pants and business shirts and strode quickly to the rear of the store and the curtained changing rooms. *If she's seen the news this morning . . .* his heart hammered in his chest. This was dangerous, stopping in one place, but given the stunt at the bank and the tightening net, he couldn't stay in the Rig jumpsuit. *The Alliance knows you're nearby*, nattered a troublesome voice in his head. *They're coming.*

As he waited, Drake took a moment to look at himself in the long mirror on the wall. His jumpsuit was wet, torn, and dirty, and a fair bit of blood from the Rig had dried into the fabric, staining the green cloth almost black. He stared at his face – mouth set in a grim line, eyes bloodshot – and dug his left hand out of his pocket. The light still danced beneath his skin, but the skin wasn't normal any more . . . it had changed over the last few days, ever since he'd started really practising what he could do with his power. The fingers of his left hand had hardened into a dark, obsidian crystal. The digits still worked just fine, but they were no longer flesh and bone – or even blood. Drake tapped them together and produced a dull ring, as if he'd tapped a fork against glass. He wasn't sure if he was imagining it, but the crystal seemed to have spread further down the back of his hand and towards his wrist, since he'd last checked on it.

19

It's getting worse the more power I use, he thought. *But what choice do I have?*

Drake cursed and shoved his hand back in his pocket. He thought he caught a brief flash of crimson in the pupils of his brown eyes reflected in the mirror, but when he looked again, he saw nothing.

You absorbed a container of that stuff. 'Shit,' Drake said to his reflection. 'Shit, shit, shit.'

The wait behind the curtain seemed agonisingly long, hours in place of minutes, but Tristan soon stepped into the stall with a stack of jeans, T-shirts, and jumpers. Shuffling in the next stall told Drake Irene was changing.

'Only two stalls,' Tristan explained. 'Irene tried to pull me into hers, but I was having none of that nonsense –'

'I can hear you, you know,' Irene's voice chimed over the wall.

Tristan grinned and threw a stack of clothes at Drake. 'Girl at the counter started watching us. Better hurry.'

Drake stripped down to his boxer shorts and pulled on a dark pair of jeans, torn at the cuffs but serviceable, with plenty of pockets. Pockets were good. Being on the run, he could only take whatever he could carry. Keeping his left hand with the crystal fingers hidden from Tristan, he pulled on a white shirt and a grey woolly jumper. The dry clothes almost felt like a hot shower, washing away the grime and the chill of the last two weeks. Almost.

'Everything OK in there?' the girl from the counter asked. 'Should only be one in a stall at a time, really.'

Drake and Tristan stared at each other for a moment, and then Drake shrugged. He picked up the backpack and stepped out of the stall.

'Sorry,' he said to the girl. *Cyndy*, her name badge read. 'Sorry, Cyndy. You guys don't have any gloves and, like, boots or something, do you?'

Drake watched her face but he saw no glimmer of recognition in her eyes. She looked only a year or two older than him, pretty, and Drake guessed she hadn't been keeping up with local events that morning.

'You going to buy those?' she asked, nodding at the clothes he was wearing. Price tags stuck up from under his collar and on the belt loops of his jeans.

'Sure are. We were painting walls all morning, me and my friends,' he said. 'And ruined our overalls. Just need something for the day.'

Cyndy shrugged. 'Gloves are over here, so are shoes. You don't sound like you're Canadian.'

'I'm not,' Drake said. 'I'm on holiday over from London.'

'You were painting on your holiday?'

'It's a . . . painting holiday,' Drake said, mentally kicking himself and fairly certain he deserved to get caught again.

'Right,' Cyndy said and chuckled. 'Just what you see on the wall here. The shoes are arranged in order of size. Gloves are tied together in pairs in that bin.'

'Thanks.' Drake made the gloves a priority and dug around in a large wine barrel, keeping his left side away from the sales girl, until he found a pair of thick leather gloves that looked big enough. He slipped his hands into the gloves and pulled his arms apart, breaking the little plastic tie holding the gloves together.

'Guess you're buying those, too,' Cyndy said.

21

'Guess so.' Drake relaxed a bit, now that his incriminating left hand – and the blue sparks dancing unbidden beneath his skin – were hidden. 'Just need a pair of shoes. Some hiking boots, or something.'

'Going hiking on your painting holiday?' she asked.

'Ha, ha.' He selected a pair of boots from the wall, simple lace-ups, and shoved his feet into them. *A little tight, but we're out of time.*

Tristan and Irene met him at the wall and selected some shoes for themselves – sneakers for Irene, and boots for Tristan. Under his arm, Tristan carried their bundled-up jumpsuits and old shoes.

'That everything?' Cyndy asked.

'Let's pay and be on our way,' Drake replied. As he walked over to the counter, following Cyndy, he pulled the tags from his clothes. Irene and Tristan did the same, weaving through the aisles.

As they passed a rack of hats, Drake snatched the first one he saw, a warm-looking beanie with flaps down over the ears. A colourful yarn bobble adorned the top of the beanie, and twin tassels, a good two feet long, swung down from the ear flaps and ended in strands of frayed wool. Drake shoved it onto his head and heard Irene giggle.

He glanced at her sideways and retrieved an old man's cap for her, black and grey, pulling it down over her auburn hair. Tristan took a bowler hat, of all things, and slipped it on. It was too big, but the tips of his ears and the rims on his glasses stopped the hat from falling over his eyes.

Arranged on the front counter was a spinning display of sunglasses. Drake picked out a pair of simple wraparound

Oakley's and shoved them onto his face. Irene and Tristan again followed suit, selecting sunglasses for themselves. Tristan chose a pair with almost comically large lenses to fit over his glasses.

Cyndy had moved around the counter, and when she caught sight of the three of them with the hats and sunglasses, she burst out laughing. 'So who are you lot hiding from?'

Drake gave her an easy grin and handed over his handful of tags so she could start ringing up their purchases.

'Good riddance,' Tristan said and tossed their old bloodstained jumpsuits and Alliance-brand shoes into the nearest trash can. 'Never again,' he muttered.

Never again, Drake agreed, making it a promise. *I'll die before setting foot in another Alliance hellhole.*

'Should we be worried that we'll stand out because of the sunglasses?' Irene asked Tristan. They strolled down the street, away from the op shop and the bank – sirens still wailing in the distance – and tried to look neither harried nor hurried. 'I mean, even to the clever cameras?'

Tristan shrugged. 'We're better off with them on.' He didn't sound certain. 'The analytics software in the camera network is clever, but clever enough to pick out three people wearing sunglasses on a cloudy day?' He shook his head. 'Maybe . . . but it'll take more time, which is what we need, right?'

'It's like we've escaped one prison for another,' Drake muttered. The tassels on his hat swung across his chest as he walked. 'We can't hide from the cameras. Nothing's ever private!'

Tristan snorted. 'Private. We gave up private twenty years ago for smart phones and social networks. Not that I'm complaining,

23

I love all this tech stuff, but if you end up on the wrong side of the Alliance . . .'

'I was thinking we should check into a hotel,' Drake said. 'You know, hide somewhere so obvious they wouldn't think to look. But now I'm not so sure. The net's tightening, isn't it? From the drone in the forest to the bank. We needed money, but they're closing in. If we don't escape this city soon – now – then we won't escape. Simple as that.'

'What should we do then?' Irene asked. 'This is kind of your thing, buddy.'

Drake shook his head. *Wish I knew . . . how the hell am I going to get back to London? And after that, what then?* 'A train out of here? Do you think we can get on without an I.D.?' He looked at Irene.

'You're asking me?'

'You're Canadian.' He kicked a brick wall with the toe of his boot. 'This is Canada.'

'I'm from Vancouver – which is on the opposite side of the country!' She shrugged. 'Will, I'm sorry. I don't know. I've never been to this province before. We never had to have an I.D. in Vancouver, unless we were using the student discount.'

'The Alliance controls the Tube in London,' Drake said. 'You can't buy paper tickets like you used to. You need an Alliance-issued rider card, with your photo and everything. It probably tracks your bloody movements, as well.'

'No, that's what your phone is for,' Tristan said. 'But there are ways to hide, if you're smart.'

The street they were on seemed to be curving towards the heart of St. John's. The crowds had thickened, and the outskirts of the city, with the apartment housing and the odd cash machine, had given way to strips of shops and taller buildings. There must be a train station around here somewhere. Drake kept his eyes peeled for a tourist information board or something. Suppose I could just ask someone.

'Lot of cameras at train stations,' Tristan said. 'And I think the Alliance will be watching them carefully. Particularly now that they know we have money.' He tugged at one of the straps on Drake's backpack.

'I don't see another option.' Drake had so far followed the web, the map in his mind that always saw a way out and that had got him and his friends off the Rig, but he couldn't just stroll into an airport and book a ticket on the next flight home. An entire ocean between here and London . . . 'Unless you want to walk.'

'Walk where?' Irene asked, voicing what they all wondered.

A few light snowflakes fell from the sky, one tickling Drake's nose. He stared absently at the flakes that melted on his woollen jumper. Where, indeed?

'I'm getting a hot dog,' he said. 'Anyone want a hot dog?'

He approached a roadside food truck, parked alongside the street opposite a supermarket with a large clock adorning its front. The hour had just struck four.

'What can I get you?' the man in the truck asked. He spoke English, but his accent hinted at French-Canadian.

'One with the lot, please,' Drake said. 'You guys?'

Irene held her stomach, and Tristan shook his head. 'I'm too nervous to eat,' Irene said, glancing over her shoulder.

Drake shrugged and slapped a twenty-dollar bill down on the truck's counter. The man handed him a white roll topped

25

with mustard, tomato relish, onions, sauerkraut, and somewhere below all that, a beef sausage. The scent of the thing was maddening, and Drake scoffed it down in a few quick bites, mustard dribbling down his chin.

'That was disgusting,' Irene said.

Tristan chuckled. 'You inhaled it, mate.'

'I'm still hungry.' Drake shoved some of his change back across the counter. 'Can I get another?' The man in the van shrugged and set about his grill again. 'And something fizzy.' A can of soda slid back across the ledge.

Drake popped the tab while the second hot dog was put together. He took three big gulps and felt the bubbles burn down the back of his throat. He winced and accepted the second hot dog. A little bit more care went into eating that one, as his leather gloves were covered in splurges of sauce and grease.

'You OK?' Tristan asked.

'Just really hungry . . .' Drake frowned and motioned them close. 'I think – I think using the you-know-what takes it out of me a bit. That's why I was being careful in the forest. Need to recharge my batteries.'

'Want to try for three?' the food vendor asked.

Drake shrugged. 'Think I could. One for the road, maybe.' He slid across a few more coins from his change. 'You know what, keep the change. There a train station nearby?'

The vendor nodded as he stuffed a third roll with onions and mustard. 'Newfoundland Railway over on Water Street. Two blocks over that way. Big thing the Alliance built a few years back. You can't miss it.'

'We're looking to get back to the mainland,' Irene said. 'Over towards Quebec.'

The vendor handed Drake another hot dog and rubbed at the back of his neck with a frown. 'Hmm . . . well, you can catch the train tonight, probably, over to Argentia. But you'll need to get the ferry across to New Brunswick or Nova Scotia. Or better yet, a flight from Bristol Field. Probably find a better route on your phone.'

Irene thanked him, and Drake took the lead towards the train station a few streets over. His stomach grumbled, and he licked the sauce from his lips. The food had hit the spot, but he could've still gone another few rounds with the food truck. *When you use the crystal, you're burning through energy or something.* Energy that seemed to replenish itself from an unfathomably deep ocean, locked away in his mind, but his body must have still been tired, worse for wear – even if he couldn't sleep. *What I need is some time to figure this stuff out. Before it kills me.*

The train station on Water Street was a modern glass building, several storeys high and built facing the cold windswept sea and St. John's Harbour. Drake hunched his shoulders against the snowy breeze and glared at the harbour. Across the water, between warehouses and loading cranes, was the holding facility that shuttled staff and inmates back and forth between St. John's and the Rig.

Drake had the strangest urge to dive over into the harbour and swim back to the dilapidated oil rig in the middle of the Arctic Ocean – hundreds of miles away. An itch between his shoulders shivered down his back, and he felt *watched*. Not by cameras, the eyes of the Alliance, but by something far crueller and . . . angry. *Something in the crystal.* He shook his head and cleared his thoughts, but the itch remained, burrowing like a tick in the back of his mind.

'We've almost come full circle back to the start,' Tristan said, recognising the lay of the land across the harbour. 'Bugger.'

'We need to get out of here,' Irene said.

'Somewhere that's not this town,' Drake agreed, as they entered the station through a set of revolving glass doors. He glanced up at the departure and arrivals board, just inside the expansive main foyer littered with fast food shops, bars, and small retailers. A steady stream of people, families, business folk in shiny suits, and station staff jostled for room in the foyer. 'What's leaving next for the coast?'

Irene had already figured that out. 'Five o'clock to Argentia. Platform Seven. The hot dog guy seemed to think we could catch a ferry from there.'

A bank of self-service ticket machines ran across the polished marble floors. Tristan found a vacant one and flicked through a few screens, as Drake and Irene tried to look innocent at his shoulders. He shrugged. 'Yeah, there's some seats available on that one to Argentia. Oh, even a private booth in first class, but they want, like, five hundred . . .' He glanced at Drake's backpack. 'Yeah, the machine takes notes. What d'you say?' he asked, already pushing buttons and confirming the tickets. 'Travel in style?'

Chapter Four

Pizza Delivery, No Pineapple

With half an hour to spare before the train departed, the three of them sat at a small café near Platform Seven and tried not to glance up at the cameras on the wall. Irene bought water and biscuits for them all, and Tristan wandered off to The Source, an electronics store, with a wad of bills and a plan. Drake kept his head down at the table, doing his best not to look too guilty while avoiding looking anyone in the eye.

I can't run forever, he thought. *But with the crystal power, I don't have to. I just have to get to London. I can make Mum well again* . . . he glanced at Irene. *With her help, her healing power.*

Half an hour later, the train departed the station on time, with Drake, Irene, and Tristan secluded away in the front carriage. The ticket inspector hadn't spared them a second glance. The compartment was lavish, complete with a small refrigerator containing all manner of delicious snacks. Twin rows of racks for luggage sat above the seats, which folded out into full-length beds. A television screen was concealed in the arm of each foldout bed, and along the outer wall of the carriage stretched a clear window.

'This definitely beats the Alliance's idea of accommodation on the Rig,' Drake said to his friends. 'A few weeks makes all the difference, eh? Especially after that shack in the forest.'

'A few weeks ago, you were bleeding to death on the floor of our cell after Brand gave you a beating,' Tristan said. 'Bloody hell, I was sure you were dying.'

'I might have, if not for you.' Drake grinned. He ran his tongue along his bottom teeth, over the gap. Brand had got him with a right hook and cost him a tooth. 'And Irene, of course, slipping you those pills from the infirmary.'

'Well, you're welcome. But I reckon we're even after what happened on the *Titan*. You saved us from going down with the ship . . . although it was kind of your fault it went down in the first place. Heh.' Tristan paused, then considered, and flicked his ticket onto the spare seat by the window. 'It's a little under three hours to Argentia. Time to work.' He riffled through his shopping bag from the electronics store and began sorting the tools and components he'd purchased on the table in front of him.

'This almost seems too easy,' Irene said, grinning from ear to ear and bouncing on the comfortable leather seats.

Drake gave her a grim look. 'We're not away yet. The Alliance has caught me every time I've escaped. Granted, I couldn't melt walls those times, but it won't be too long – will it, Tristan? – before they know we're on this train.'

Tristan raised his palms towards the roof and shrugged. 'Depends how cautious you want to be, Will. They might not know we've switched clothes yet, but they'll certainly be sifting through all the footage from the train and bus stations. We might get stopped just because we're three people travelling together, wearing hats and sunglasses, who bought last-minute train tickets.' He sighed. 'I mean, we might fool the camera algorithms – and I say *might* – but if anyone is actually watching the footage then . . . well, we stick out like sore thumbs painted neon pink.'

Drake pressed his sore thumbs together. 'Hmm . . . bother.' He let his shoulders slump a little. 'I really, really want to avoid a fight, but we can't be recaptured. You guys know that, right? With what we know, the Alliance isn't going to send us back to one of their prisons.'

'They'll kill us,' Tristan whispered. He crossed his arms and glanced out of the window as the train cleared the station. Light snowfall was settling over St. John's. 'It's getting dark.'

'We could ride the train out to one of the smaller stations,' Drake suggested, trying to follow the web a few strands further down the line. 'Somewhere out of the way, rural, with no cameras. Change trains, maybe, throw them off that way.'

'If we get that far.' Irene bit her lip. 'But Newfoundland is still one big island. We'll need to use a ferry or something eventually. Oh, I've got a bad feeling about this.'

'That's just normal post-escape blues,' Drake said. 'I get them all the time.'

Irene rolled her eyes. 'That's not encouraging.'

Drake squeezed her knee and shrugged, stifling a yawn. 'Ah, can you believe that? Haven't felt tired at all and now . . . we're comfy.' He leant back in his seat and stretched his arms above his head. 'Might see if I can drop off for a bit. Wake me for *anything*.'

* * *

'I think he's actually asleep,' Irene said, about fifteen minutes into the journey to Argentia. She sighed. The knot of worry, wrapped around her heart, loosened a bit. 'That's a relief. He was awake for too long.'

Tristan fiddled with the stolen search drone on the table, a mess of tangled wires and tools within arm's reach. He glanced at Drake and then back down at his work. 'So are you going with him?'

'Sorry?'

'To London,' Tristan said. 'He hasn't brought it up yet, since our escape, but that's where he's going, you know. All he bloody talked about in our cell, when I could get him to talk. To find his mother and help her, if he can.'

'I don't know,' Irene said, pulling her feet up and hugging her knees. She swayed slightly in her seat, to the motion of the train. 'How would we get there?'

Tristan shook his head. 'Don't tell him I said this, but we won't.' He shrugged and unscrewed what looked like a circuit board from within the drone. 'And even if by some unholy miracle we manage to cross the entire North Atlantic and find his mum alive, she won't be alone.'

'The Alliance,' Irene said.

Tristan nodded. 'The moment Storm reported our escape, the Alliance would have sent someone to watch her. We won't get within a mile of wherever she lives.'

If she's alive. Irene cast a quick look at Drake, still asleep upright in his chair under that silly hat. 'I don't think they can stop him getting to her without . . .'

'Without killing him, yeah.' Tristan said. 'Christ, two weeks ago he sank a supertanker and his body healed a gunshot, broken leg, and one *helluva* beating from Marcus Brand. Today he read your mind. What will he be doing tomorrow, Irene? Seeing the future? Shooting lasers from his eyes? Flying? What if he wakes up from his little nap and he's Superman?' Tristan pointed two fingers at Irene and shook his head. 'Never mind if he's insane or not, like Carl. Will he stay with us, you think? If he can just fly away? I don't know if I would.'

'He'd stay,' Irene said, but her voice quivered and betrayed her worry.

'What if . . .' Tristan sighed and removed his glasses, cleaning the fractured lens carefully with the hem of his shirt. 'What if he's better off on his own?' he whispered.

Irene raised an eyebrow and glanced at Drake, checking that he was still asleep. His even breathing said that he was, but he was frowning, and his eyes darted beneath his lids.

Bad dreams, she thought. *I hope that's all it is.*

'Are you saying you want to leave him?' Irene asked.

Tristan shrugged. 'No, no, I'm not. But it's only going to get more dangerous as the Alliance close in.' He secured a panel on the drone and picked up a small screwdriver, waggling it at Irene. 'And they are closing in, Irene. Like a noose around our necks, pulled tighter the harder *he* runs. All I'm saying is having Will Drake around is dangerous.' He held her gaze for a long moment before returning to the drone. 'That's all.'

You may not be saying it, but you're thinking about leaving him. Irene squirmed in her seat and glanced at Drake again. *What are we going to do?*

* * *

33

Drake awoke to find an Alliance search drone hovering in the air above the table. He cursed and jumped up in his seat as all vestiges of a rough, restless sleep washed away in an instant.

'It's fine – it's fine!' Tristan said, eyeing Drake's gloved hands. 'Don't shoot. I've reprogrammed it.'

Drake relaxed and rubbed at his forehead. 'Headache,' he muttered. 'And a strange dream about . . . how long was I asleep?'

'A little over an hour,' Irene said. 'But you tossed and turned a lot. Candy?' She held a bag of colourful gummy sweets. 'I swiped these from the little refrigerator.'

Drake accepted one and popped it into his mouth. He stared at the hovering drone, the internal engines humming softly, and worried. The engines had a slight tick to them, skipping a beat, as if someone had recently damaged them with a bolt of magical lightning. 'You sure that thing isn't beaming our location back to the Alliance?'

Tristan scoffed and tossed him something across the table. Drake caught it and eyed what looked like a complex circuit board, with dozens of little microchips coating its surface.

'That's basically the transmitter,' Tristan explained. 'Without that, the drone can't report home unless I tell it, or receive any external commands from the Alliance. Trust me, I know what I'm doing.' He tossed Drake something else.

'What's this for?' Drake asked, gazing at a smart phone. He pushed the home button, and the screen illuminated with a handful of apps. 'We can't use these – they'll be on us in seconds.'

Tristan crossed his arms and smirked. 'Not if we route the signals through the fluidmesh wireless network – the old microwave channels – on the drone. Pick the camera app.'

34

Drake hesitated and then shrugged. He hit the camera icon, and the screen flicked to an image of . . . of himself, in his seat in the cabin. He glanced up at the drone, to the lens on its underside, and back down at the screen. The phone was receiving footage from the drone in real time. 'OK, that's pretty neat.'

'I bought phones for all of us,' Tristan said and gave Irene a look Drake couldn't read. 'In case we get split up or something. Numbers are keyed in.'

Drake scanned his contact list and saw two numbers. Irene Finlay and Michael Tristan. That made him grin, how Tristan had used full and proper names. *He likes the little details.*

'One more thing.' Irene slid a piece of paper along the table to Drake.

He picked up the slip – torn from one of the phone manuals, from the look of it – and saw a bunch of numbers. 'What's this?'

'Irene's idea,' Tristan said. 'International dialling codes for London. Thought you might want to call home.'

Drake froze for a long moment, considered, and then chuckled. 'Blimey . . . after so long, it's that easy? I can call home, just like that?'

'Hell, you could post a status update about escaping from the Rig or take a selfie, if you want, but yeah – if you remember your home number,' Tristan said. 'I'd be quick, though. Routing the call through the drone means the Alliance won't be able to tag our location, but they'll be able to listen in if they've bugged your mum.'

Drake removed the glove on his right hand and was happy to see his fingers weren't aglow and no blue light danced beneath his skin. He slowly punched in the numbers on the touch screen, as if he were afraid that the phone would shatter or disappear – or that he was still dreaming.

He dialled his home number from memory, sure it was right after the better part of two years away, and pressed the call button. The screen changed to a picture of a telephone with signal bars rippling out from it, and Drake held his breath. As the train zipped across the snow-swept plains of Newfoundland and Labrador, a tiny burst of signal from Drake's phone bounced through the Alliance drone and shivered over the global wireless network.

The phone beeped.

The phone *connected*.

And the dull sound of a ringtone, travelling from over five thousand kilometres away, rang in the silent cabin.

Drake pressed the phone against his ear, heart racing, as someone picked up on the other end.

'Little Caesar's Pizza,' said a man with a thick London accent. 'Pickup or delivery?'

Drake blinked and pulled the phone from his ear. He read the number on the screen and cursed. 'Misdialled,' he muttered and ended the call. 'Food on my mind. Don't think they'd deliver this far out, anyway.'

He dialled the number again, more slowly, and switched the two last digits to match his actual home phone.

The tone rang twice before his mother picked up.

'Hello,' she said, her voice frail but unmistakable.

Drake paused, felt a wild chuckle rising in the back of his throat, and couldn't think of a thing to say. *She's alive!*

'Hello,' his mother said again. 'Is anyone there?' She sounded sick, to Drake's ears. She was sick.

Drake felt a hand on his shoulder and glanced at Irene. Given the comforting look on her face, he probably looked like a deer in headlights. His gut churned as if he'd blown up a supertanker on a full stomach.

'Will?' his mother asked. 'Will, is that you?'

Drake took a deep breath and exhaled. 'Hey, Mum. Yeah, it's me. Um . . . hello.'

'Oh, Will, what have you done? The news is saying such terrible things about you –'

'Mum, don't believe them –' The line squealed, and Drake pulled the phone from his ear with a hiss of pain. He checked the screen – still connected – and gently put the phone back to his ear. 'Hello? Mum? Are you there?'

'Good evening, Mr. Drake,' said a deep, smooth voice. 'Do you know who I am?'

Drake recognised the voice – most in the world would. He clenched the phone almost hard enough to snap the battery cover from the device.

'Lucien Whitmore,' Drake said. 'King of the Alliance. Looks like we've got a crossed line . . . sorry, I was trying to order a pizza.'

Whitmore chuckled, and Drake pictured him behind some massive mahogany desk, dressed in an expensive suit, in an office overlooking New York City – the headquarters of the Alliance – at dusk. Or, as Drake had first seen him, deep below the Rig, staring up at Carl Anderson in his glass cage, from behind the tinted sunglasses Whitmore wore in every picture and interview. The man was a monster who bred monsters.

'Are you hungry, Mr. Drake?' Whitmore asked. 'It is well within my means to provide pizza, if you just tell me where you are.'

Across the table Tristan had clenched his fists hard enough to turn his knuckles white. '*Hang up*,' he whispered.

Drake raised a finger and shushed him. 'Have you hurt my mum?'

'Quite the opposite. I'm seeing she gets the care she needs, given her condition. You gave the Alliance quite the black eye with your recent escape.' Whitmore tutted, his voice like silk against sandpaper. 'What better way to protect our reputation than by caring for the mother of the young and misguided William Drake?'

'Misguided?' Drake scoffed. 'Your news channel is calling me a terrorist.'

'What you did on the Rig was cause for great terror,' Whitmore said. 'And public opinion is all about perception, Mr. Drake.'

'Yeah, but I didn't kill anyone!'

'No? What of the boy you let out of his cage in my facility beneath the Rig? Carl Anderson? Why did you let him out?'

Drake swallowed and said nothing.

'Was it because you knew what he was going to do with his brief freedom? You loosed that particular arrow from the bow, and it struck the spark that caused the wildfire. He died so you could escape, and he took a great many of my staff with him.' Whitmore's tone suggested unshakable confidence. Drake was dealing with the man who controlled the world, and Whitmore knew it. 'Not the first young man to die for your cause, though, was he? Haven't enough died for your freedom, Mr. Drake?'

Aaron . . . Drake still felt the heat of those flames from his unsuccessful escape attempt at Cedarwood. 'Goodbye, Mr. Whitmore.'

'How did you escape Harronway?'

Drake hesitated. 'I walked right out the front door, whistling a merry tune and clicking my heels together.'

Whitmore laughed. 'No, no, you didn't,' he said, with such sincerity that Drake's shoulders slumped. 'You cannot run forever, Mr. Drake.'

'Just watch me.'

'I have been, lad, and now I'm afraid you've reached the end of the line.'

Drake's heart leapt into his throat. *End of the line* . . . he ended the call and slapped the phone down on the table. 'He knows where we are. We need to –'

The train lurched. The momentum tossed Irene and Drake back against their seats, and it threw Tristan chest-first into the table. The brakes squealed against the tracks and spilled Irene's gummy sweets on the floor.

Outside, a sudden beam of light swept along the ground, making the snow sparkle, until it lit up the compartment. Heavy, sharp helicopter blades buffeted the air, and Drake watched, grim-faced, as masked men descended from two Alliance-branded attack helicopters on cords of black rope.

The chopper swung over the train, out of sight, and the thump of heavy boots clunked against the roof.

Drake got to his feet and clenched his fists. 'End of the line, is it? We'll see about that.'

Chapter Five

Derailed

'Tristan,' Drake said, 'you carry the pack – what's that drone going to do?'

'Follow our signal,' Tristan said, hoisting the pack of money and supplies onto his shoulders. Without the drone, the pack looked heavy but manageable for his small frame.

Drake shifted his beanie and slipped his sunglasses into his pocket. 'Right. Follow me.'

'What are we going to do?' Irene asked, fear written clear across her face.

'Follow the web,' Drake said. 'Keep following the silly old web. Trust me, we're not caught yet.'

'But they're soldiers *with guns*!' Tristan clutched his phone hard enough to turn his knuckles white.

Drake nodded and removed one of his gloves. 'Yes, they are.' He held up his right hand and concentrated. Hot blue flame burst from his fingers, singeing the cuff of his jumper. 'But they're not ready for this.'

'How the hell do you know what you're doing with that?' Tristan asked.

Drake shrugged and stepped out into the corridor. 'I don't, but it's worked so far, and it's working now. Let's keep at it, eh?'

'What about . . .' Tristan hesitated. 'What about the warden's revolver?'

'No,' Irene said.

'Best not,' Drake agreed. 'More likely to shoot ourselves – not that we should be shooting anyone.' *Haven't enough died for your freedom, Mr. Drake?* 'Come on. We need to hurry.' He set off along the corridor at a steady clip, heading for the rear of the train.

Confused travellers stuck their heads out of their compartments as Drake dashed past, the tassels on his hat swinging. His glowing right hand left a trail of sparks floating in his wake. He entered the dining car, the smell of roasting coffee on the air, with Irene and Tristan at his heels.

The next carriage was sparsely populated, with twin rows of seats running the length of the car. Drake slowed his run to a brisk walk. He ignored the strange looks he was getting from the other passengers. When he was about halfway down the aisle, the door at the far end of the car burst open. A tall soldier, dressed in black combat fatigues and a familiar gas mask, stepped into the carriage with his sleek rifle raised. He swept the gun across the carriage and settled it on Drake.

A long second passed, and the soldier's finger twitched on the trigger of his rifle at the same moment Drake raised his hand. The rifle hissed. Drake staggered back.

41

A dart slammed against an invisible barrier in front of his face. It stuck in the air for a moment, as if crumbled against a sheet of thin glass. The tranquilising agent in the dart dribbled down towards the floor. Drake felt his shock mirrored behind the soldier's mask.

Before the soldier could fire again, Drake stepped forward – acting purely on what he'd been able to figure out in the past two weeks – and cut his hand down through the air. A wave of concussive force shot down the aisle, shattering windows, splintering the wood panels on the walls, and forcing the passengers back against their seats. The soldier took the brunt of the wave and slammed into the rear of the carriage. He slumped, head against his shoulder, and the rifle fell from his grip.

'Let's keep going.' Drake started to run again. He removed the glove from his left hand, but hid the sparkling mess from sight in his pocket. 'There'll be more than one.'

Stepping over the unconscious soldier, Drake pushed the carriage door open. A cool, biting breeze carried in flurries of icy snow, as well as the harsh sound of the hovering helicopters. Bracing himself against the cold, Drake stepped down off the train – sweeping his head left and right for the Alliance soldiers – then turned back to make sure Irene and Tristan were keeping up.

'Cold out here, isn't it?' he said, as if the weather were the most important thing on his mind. The train had stopped in a wide, snowy clearing surrounded by dark silhouettes of trees – another forest.

'Bit brisk, yeah,' Tristan agreed. A half-dozen darts pinged off the carriage, the three of them bright targets where they stood highlighted against the light from the train. Irene shoved Tristan from the carriage and fell with him into the knee-deep snow.

Drake spun and saw three soldiers crouched against the snow, the muzzles of their rifles flaring as they fired at Drake and his friends. Drake raised his hand, and an invisible shield formed in the air. He couldn't feel it, but the crumpled darts showed him it was working.

I need the shield to follow us. Can I do that?

'Only one way to find out,' he muttered. 'Come on. We can lose them in the trees.'

Drake hauled Tristan up from the snow with his left hand, keeping his ignited right out of harm's way, and set him on his feet. One of the helicopters swooped over the train, and gusts of wind and snow buffeted the three of them. At least, the wind and snow tried – but the invisible shield forced the gale to split around them.

'That's so cool,' Irene marvelled.

'I know, right?' Drake chuckled and began to take wide steps through the knee-deep snow. 'Just hope it isn't frying my brain.'

'I think that was fried long before the Rig,' Tristan quipped. He was covered in snow from his dive off the train and shaking – whether from the cold or the adrenaline, Drake didn't know. He had his phone out and was recording as best he could.

'Three Alliance psychologists and a court in London would agree.'

Trudging through the snow was slow work, and the soldiers were having trouble closing in, keeping their distance but also keeping the three of them in sight. Drake's shield was stopping their darts, but he wasn't certain why the shield had popped into existence at all – just that he'd wanted it to happen – or why it hovered level with him as he broke through the snow.

The power bleeding through his arm and out of his hand felt warm, inviting. *And something else. Vast . . . no, not vast. Deep. Old.*

The second chopper had moved from over the train and hovered above the dark line of trees, buffeting the tall branches of the white pines and shaking loose fallen snow. Drake slashed his glowing arm upwards, and wicked energy arced along the snow – digging a deep furrow – and curved up towards the chopper.

The pilot veered the chopper away, but not quickly enough. The crescent of white energy sliced cleanly through the tail, severing the rear rotor. The chopper spun out of control above the trees – the spotlight underneath scattering light wildly across the edge of the forest – and crashed against a drift of deep snow. The blades snapped and flew across the clearing, ultimately embedding themselves in the ground and the trees. A chunk slammed against Drake's invisible shield with a resounding *thunk* of crumpling metal. The other chopper swung away from the crash, away from Drake.

Glittering crystal as blue as the sky had formed along the path of Drake's crescent bolt of energy. He marvelled at the crystal – like a frozen wave forever about to crash against the shore – and touched it with his fingertips. The crystal *sang*, with a chime like church bells, and shattered.

Irene and Tristan dived for cover but Drake watched the shards fall like sparks of electric-blue snow mixed with white. They disappeared into the actual snow and *melted* the hard-packed powder beneath. The lighter sparks were swept away on the wind, marking the pristine snow with hundreds of tiny burns.

I did that. Whatever it was, it was beautiful, and I did it.

'OK, that's one chopper down,' Drake said. Dozens of tiny darts, the Alliance's favourite weapon on the Rig, were still striking his shield. 'Think I can get the other?' He rubbed his hands together, and a waterfall of blue sparks fell to the ground, as if his palms were a spinning grinder wheel striking metal.

'Will, don't!' Irene said. 'Just don't!'

He blinked and looked down at her. She was on her knees in the snow, terrified. Not terrified of the soldiers – at least, not only of the soldiers, but also of him and what he was doing.

The other chopper had pulled back beyond the soldiers and landed next to the train. A man emerged from the belly of the steel beast and . . .

Drake blinked. Something wasn't right about the man. His proportions were . . . off. He was tall – at least seven feet tall – and his arms were elongated, thin, and pale. His face was half-concealed behind a breathing mask, but the eyes, above the mask and a slit of a nose, looked as black as coals. An intense *wrongness*, an invisible aura of malice, clung to the man. Drake fought an urge to scream in horror – and run.

Just a trick of the light. This can't be what I'm seeing.

The image of a skeleton geared up in Alliance solider armour wasn't far from what Drake was seeing in the pale light from the chopper reflecting off the snow. The soldier stared at him, across the distance, and waved at Drake as if they were old friends. The wave felt almost like a blow to the gut. Every instinct in his body told him to run and hide – to flee – even as the hair on his arms and the back of his neck stood rigid.

Twin blades of crimson fire burst from the man's arms, and he thrust both limbs forward. Rippling flame spiralled a rough course through the air towards the three of them. Some gut instinct told Drake his shield wouldn't withstand the blast. He mirrored the soldier's move, right palm blazing.

The electric-blue and ruby-red light struck in mid-air. A colossal *boom* echoed across the clearing, melting snow and rocking the train on its tracks. The flames melded together, red bleeding into blue, and blended into white. A thin spire of hot energy raced towards the clouds. At its base, the fire *split* to reveal a space of dark air that should have shown the snow and trees beyond, a gap through the blaze. Instead, surrounded by flames, the gap seemed to *bend* inwards against the air.

A consuming rage hammered in Drake's chest, as he lost all feeling in his left arm – save for the rush of crystal power. *What was that?* A terrifying thought ran through his mind but he pushed it aside.

'Are you seeing this?' Tristan held up his smart phone, watching the firestorm through the lens of his drone, which hovered above their heads. 'What the hell is *that*?'

'I've no idea,' Drake whispered.

'The drone . . .' Tristan took a deep breath. 'The drone is picking up all sorts of weird readings. Bloody hell.'

The gap beneath the column continued to bend, to twist, and formed a tunnel back through the blaze, like a drill bit burrowing into thick wood. A cone of fire surrounded the tunnel, cascading inwards towards something impossible. Drake glimpsed blue crystal and felt a rush of air colder than the Canadian weather. A rush of air that stank of stagnation and decay.

Glimpsed within the depths of the tunnel was a world of grey ash and storm clouds flashing red lightning. The view was lost as, from within the tunnel, a creature of dark, obsidian stone, with at least half a dozen long legs bristling with barbs, clawed towards the snowy clearing. The white light seemed to fail against its hide. *Not stone*, Drake thought.

'Oh, it's made of glass!' Irene said.

'Crystal,' Drake muttered, holding his head. 'It's made of crystal.'

'*What is it?*' Tristan managed, his voice rough and choked. 'What is it? What is it? What is it?'

It looked like a spider the size of a small car. The creature pulled itself out from within what Drake could only think was a portal to . . . somewhere else. A tear in reality caused by the conflicting, unnatural power. Its bulk left a deep furrow in the snow. Twisted legs as thick as bollards, a nest of blinking eyes, and a maw of sparkling silver teeth dripping with some clear substance; the crystal spider clawed from the maelstrom of blended white fire. As the creature emerged, the spire of flames flickered and died – whatever energy powered the light had been expended – and the portal snapped closed with a sound like tearing paper.

Two crystals, glowing blue and red, hung in the air above the bulk of the creature. The crystals hovered for a moment, sparkling, and then the blue one shot through the air towards Drake and the red went the other way, towards the tall soldier with impossible power of his own. Acting instinctively, Drake snatched the crystal, which was about the length of his forearm, out of the air. He tossed it to Tristan who gave a cry and let it fall into the backpack.

The spider screeched.

Drake winced, and Irene clapped her hands over her ears. The sound was somewhere between nails on a dusty chalkboard and metal scraped against metal. Tristan stared, slack-jawed, holding his phone between him and the beast as if it offered some sort of protection.

The soldiers across the clearing turned their weapons upon the creature and fired. Dozens of tranquiliser darts chimed against its glassy hide. Some of them switched to sleek black pistols, real bullets, lethal, but the rounds ricocheted off the spider. The tall soldier who had fired the crimson bolt of power threw his head back, laughed, and offered Drake two thumbs up.

The spider creature, whatever it was and wherever it had come from, shook its bulbous head, blinked a hundred black eyes, and turned towards the Alliance soldiers. It moved slowly, eight legs digging through the snow and kicking up chunks of hard-packed ice in its wake.

The man with the black eyes and red fire clenched his fist, and the soldiers fell back behind the chopper. At the same time, a great wrenching of metal echoed across the forest's edge, of couplings tearing apart and steel straining to its breaking point.

The engine car broke free from the rest of the train and rose fifteen metres into the air above the tracks. The horror-struck passengers in the next carriage clung to their seats as the engine car spun on its side, as if on a pivot, and shattered glass rained from above.

'What are you doing?' Tristan shouted.

'It's not me.' Drake's heart pounded against his chest. 'It's . . . it's him. The skeleton man.'

Skeleton Man removed his breathing mask, raised his thin arms above his head and gave a high, shrieking laugh that pierced Drake like a rusted fish hook. He held his forehead, pain pulsating in his skull.

'Oh my . . .' Irene gasped. 'Who is – ?'

Skeleton Man *threw* the train at Drake, over the slow crystal spider, as easily as throwing a tennis ball.

Moving with an almost casual grace, as surreal as the sight of the train hurtling through the air, Drake raised his arms and clapped once. On some sort of insane autopilot he didn't understand, he *caught* the train in an invisible net. A few metres above the snow, the engine car bounced, as if on a bungee cord.

Now what?

Drake snorted, and he couldn't help the mad giggle that escaped him. He clapped his hand over his mouth to stop it and dropped half the train. The closer end of the carriage slammed into the bulk of the crystal spider. The creature shattered as if it were a fine crystal glass, and a clear ichor burst from its innards before it was lost under the carriage.

'Whoops,' Drake said, tears in his eyes, still fighting the giggles. He carefully lowered the other end of the train into the snow, blocking his view of Skeleton Man and the chopper, and making sure no passengers were underneath it. 'We have to go now,' he said. 'And yes, I think that did, in fact, just happen.'

Irene and Tristan stood either side of Drake, but they nodded as one and turned towards the dark forest of snow-covered trees. The heat from the blasts, the portal, and the downed chopper had melted a rough, slushy path through the snow. Drake cast a quick glance over his shoulder as his friends entered the forest, back towards the soldiers, just as they appeared from around the far edge of the derailed carriage.

Darts whizzed through the air around them, and one bit Tristan just below his hairline on the back of his neck.

'Ah!' he cried and stumbled forward, the tranquiliser in the dart knocking him out cold.

Drake cursed. His shield had dissipated, most likely when he was playing catch with the train. He caught Tristan under his arms, slung him over his shoulder, and dashed after Irene deeper into the forest.

The trees soon provided cover from the darts. Drake let Irene lead them away – away from the train, the soldiers, monstrous spiders, and . . . Skeleton Man.

He's one of the Alliance's Crystal-X soldiers, Drake thought. *Has to be. Christ, look what it did to him . . .*

Visibility beneath the trees was dark, barely better than washed-out greys. Shadows cast by the trees crossed the snow. Irene stumbled on a knot of tree roots and landed hard on her knee. She cried out, stifled a sob, and hobbled back onto her feet.

'Keep going,' Drake breathed. He wasn't using any power to carry Tristan, but his small friend was light enough not to weigh too heavily on his shoulders.

Irene retrieved the smart phone Tristan had given her from her pocket. She spent precious seconds fiddling with it. Drake was about to hurry her along when a beam of light shone from the camera flash on the back.

'Flashlight app. Michael thought it might be a good idea,' she said and winced. 'Damn it, my knee's bleeding. We should risk the light so we don't fall into a ditch or something.'

'Right.' Drake thought he could hear boots against snow behind him, but that could have been the pounding in his ears. He trusted Irene to find the right path – any path – deeper into the forest and away from the Alliance soldiers.

What the hell are we going to do? The net was closing fast. Sooner or later, they'd be cornered. *Even with my power and however the hell I'm using it, the bloody Alliance is everywhere and controls everything!*

Drake pushed his sour thoughts aside and concentrated on the present – and on not snapping his ankle thanks to a malicious tree root.

After what felt like hours but was probably only the best part of forty-five minutes, the trees thinned and they reached a gravel road under a thin coating of fresh snow. Sand and grit had been thrown down recently – earlier in the day, most likely – to melt ice, which meant the road had to lead somewhere populated. No soldiers had followed them through the forest, but they wouldn't be far behind.

Favouring her left leg, Irene limped across the road and into the trees on the other side.

'Let's head in here a bit and then stop,' Drake said. His shoulders were burning from Tristan's weight, but he didn't

51

want to try using his power again. So far he'd been able to swing it in his favour, but at no point had he felt in control. *Where the hell did that spider thing come from?*

Irene didn't reply but disappeared around a copse of trees. Drake followed, down a narrow hollow just beyond the trees. About fifty metres away from the road, the hollow opened up into a glade alongside a frozen river and a barrier of trees and shrubs that looked, in the poor light, impassable.

'Either we stop here,' Irene said, gasping for air, 'or we have to climb back up the way we just came and look for another way through.'

Drake glanced around the glade, shielded away from the road, and tried not to think what a fine spot it would make for a last stand. The thought made him smile and forced another chuckle from him. *Quit laughing. Nothing about today is funny!*

He couldn't help it – the laughter was coming, and he was about to drop all sixty kilograms of Michael Tristan.

He placed Tristan down against the trunk of a tree. His shoulders screaming relief, he fell to his knees in the light snow and let the laughter out. Drake laughed up at the night sky – a million stars twinkled far away, between wisps of grey cloud – until tears streamed down his face.

'Will?' Irene asked, not quite approaching him. 'Are you OK?'

'She's alive, Irene!' Drake stood up quickly and swept Irene into a quick embrace, spinning her around in his arms. 'My old mum, bless her, she's still alive!'

A smile blossomed across Irene's face and turned into a giggling fit. She pulled Drake's hat back from his forehead and kissed him squarely between his eyes.

Chapter Six

Veiled Light

Irene sat against the cold tree trunk next to Tristan and rolled the leg of her pants up and over her knee. She was covered in sweat from the dash through the forest, but it was drying cool against her skin and making her shiver. *This cold will kill us faster than the Alliance, if we're not careful.* She kept her ears pricked for the sound of heavy boots or the click of assault rifles. For now, it looked like they'd lost the soldiers.

Her knee was a bloody mess from the fall in the forest.

'Ouch,' Drake said. 'Do you want me to try to heal . . . ? No, you should do it yourself. Blimey, I'd probably just end up cutting the whole leg off.'

Irene pressed her palm against her knee. The wound was throbbing. She concentrated and brought her own power – meagre compared to Drake's – to bear against the pain. Back on the Rig, they'd given her a drop of the blue crystal, barely enough to cover the head of a pin, but enough to result in an ability to heal, among other tricks. A few dozen sparks

53

ran down her arm and pooled under her palm. A cool balm spread over her knee, drops of liquid light, and tendrils of bright smoke escaped from between her fingers. When Irene removed her hand, her knee was still coated in blood, but the wound was sealed.

Drake was tapping Tristan on the cheek, trying to wake him up. Irene watched him carefully. More than once during their mad dash from the train and through the forest, she'd seen pinpricks of crimson light shining in his pupils. *Did you really see it?* she wondered. *Yes, it was there. His eyes are starting to shine red ... which isn't good.*

'Tristan has bad luck when it comes to the Alliance and their stunning darts,' Drake said. 'He took one to the chest on the Rig, too. Remember? That's when we met in the infirmary.'

'Is he OK, d'you think?'

Drake nodded slowly. 'He's breathing fine.'

'Do you think they're far behind?' Irene strained her ears, but apart from the whistle of the wind and rustle of leaves, she heard nothing to suggest they were being pursued.

Drake glanced back up the rise through the hollow and towards the road. 'What time is it?'

'It's not late. Six-thirty, maybe.'

'We've got a lot of darkness to hide in then before morning.' Drake hugged his chest and sighed. 'Did you see that man back there? The one that threw the train?'

'No, I missed that,' Irene said sarcastically. 'He didn't look ... normal.'

'Human,' Drake said. 'It sounds absurd, I know, but he didn't look human. And it felt like ... but how could I?'

Irene stood up, tested her healed knee, and unrolled her cuffed pant leg. 'How could you what?'

Drake shrugged. 'Felt like I knew him, somehow. Skeleton Man.'

Irene shuddered, and not from the cold. 'Skeleton Man . . . that's an awful name, but it suits him. Do you think you could make a fire?'

Staring off into the distance, Drake seemed lost in his own little world. *His eyes are fine now.*

After a long moment, he blinked and gave her half a smile. 'Sure, fire I can do.' He looked down at his right hand as it started to glow. 'That one's easy.'

A half hour later, Tristan had woken up. Irene felt close to normal again, despite the aches in her limbs and the edge of biting cold that couldn't quite be overcome by the warmth from the two spheres of rippling energy Drake had hung in the air against the edge of the hollow to help shield the light from the road above.

'That crystal thing you made,' Tristan said, shivering near one sphere. 'The one that took down the helicopter.'

Drake nodded, picturing the glittering crystal that had stretched up from the ground to above the trees. 'I thought it looked like a wave about to crash.'

'Yeah, that thing. What was that?'

'Honestly?' Drake paused, and his eyes drifted over the frozen river, as if searching for something. 'Buggered if I know, mate. It felt . . . good. Like, I didn't mean to do it, but I couldn't have done anything else, you know? That made no sense.'

Tristan swallowed, and Irene watched him shiver from the knockout juice working its way through his system. His groggy movements reminded her of her stepfather after he had too much to drink. Thoughts of that man could only lead down one road, so she shoved them aside.

'No, that didn't make much sense.' Tristan sighed. 'Irene? What do you think it was?'

She tried for a smile. 'It looked pretty cool, whatever the hell you did, and it was a lot nicer than what came next. That . . . tunnel with the enormous spider.'

'It didn't explode,' Drake said. 'You know, like the crystal they pulled up from under the Rig would explode when it was exposed to air. This stuff didn't.'

'What does that mean, d'you think?' Tristan asked.

Drake, leaning against the tree with his knees up, rested his chin on his hands. 'Wish I knew.' He eyed the backpack, full of cash, the revolver, the strange crystal that had been created by the spider-portal, and a dwindling supply of snacks. 'Bloody hell, I'm hungry.'

'Using so much of the power takes it out of you,' Irene said. 'That's why you devoured all those hot dogs after tearing apart the cash machine.'

Drake shrugged. 'Guess so.'

Tristan pulled out his phone and fiddled with it for a moment. 'The drone's catching up,' he said. 'It got a little lost in the forest. Removing most of its tracking hardware has slowed it down. Should be here in a few minutes. Be interesting to see what it recorded about that portal and the spider.' He scratched the top of his head. 'Oh, I left my hat back on the train. I liked that hat.'

'How'd they find us on the train?' Drake asked. 'Was it the phones?'

Tristan shook his head. 'Not possible. Believe me. They must've tracked us back at the station. On a camera or something. Think how quickly those soldiers showed up. The phones had barely been switched on five minutes. No, some clever analyst caught us on the cameras.'

Drake slipped his own phone out of his pocket and stared at the dark screen for a long moment. Irene guessed he wanted to make another call. But if he called home, the Alliance would just intercept it again.

With a sigh, he returned the phone to his pocket and warmed his hand around the orb of crystal fire. His right hand.

'Wouldn't work anyway,' Tristan continued, 'at least not until the drone is in range. I could set it to patrol tonight. Might give us a bit of warning if the Alliance is getting close again – what are you staring at?'

Drake was frowning at a small boulder on the edge of the frozen river. He blinked. 'Sorry, what?'

'You keep staring at the ice and . . . scowling,' Irene said.

'Do I?'

'Are you feeling OK?' she asked. *Are you going mad?* When she'd screamed at him to stop during the fight back at the train, for an awful moment Irene had been certain he was lost – that whatever control he had over his power had slipped.

'Yeah, I'm fine –' Drake jumped to his feet, keeping the tree at his back. 'No. Who's there?' he demanded. 'I know you're there!'

Irene exchanged a look with Tristan and stood up to calm Drake down. He glowered at the river, at the far bank of thick trees and shrubs, with his fists clenched.

'Will,' she said gently. 'Oh, Will, there's nothing there.'

Drake licked his lips and swallowed hard. 'No, look. Just *look*.'

Irene sighed and followed his gaze to a small boulder, two metres away. She swept her eyes up and down the icy river, a feeling of utter helplessness gripping her. The only people on earth who could possibly understand what Drake was going through had drowned under the Rig – and those people had been just as likely to cut him open and experiment on him. He had no one who could help as his condition . . . *worsened*.

'Will, really, there's nothing –'

The air above the boulder shimmered, as if it were a clear plastic curtain caught in the breeze.

A teenage girl appeared, standing on the boulder.

As if she had been there all along and *not* invisible.

'Ha!' Drake said, suppressing a rough chuckle. 'Told you.'

'Who the hell is that?' Tristan breathed. 'She . . . she was . . . not there.'

'Good evening,' the girl said, smiling softly. 'My name is Noemi, and I am not here to harm you.'

'S'up, Noemi?' Drake said, as if he'd been expecting her this whole time. The set of his shoulders and the hard line of his jaw told Irene he hadn't been.

Not seeing the future just yet.

Irene stared at the girl on the boulder. She was young, perhaps around the same age as they were, and Asian. Her dark hair was pulled back in a loose ponytail, and her olive skin blended well with the white, snowy backdrop of looming trees and the cloudy night sky. Her breath shimmered on the air, obscuring dark eyes. She wore knee-length leather boots over black pants and a loose, V-necked blouse. Around her shoulders, clasped below her neck, was a strange silvery cloak that tricked the eye as if it were made of grey stone cast with moonlight. At her hip, half-concealed by the cloak, was the hilt of a sword in a long, curved sheath. She held the hilt in a hand wearing a thin glove.

As Noemi stepped down from the boulder, Irene's eyes had trouble following her movement, as if she was about to fade as quickly as she had appeared. *She's been exposed to the Crystal-X, too.*

'William Drake,' said the girl, Noemi. 'I've been searching for you for some days.'

Drake raised a hand, and she stopped moving. 'Please, just stand where you are. How did you do that . . . disappearing trick? I knew you were there,' – he tapped his forehead – 'but it was like an itch I couldn't scratch. You've been watching us for at least ten minutes.'

Noemi inclined her head. 'Like you, I am gifted.' She smiled, as if she and Drake shared a secret Irene wasn't supposed to know. 'However, I have never met anyone capable of piercing my veils. You should not have been able to sense my presence at all.'

'You were like a bee buzzing in my ear . . .' Drake muttered and scratched at his head beneath his hat. 'I could, like, see you out of the corner of my eye and sort of . . . taste it.' He licked his lips and frowned.

'Cool sword,' Tristan said. 'What's it for?'

59

Noemi's eyes flicked from Tristan to Irene, as if she were seeing them for the first time. She settled on Drake again. 'You are hunted. I can offer you means to escape the Alliance.'

'Where did you come from?' Drake asked. 'And how the hell did you find us all the way out here in the middle of snowy nowhere?'

'I followed the trail of destruction.' She grinned and shook her head, brushing a loose strand of dark hair back behind her ear. 'To those who know how to look, William, you blaze like a bonfire from half a world away. We could be separated by vast oceans and tall mountains, thousands of miles, and I'd still be able to point straight to you.'

With his back against the tree, Drake folded his arms and said nothing.

'Shall we sit?' Noemi asked. 'We have much to discuss, and the Alliance will burn this forest to less than ash come morning to flush you out.'

Irene felt wary of the newcomer and gave Drake a look that said as much. He nodded slightly, not about to lower his guard, and gestured to one of the spheres suspended in the air, radiating warmth. 'Stay on that side of the fire and we'll chat.'

Noemi nodded. She stepped across to the fire, her footfalls so light she barely left a mark in the snow, and entered the ring of light from the orb. Irene again thought she was about to disappear.

With movements like a cat's, lithe and certain, Noemi folded her legs and sat, her back straight and her head inclined at a graceful angle. Her sword she placed carefully in her lap, to avoid digging a furrow in the snow.

'It is an honour to meet you, William,' she said. 'A great many people have been waiting a long time for someone like you.'

Drake raised an eyebrow and shifted his hat on his head. 'Yeah?'

'Yes,' Noemi said, and she rocked with excitement. 'By destroying the Rig, you hurt the Alliance – bloodied the giant. You struck a fierce blow in the Shadow War.'

'The what war?' Tristan asked. 'Whose war?'

Noemi looked irritated at his interruption. 'The war against the Alliance. And the things controlling the Alliance.'

Things? Irene's gut squirmed as she thought of Skeleton Man.

'What war?' Drake echoed Tristan. 'There's no war – the Alliance controls the world, Miss Noemi.'

Noemi held his gaze for a moment, giving him a look that Irene thought might have been a touch pitying. 'As of a few hours ago,' she said, 'your friends here have also made the news.'

Tristan frowned. 'Yeah? What are they calling us?'

'Followers of the terrorist William Drake.'

Tristan scoffed and glared at Drake. 'Followers? So we're, like, your minions or something now,' he said, a touch bitterly. 'Followers of the Dark Lord Drake!'

Drake laughed. 'You're a minion. Irene is more . . . did you ever watch *Doctor Who*? Irene is my loyal human companion.'

'You're not the Doctor,' Irene said patiently and patted his shoulder.

Drake glanced down at his hands and shrugged. 'If they were right about the crystal, then there's a little bit of alien in me.'

Irene squeezed his shoulder, worried, and asked Noemi, 'So what do you want? For us to come with you, I take it.'

'No, not you. Just him.' She pointed at Drake. 'We have a . . . training facility,' she said. 'Of a kind. In English, you would call it Haven. A place the Alliance cannot go, where they *dare* not go. William Drake, you can be free there, away from the Alliance, and learn how to harness your gift. In Haven, you would never have to look over your shoulder, fearing soldiers or isolated prisons.'

A knot of fear tightened in Irene's gut at the brief flash of longing on Drake's face. *For him, freedom is all he wants. So he can help his mum.* He gave a dismissive snort, and she relaxed a little.

'I've no reason to trust that. For all I know, you're an Alliance spy. You're young like us, I suppose, but they were using kids on the Rig for worse. So go on then, tell me, where is Haven?'

Noemi hesitated. 'Japan.'

Drake nodded, as if he'd expected her to say the moon. 'Right. Well, I'm sure I'll fit right in.' He cleared his throat and played with the tassels on his hat. 'Two things. First and foremost, you don't get me without Irene and Tristan. We run together. And second, how are we supposed to believe anything you say?'

Noemi smiled. 'A fair point.' She sighed and removed her hands from within the folds of her silvery cloak. On her left hand, she wore a black silk glove, which she removed slowly, watching Drake's eyes. 'Does this suffice for belief?' Noemi asked, holding up her hand for them to see.

Irene gasped.

The thumb and index finger on her left hand were pure crystal.

62

Chapter Seven

The Path of Yūgen

Drake stared at Noemi's fingers and felt a wild thrill rush through him. *I'm not the only one!* Whether her hand was a glimpse of salvation or he and the Japanese girl were merely drowning together remained to be seen. Sparks of blue light danced within her crystal fingers, disappearing into the actual blood and bone of her hand.

He glanced at Irene, whose face was unreadable, and Tristan – Tristan looked as if he might be sick.

'You were never on the Rig, were you?' Drake asked.

Noemi smiled. 'Haven, hidden away in Japan, has its own source of Yūgen.'

'Of what?' Tristan frowned and tasted the word. 'Y*oo*gahn?'

'Close. Yūgen,' Noemi corrected softly. 'I believe the Alliance call it Crystal-X, and they have no idea just what it is they found under that despicable oil rig.'

'Bugger,' Drake said. 'You mean there's more of it? Other sources out there in the world? On the Rig, if the crystal was exposed to the air, it exploded – quite spectacularly. I mean, I sank a cargo ship with it, and I'm pretty sure it's still burning on the ocean floor now. If there's more of it out there, then you're sitting on a time bomb.'

Noemi shook her head. 'No, the Yūgen we receive from the Silver Tree does not erupt.'

'From a tree?' Irene asked.

'Oh yes. A grand tree, as bright as polished silver, its branches bursting with clear leaves as sharp as twice-cut glass. Once every generation, the tree bears fruit, and spheres of pure Yūgen fall like cherry blossom petals to the bottom of a vast pool surrounding the tree. The spheres, each about the size of a marble, are offered to a handful of chosen children from families all over the world. Secret families that hold true to the Path eat the fruit of the tree. We must dive deep for the gift.' She grinned. 'The Silver Tree is due to blossom again soon.'

'I take it you were one of the children?' Drake asked, nodding at her fingers. 'And then they teach you how to . . . how to *use* the Crystal-X? The Yūgen?' The Alliance had been doing the same thing on the Rig, kind of, with mixed but cruel results. They hadn't been teaching so much as poking the inmates with sticks and seeing what happened.

'Those who follow the Path of Yūgen can learn to control their gift, William,' Noemi said, and pinpricks of neon blue excitement danced in the calm of her pupils. 'I'm sure you've seen the power manifest itself in the eyes. Without the Path, without control, even a small drop can overwhelm the mind and –'

'Drive a person insane?' Drake offered. 'Oh, trust me, we've seen our share of that.' He tried not to think about his own eyes and the worry that felt like the weight of the world shackled around his neck.

'Yes, the gift can wound.' Noemi shivered, and Drake guessed she was remembering something unpleasant. 'But Haven can offer a light through the dark.'

'You sound far too good to be true,' Drake said. 'And as I said, you don't get me without Irene and Tristan.' He took a deep breath and exhaled slowly. 'But if I were to agree – and I'm not saying I do – but if I wanted to come with you, how the hell would we get to Japan?'

Noemi nodded. 'My partner, Takeo, is parked nearby in a car, about half a mile down the road. We thought it best to approach you carefully, given your current circumstances. And not far by the road, on the coast of Argentia, there is a private jet at Bristol Field Airport waiting to take us back to Haven.'

'A private jet?' Tristan whistled low under his breath. 'Bloody hell.'

'My family,' Noemi said, with a note of deep pride in her voice as she maintained her perfect posture, 'is one of the oldest and richest in the world. We care for the Silver Tree and command enough wealth and resources to make even the mighty Alliance blink.'

Drake chuckled softly to himself. 'All this for me, huh?'

Noemi stared at him. 'Understand, William Drake.' She raised her crystal fingers. 'The mark of a Yūgen user, you see. One flower per child, and the Yūgen affects them all differently.' She hesitated. 'Two of my fingers bear the mark, and I am considered one of the strongest among Haven's students. Some who absorb the flowers do not even develop a mark or talent.

But if I could sense your strength from Japan . . .' Noemi shook her head, and the mask of calm composure she wore so well cracked just a little. Underneath that mask she was terrified. 'I have no idea what you may be capable of achieving, should you decide to follow the Path. I only know that it will be beyond what has been possible before.'

Drake didn't know what to make of that, but before they went any further, the gloves were going to have to come off, so to speak.

'I've shown you mine,' Noemi said, and Drake almost jumped. *Is she reading my mind?* 'Perhaps you should show me yours.'

He nodded, steeled himself, and cast an apologetic glance at Irene. 'Sorry,' he said, 'but I've been keeping a secret.'

Drake stood and pulled his glove from his left hand, shrugging out of the leather and rolling his shoulders. Before any of them could get a good look at his hands, he slipped them into the sleeves of his jumper and pulled on the woollen fabric. Hesitating a moment, he lifted his jumper and shirt over his head and exposed his bare chest to the cold Canadian air.

Irene gasped.

Tristan made a strangled noise, as if an invisible boot had been pressed down on his throat.

A tear cut down Noemi's face, and she clasped her hands together.

Drake's entire left arm was made of dark crystal.

In the flickering light from the fiery orb, Drake's crystal arm looked almost obsidian, dangerous – like the spider creature that had emerged from the portal back at the train. Dozens of sparks of blue light spiralled along its length, from the tips of his fingers and up into his shoulder.

Irene's mind raced through the implications. *Oh, God, what is it doing to him?*

The pure crystal ended at his shoulder, blurring into the flesh of his neck, but thin veins ran down from his shoulder and over his chest towards his heart. A dozen crooked, gaunt fingers clawing across his skin. The occasional blue spark shot through the veins. Irene thought it looked like an infection.

'Holy shit,' Tristan said, summing up Irene's thoughts nicely.

'It started after we escaped,' Drake said. 'During the days we spent in the forest, it got worse. That first night I was worried it wouldn't stop, but after today . . . it was only my fingers this morning. Using the power has made it this much worse.' He faced Noemi. 'What's happening to me?'

Noemi stood and stepped around the fire, a hand to the hilt of her sword. She approached Drake slowly, as if he were snarling at the bit instead of standing in the half-light, shoulders slumped and tired. She touched his chest with her crystal fingers, and the sparks flowing along his arm became hundreds, *thousands*. A clear chime, like two Baoding balls swirled in the palm of the hand, sang just on the edge of hearing. The sound made Irene think of wide open plains and forests of trees disappearing over the horizon. *Distance*, she thought. *Or size . . . something deep and old.*

Drake shivered at Noemi's touch, and Irene struggled to keep an icy glare from her face.

'You still have full function in the arm?' Noemi asked.

Drake raised his crystal arm above his head and wiggled his fingers. He clenched his fist and gave Noemi a thumbs-up. 'Have you seen this before? At your . . . what, is it, like, a school?'

'Haven is . . .' Noemi stared at his arm. 'Haven is a school, yes, an academy – and the only safe port in the storm to come.'

'Storm to come?' Irene asked.

'Against the Alliance and the creature beneath the sea.'

Drake stepped away from Noemi and slipped back into his shirt and jumper, readjusting the tassels on his hat so they hung over the back of his shoulders. 'The creature beneath the sea?'

Noemi stared at him solemnly and clasped her hands over her heart. 'You've already met it, William Drake, after a fashion. To gain the power you have, you bathed in its blood.'

Chapter Eight

Lift-Off

Drake asked Noemi to wait on her boulder by the river while he spoke to Tristan and Irene, huddled together around one of the dwindling spheres of pale blue flame for warmth.

'What do you think?' he asked, once the girl had gone to wait.

'I think she's, like, a witch-ninja or something,' Tristan said, shaking his head. 'Seriously, secret schools for magic in some old world location? I've read this book before, Will. Next stop is the hidden market to pick up your owl and spell books. It's too good to be true. We can't trust her.'

'I'm wondering if she can hear us . . .' Irene said. 'She's absorbed the Crystal-X. Who knows what her tricks are? Invisibility, for one. That scares me more than . . .' She bit her lip.

Drake grinned. 'More than I do?'

'Well, yes, but I didn't mean –'

Drake waved her words away. 'It's OK. I'm pretty scared of me, too, and that was before I "bathed in the blood" of some alien sea creature.'

Tristan pushed his glasses up the bridge of his nose. 'That was pretty dramatic. Question is, do we trust her?'

'What's our other option?' Drake asked. 'No, seriously, what other options do we have? The Alliance won't be far away, and when they come again, they'll come with more than just two helicopters. Our immediate future looks like another bloody night spent huddling for warmth around these fireballs. And I'm not entirely sure they won't explode.'

Tristan took a step back from the orb. 'What? Really?'

Drake shrugged and offered him a smirk. 'There's no manual for this, mate. I'm just thankful it doesn't burn my eyebrows off whenever I use it.'

'Singed the cuffs of your jumper, though,' Irene remarked and pulled at the frayed and burnt thread around his wrist. He had put his glove back on over his crystal left hand. She grasped his right and squeezed his fingers with all the reassurance she could muster.

'Here's what I think,' Drake said. 'I think Noemi is telling the truth. Or at least a truthful version of some bigger truth, if that makes sense. Letting us glimpse, like, a bit of the bigger picture.'

'She's not Alliance,' Tristan said.

'Yeah, I don't think she is.'

'And she's got a car,' Irene said. 'Supposedly.'

'Private jet to Tokyo?' Drake asked his friends and couldn't help but laugh. 'Who saw that coming?'

'So we're going along with it?' Irene let go of Drake's hand and looked over her shoulder.

Drake followed Irene's gaze. Noemi stood serenely by the river, her eyes cast towards the sky. She looked like a statue, carved from pale marble, untouched by the snow. *She's quiet and unassuming*, he thought, *but I reckon she knows how to use that sword*.

'I guess it comes down to ninja-witch tonight or Skeleton Man tomorrow,' Drake said. 'And so far, she hasn't thrown a train at us, so I say we take our chances with Noemi. Agreed?'

Irene and Tristan looked at each other and then nodded.

It was a walk of five minutes back up on the road, and Noemi led the way, hugging the edge of the treeline in case of any unexpected traffic. Drake and his friends followed closely, but not too closely. After all that had happened, and given the global reach of the Alliance, trust didn't come easily. Especially for girls who appeared out of thin air toting a katana of folded Japanese steel.

'So this person you're travelling with,' Drake said. 'He got any special talents?'

'Takeo follows the Path of the Warrior. An apt path for him, I think. You will see what I mean when you meet –'

The familiar hum of an Alliance search drone echoed along the empty road.

Noemi crouched, her hand flying to the hilt of her katana, and spun on her heels. The blade was halfway out of the sheath in less time than it took Drake to blink.

'Wait!' Tristan said. 'It's not Alliance – it's mine.'

Hovering two metres above the road was Tristan's rewired drone, having finally caught up after the debacle on the train. He whipped out his phone and drew the drone in close. An image of the four of them appeared, lit up by the eerie green glow of night vision, as he showed Noemi the screen.

'I reprogrammed it,' he said quickly. 'Please don't stab it. The Alliance can't track us using it.'

Noemi regarded him for a long moment and then let her katana fall back into her sheath. 'You are certain?'

'No ninja swords! I ripped the locator beacons out of it back on the train, after Drake shot it down with a bolt of lightning.' Tristan blinked, perhaps wondering when in his life he'd have to say something like that again. 'Right, guys?'

Drake shrugged. 'Tristan's a whiz with computers. Back on the Rig, he got these bloody tracker things off our wrists with fridge magnets.'

'Well, not quite . . .' Tristan muttered, but he looked pleased.

Noemi relaxed, glanced at the drone, and then looked back at Drake. 'Very well. Hurry along now. Takeo is just around the bend in the road ahead.'

The car idling by the side of the road was more of a van, dark blue with tinted windows. The driver's door swung open as they approached, and a man the size of a small mountain stepped out and crossed his arms over his chest.

'Apparently we should not be concerned about the drone,' Noemi said to the man.

'Three, Noemi?' he asked. A severe furrow cut his brow in half below a shaven head of what looked like black stubble, in the poor light. His skin was tanned, and his eyes, as severe as his frown, were blue. He pointed at Drake. 'We only came for him.'

'He will not leave his friends,' Noemi said. 'Nor should he have to, Takeo. Think on the path, brother.'

Drake realised after a moment that Takeo wasn't so much frowning as his face naturally formed a series of disappointed angles. His arms were about the width of tree trunks, and his chest, under a tight-fitting white shirt, bulged with muscle. He carried no sword, but a holster on his waist held a sleek black pistol that probably wasn't loaded with anything so kind as stunning darts.

'Nice car,' Drake said.

'Get in,' Takeo said as he got back behind the wheel. 'The Alliance will be patrolling this road soon, if they're not already. But luck is with us this night, it would seem. There was some sort of train derailment nearby, which means we may have a chance to slip through unnoticed.'

Noemi slid open the side door to reveal a spacious cabin, with seats enough for six. She stepped up into the vehicle. Drake looked at his friends and shrugged. He got into the van and buckled up his seat belt.

Five minutes later, they were zipping by white trees illuminated only briefly from the van's headlights, as a fresh light snowfall coated the world.

'How far are we from Argentia?' Drake asked.

'About forty-five minutes,' Takeo answered from the front.

'You mind cranking the heat up a bit?' Drake rubbed his hands together and breathed warm air into his palms. The heat didn't touch his crystal hand, but it helped with the flesh of his right. 'It was nippy out there.'

'I am glad you agreed to join us, William,' Noemi said. 'There's a lot you need to learn, and only Haven can teach it to you.'

'Yeah, we're not going to Japan,' Drake said as a blast of warm air came out of the heating vents near his feet. 'Oh, that's good. Isn't that good?'

Irene chuckled. 'It's the little things.'

Tristan had powered down his drone and settled the device on his lap. He was staring at a screen of numbers and data on his phone. 'The readings from that portal are amazing. I . . . don't know what it all means, but it's amazing. Any chance of burgers and milkshakes in Argentia?'

'Forgive me,' Noemi said, 'but you do not wish to come with me to Japan? To Haven? William, you know what will happen to you without the guidance of the Path of Yūgen. Madness and pain. You must choose a discipline and devote your life to maintaining the balance. For you, more than any who have sipped from the crystal waters, to ignore this calling will spell catastrophic disaster.'

'Crystal waters now, is it?' Drake muttered. 'Quarter of an hour ago you were telling me I'd bathed in the blood of Cthulhu or something.'

'Ca-two-what?' Irene asked.

Tristan snorted. 'You've read Lovecraft, Will?'

'I've spent the better part of the last year and a half incarcerated by the Alliance. When I wasn't escaping, I was reading. The prison at Cedarwood had a pretty cool library.'

Noemi seemed a touch perturbed by their banter. Drake grinned. 'I'll come with you,' he said. 'All the way to Japan, if that's what gets me on your plane, but if you want me to play along, then we're going to have to make a slight detour.'

'A detour?' Noemi's sharp eyes glinted in the half-light. 'Where?'

'London.'

Noemi shook her head slowly. 'William –'

'Call me Drake.'

'Drake,' she said. 'London is not on any convenient flight path between here and Japan.'

'Sure it is,' Irene said. 'Just gotta go round the long way.'

'The Alliance control the majority of the world's airspace,' Noemi whispered, as if explaining herself to a group of five-year-olds. 'It will take them mere hours, perhaps less, to learn you are aboard one of our jets. Once they do – once the betrayer Lucien Whitmore knows where you're going, Drake – he will do everything in his considerable power to stop us. We're going to have to outrun the devil as it is, and I cannot guarantee we will make it to Tokyo.'

Takeo grunted from the driver's seat. 'Grace and Toby won't fly to London,' he said.

'Your pilots?' Tristan asked.

Noemi nodded. 'Prepping the jet as we speak. Why do you want to go to London?'

Drake rubbed at the wiry stubble coating his cheeks. At fifteen and a half, he didn't need to shave properly yet, but two weeks of fuzzy growth had him itching his chin. 'I've been gone nearly two years, and I'm feeling a touch homesick. Also I promised Irene and Tristan the best fish and chips with mushy peas and curry sauce they'll ever find.'

'The Alliance's influence in the United Kingdom is . . . considerable,' Noemi said.

'That it is,' Drake agreed. 'I still need to go to London.'

Noemi sighed. 'We will need to discuss this once we're on board.'

Drake folded his arms and nodded once.

75

The drive into Argentia was uneventful, for which Drake and his friends could only be thankful. After the best part of two weeks on the run – not to mention the madness involved in actually escaping the malevolent Rig – he wanted nothing more than to sleep and forget *everything* for a while, to bury his head in the sand and pretend everything was OK.

But sleep was hard to come by, these days. As Takeo drove past a strip of fast food restaurants, the roads practically empty, Drake made him pull over to the drive-thru and order a bag of cheeseburgers. Back on the road, he immediately devoured half a dozen of the greasy burgers, feeding the monster blood flowing through his veins and turning him, at least in part, to crystal.

'Without the proper guidance,' Noemi said, watching him eat, 'you will burn yourself away.'

'Stop being so cheerful,' Drake muttered, as they headed through the town of Argentia. Signs on the roadside told Drake they were about five kilometres away from the airport. He lay back in his seat and rested his head on his normal hand, eyes closed, and tried not to think about how things were going to work out in the end.

Just follow the web, he thought and yawned. *There's always a way out . . .*

Takeo hit a bump in the road, and when Drake snapped his eyes open, he was no longer in the car. He stood on a crest above a vast plain under a burnt orange sky, looking down at what had once been a vibrant city. A violent wind whirled pockets of ash and dust all around him, and the acrid stench of smoke hung on the air, with a taste that was almost stale.

'OK . . .' Drake said. 'This is . . . something.' His voice echoed in his ears, but it was no more than a whisper stolen by the hot wind.

Ruins of once mighty skyscrapers marred the landscape, fallen and decayed like the rotten teeth of some massive skull buried in the earth. In the heart of the ruined city – which Drake knew was London as sure as he knew his reflection in the mirror – a great spire of pulsating blue crystal pierced the clouds. Bands of thick grey cloud swirled around the summit of the spire, and crimson veins ran within the crystal.

And if that wasn't awful enough, Drake *felt* more than saw a pair of cruel eyes staring down at him from the top of the spire.

An awful, high-pitched laughter seemed to echo in his head and shake the whole world. In the distance, crystal towers toppled, and roiling storm clouds struck red lightning upon the ruins. Creatures that looked an awful lot like monstrous crystal spiders covered the ruins. Hundreds – no, thousands of the beasts.

Well, this is shit, Drake thought, holding his head as the calamity vibrated through his mind and into his bones. *I don't –*

Someone was shaking him. He leant forward, startled, as his vision wavered. He blinked, frightened and confused, until he saw Irene's kind eyes looking down at him. He was back in the van, the world wasn't ashes, and no crystal demon spire marred the horizon.

'You nodded off for a few minutes there,' Irene said. 'We're here at the airport. You OK?'

Drake took a deep breath, considered, then shook his head. Cool sweat clung to his skin. 'No, Irene, I'm not sure that I am.'

He caught Noemi watching him carefully from the taxiway, her green eyes all too knowing.

'Bad dreams, William Drake?' she asked.

Drake stepped out of the car and stretched his tired limbs. The scent of aviation fuel hung in the air, sweet and nauseating. Some snowflakes landed on his shoulders, and the lights of the small airport and on the underside of the private jet parked twenty metres away were enough to ward away the dark – but not the memory of what Drake had seen in his dreams.

'I saw something,' he said. 'Something that didn't feel like it belonged in my head.'

'We are all of us susceptible to the balance in the ether,' Noemi said. 'The soothsayers and prophets at Haven have shared their visions of the world to come, should the Alliance be left unopposed to carry out its work. Perhaps you glimpsed something of the same.'

'What I saw . . .' Drake shook his head. The finer details of his dream – nightmare – were already fading, as was the way of most dreams, but he recalled enough to know there was trouble ahead. 'Let's just say I'm not sure what the hell is going on.'

Tristan laughed. 'You only just figured that out?'

'There's more,' Drake insisted. *How can I explain the spire, or the . . . presence at the top of it?* 'But let's get out of here, eh? Somewhere . . . heh . . . somewhere safe.'

The stairs up to the jet were deployed, and a small square of red carpet, bearing the crest of *SkyWest Airlines*, had been laid out on the ground. Takeo stood on guard at the base of the stairs as Noemi boarded, followed swiftly by Drake, Irene, and Tristan.

The jet wasn't big, but what it lacked in size – it only seated about eight – it made up for in luxury. Drake had flown little in his life, but he knew most commercial airliners didn't offer their passengers such comforts as reclining leather seats, stocked kitchens, widescreen televisions, and video game consoles – save, perhaps, in first class.

Drake marvelled at how quickly his fortune could change. Sure, he was being hunted by men and monsters, his arm had turned to dark crystal, and the Alliance had his mother under their 'care', but right now he had video games and fizzy pop.

Given the ups and downs – mostly downs – of the past two years, he took time to appreciate the small things whenever he could.

More importantly, he was making progress towards home.

'Ready for departure,' said one of the few grown-ups Drake had met recently that either didn't know him or didn't want to slap him in handcuffs. He was dressed in black trousers and a white shirt, with three of those yellow stripes pilots wore on their shoulders, and he sported a scruffy beard that made him look a touch older than he probably was. Drake put him in his mid-twenties.

'Thank you, Toby,' Noemi said as she took a seat on the left-hand side of the plane down the front, near the small kitchen, which followed the single aisle to the cockpit. 'Could you source fuel?'

'Negative,' Toby said. 'Not without the Alliance knowing about it. They own this airport. We'll have to land somewhere privately owned on the way. Grace suggested the airstrip just outside of Niagara Falls, on the Canadian side. Only about ninety minutes away.'

Noemi looked troubled. 'Very well.'

'How long is the flight to London?' Drake asked, letting the Japanese girl know he hadn't forgotten.

Toby blinked and shook his head. 'Flight time to Tokyo, after we refuel, is thirteen hours, give or take half an hour for the weather.'

Takeo stomped up the stairs, ducking his head to squeeze onto the plane. He retracted the stairs and pulled the door closed, sealing them all aboard. 'We cannot afford a detour to London,' he said, with a certain edge to his voice Drake had heard before – from the bullies and guards in the Alliance prisons.

'What are you going to do?' Noemi asked. 'Are you and your friends going to abandon this plane and spend the next few days running around this small town, hiding from the Alliance and getting absolutely nowhere?' She smiled. 'This is better. We can talk about your reasons for wanting to go to London once we're away from here.'

Drake felt a shiver run down his crystal arm, and he clenched his fist to stop whatever was about to happen. His palm burnt as if he was holding his hand over an open flame. As he took measured, controlled breaths, the heat subsided. *What the hell was that?*

'What do you think, guys?' he asked Irene and Tristan. They had taken seats together on the opposite side of the aisle to Noemi, while Drake stood at the edge of the kitchen, overlooking the cabin.

'I think you should buckle up,' Tristan said. 'Will, what were the odds of an opportunity like this one? We might actually get away!'

Irene tightened her seat belt and shrugged. 'Better than the cold and trying to cross on the ferry, isn't it?'

Drake cursed and glared at Noemi and Takeo. 'Fine. But don't think for a moment you're locking me away in this compound of yours in Japan.'

'Haven is a safe place, William Drake. Secure.'

Drake took a seat and snapped his seat belt into place with a grunt. 'Ask the Alliance what happens when they put me in secure places, Noemi. I won't be caged – just you remember that.'

Chapter Nine

The Fine Balance

The plane departed Argentia without incident, for which Drake was supremely grateful. Images of attack helicopters and supercharged soldiers wrenching their plane from the sky during take-off had settled in his mind as soon as the engines whirred to life. For a moment, he'd been certain the Alliance would blow them out of the sky.

But as they climbed through ten thousand feet, according to the display on the screen in front of him, he allowed himself to relax as his ears popped from the change in pressure.

Sitting by himself near the rear of the plane in a wide, comfortable leather chair that had a drinks cabinet built into the arm, Drake helped himself to another bottle of fizzy cola, pouring it into a glass tumbler. He was tempted to pour one of the mini bottles of vodka or scotch into his drink, but his one and only real experience with alcohol over two years ago, just before he burnt down Alliance warehouses and landed in his first prison, made him think better of it. Drinking a cheap 'champagne', two quid a bottle, in the park with his mates and going on the merry-go-round had resulted in a dizzy kind of vomiting in the sandpit.

Drake snorted at the memory. He missed his old mates, Gaz and Jordan and Owen. He wondered, as he sipped his soda and sighed, what they thought of all the stories about him on the news. *The terrorist William Drake*.

'Using fear to control people . . .' Drake muttered. 'Rule one in the Alliance playbook.'

He finished his drink and removed the leather glove from his left hand. He stared at the dark crystal and tried to swallow his fear. He tapped his fingers against the arm of the chair, striking delicate chimes from the crystal digits . . . and igniting a few sparks of blue light from deep within his palm. With his good hand, Drake ran his soft fingers over the hard crystal, feeling for imperfections or defects.

The hand was as smooth as polished glass, as cold as the Rig in winter, and he couldn't feel anything. He tickled the back of his crystal hand and felt nothing. He clenched and unclenched his fist and got no sensation in return. The limb still worked like a limb, but for all he could feel, someone might as well have lopped the whole arm away at his shoulder.

'You'd do best to keep that a secret at Haven,' Noemi said, claiming the seat next to him and pulling her legs up under her. She leant in close, and Drake caught a scent of something like pear and blackberries that made him think of Christmas morning, of all things. 'For as long as you can, at least. There will be many who resent your inclusion within the academy, as well as your strength. The Path of Yūgen is a subtle discipline, a devotion to something close to the divine. We're supposed to worship the power of the gods and accept a small boon of that power – not possess an ocean of it.'

Drake slipped his leather glove back on and pulled his sleeve down over his wrist, concealing his crystal limb. 'I felt something,' he said. 'Well, I had a dream and . . . I've no other word for it, Noemi, but it felt *alien*. Not at all how I imagined a god would feel.'

'We sometimes can feel a . . . presence,' Noemi said, hugging her legs and smiling fondly. 'From the Silver Tree. A source of warmth and kindness buried within its heart. Members of Haven have spent decades in quiet contemplation, hoping to converse with the force within the tree.'

'Yeah, I didn't feel that, but I kind of . . . heard something laughing,' Drake said. 'When I dozed off in the car back there. But the one in the ocean, the creature under the Rig, it's pissed off and *screaming*. No warmth. No kindness. I think I annoyed it when I dropped a supertanker on it.' Drake shivered and scratched at the back of his neck. 'Noemi, whatever's down there in the crystal . . . it's not our friend.'

She nodded and released his hands. 'This we have known for many centuries. There is a balance to the world, Drake, and the creature buried in the cold waters of the Arctic Ocean violates that balance. The scales tip towards darkness.'

Drake licked his lips. 'OK . . . is this what they teach you at Haven? Blimey. Don't take this the wrong way, but I'm getting a rather strong cult vibe from you at the moment.'

Noemi ignored him. 'For centuries it has slept undisturbed, menacing but silent, and then the Alliance started *drilling*. Worse, they started experimenting with its essence, forcing rapid change in you and the other inmates that should've happened over time. The creature in the crystal has awoken.' She tapped the hilt of her sword, which poked out into the aisle in its sheath. 'And it has had centuries to grow old in its hate. We must be ready.'

'The Alliance said the Crystal-X was a meteorite that crashed to earth a long time ago. At least, that was the leading theory I heard from a man named Doctor Elias.' Drake found he didn't care so much that Elias had drowned below the Rig. The man had been experimenting on kids and disposing of failed experiments using mutant sharks.

They're not going to get away with what they did to Doctor Lambros, Drake thought, not for the first time and not for the last.

Noemi shrugged. 'Perhaps, but I think it is something more. Something . . .'

'Divine?' Drake offered.

Noemi smiled.

'How old are you, Noemi?'

'I am seventeen,' she said.

'Same as Tristan. And how long have you had, you know, magic powers?'

'I have been cultivating my gift for seven years.'

Drake bit his lip and flicked the tassels on his hat over his shoulder. 'Does it ever . . . overwhelm you? Or, like, do things you don't want it to or . . . give you headaches? Stop you sleeping? I'm too new to this to know what's normal.'

'Balance is normal,' Noemi said. 'Whether you're gifted with just one flower or exposed to an ocean of Yūgen, the balance must be upheld.'

'You keep saying that,' Drake said, trying to keep the edge of desperation from his voice. 'But I don't get it.'

Noemi nodded, as if she'd expected as much. 'It's not something you "get", so much as something that finds you, in time.'

'I'm worried I don't have time. I absorbed a *helluva* lot of the Crystal-X, Noemi.'

'How do you use your gift?' she asked.

'What, like, for good or evil?' Drake chuckled.

'No, not quite, although we'll talk more on morality in a moment. How do you physically access the power and impose your will upon the world?'

Drake was already shaking his head before she finished speaking. 'Wish I knew. I really do. I've only been at this two weeks. The things I did on the Rig to escape, healing myself, and what we've done since . . . it kind of just *happens*. I spent two weeks in the forest tinkering with it, and I learnt how to do some simple tricks, like start fires, but sometimes I don't even notice the power happening until my hands are moving and blue fire is spewing from my fingers.'

Noemi nodded again. 'Understand, William Drake, my studies have afforded only a surface grasp of the Path. I often feel as if I am stumbling in the dark myself, but the balance is there to guide us. A handrail in the dark, if you will. Your subconscious mind, the part of you that reacts quicker than thought, understands the balance. Even if your surface mind does not. Which is why, in all things, you must ground the balance in morality. A morality you *believe* in.'

Drake rubbed at his temple, trying to keep up with what Noemi was saying. Her soft accent and warm voice were distracting. 'Good and evil, then? You're saying, what, that it all depends on what I'm using the magic for?'

'"Magic" is an ugly word to describe Yūgen,' Noemi said. 'One that suffices, I suppose, but think of it more as a power source. You said you'd seen your fair share of people going mad from being exposed to the Alliance's source of Crystal-X. Who were they?'

Drake shrugged. 'Kids on the Rig – prisoners the Alliance had sent to the "inescapable" prison.' A slow smile spread across his face. 'They're going to have to build one on the moon to stop me.'

'Do not give them ideas. So these kids on the Rig had committed crimes?' Noemi asked. 'And not just any crimes, yes? Murderers? Rapists?'

'Not all of them,' Drake said and grimaced. 'Irene had her reasons, and Tristan . . . Tristan made a mistake. But yeah, a great lot of them were sent to the Rig because they were the worst of the worst. There was this one nasty piece of work, Alan Grey. I heard he killed people for fun with chains. That he liked to peel skin off people while . . . while they were alive. He was a messed-up kid.'

'And what happened to him?'

Drake's mind flashed back to the *Titan*, to his fight with Grey as the ship flooded and began to sink below the freezing waters of the Arctic Ocean. Drake had tried to save him, in the end, but Grey hadn't wanted to be saved.

'The Alliance gave him a lot of Crystal-X, and it drove him batshit insane. Powerful, too. He could leap between the platforms. Almost fly . . .' Drake shook his head and chuckled.

'Damn, he was a jerk. Are you saying because of who he was, a murderer, the Crystal-X caused him to go insane? That's why the Alliance was having trouble – because their test subjects were, what, evil?' He clicked his fingers. 'Is that the balance you're talking about?'

Noemi shook her head. 'No, you're not seeing the whole picture, William Drake.'

'Just Drake,' he said. 'So help me see it, then. What am I missing? Grey was a bad guy, so the crystal just made him worse?'

'Alan Grey had as much chance as you of maintaining the balance.' Noemi raised her hands and tapped her crystal thumb and index finger together. 'It's not about good and evil – there is no good and evil.'

Drake nodded along and sighed. 'You've lost me.'

Noemi lunged forward and grasped the sides of Drake's head. Her grip was firm, and she held her eyes on his. 'What I'm about to tell you is something you must think about, if you're to have any hope of maintaining your mind and your sanity, Drake. Fear will not save you. In this, hope and courage are for fools. I don't believe it dramatic to say a great many lives, including my own, may rely on your understanding of the balance. Do you hear me?'

'I . . . yes.'

'Say it.'

'Noemi, I hear you.'

She relaxed her grip. 'Then listen well. To find the balance, to *preserve* the balance, you must see the good in that which is evil . . . and the evil in that which is good. No one person is wholly good or, whatever you may think of yourself or people like Alan Grey, wholly evil. The balance exists between good and evil, because those two states are flawed ideals, never truly reflected in reality.'

Drake took her wrists and gently removed her hands from the sides of his head. 'So the balance is the middle ground?'

'No.' Noemi grinned. 'And yes.'

'You enjoy being cryptic, don't you?'

'We've spoken with clarity, Drake.' She glanced at his crystal arm and grinned. 'If you've the wit to see it. You won't find true balance if I'm holding your hand along the Path.'

About an hour into the flight, Irene went and sat next to Drake. He was hunched over in his seat, his head in his hands, mumbling to himself about something.

She tried to make herself a comforting presence for a few minutes, not saying anything, but glad that she was near if he wanted to talk. In all her life, Irene had never met anyone quite like Will Drake. He was clever and knew it, but more than that he was kind when he had every reason not to be. The men in Irene's life had always been the opposite, selfish and cruel.

After about five minutes, Drake let go of his head and gave her a forced smile. 'Hello, Irene.'

'Hello, Will. What are you doing on your own back here? We've got cookies and TV up the front.'

'Just thinking about things,' he said. 'What I said back in the car, by the way, about you coming with me to London . . . I'm sorry I just assumed you'd be coming along. I know we haven't talked about it, but you know I need you, right?'

Irene nodded slowly. She had held some vague idea about travelling to Moraine Lake, in Alberta, but this was more important. She wanted to help Drake. 'It's not as if I've got anywhere else to go . . . but I know. You don't think you could heal your mother by yourself?'

Drake shook his head. 'Look at what I've done so far, Irene. I've been able to heal myself – not so sure how, as it just kind of happens – but everything else I've done with this blasted power has either melted stuff or blown it up. I don't even know if it's possible, healing my mum of her cancer, but if anyone can do it . . .'

Irene swallowed and felt a flutter of nerves, butterflies, take flight in her stomach. 'Something like what your mum has . . . cancer? Will, I wouldn't even know where to begin.'

Drake surprised her with a gentle smile. 'I know. I worry about that a bit, but I think I know you well enough now to know you'll try your best.'

'Do you?' Irene leant in close, so their arms brushed together – hers against his crystal limb – and kicked his boot with her sneaker. 'You said something, back on that train when the soldiers attacked, that confused me.'

'What?'

'You said "follow the web", or something like that.' Irene glanced past Drake and out the small window, down at the lights of some town far below. 'What does that mean?'

Drake stared at her, and his expression softened. 'It's nothing, really. Just something I tell myself.'

'Oh?'

'Sounds embarrassing, saying it out loud,' he said. Irene poked her tongue out at him. 'Oh, whatever. Every time I've escaped from one of the Alliance's prisons, the plan I make in my head, I always see it as like . . . like a spider's web, you know? At the centre is the goal – to escape or whatever – and there's, like, dozens of ways to get there. It's what I tell myself, when they put walls or barbed wire in my way.'

'Or strand you on an oil rig.'

'That one almost had me.' Drake ran the fingers of his good right hand in slow circles on Irene's palm. She suppressed a shiver and a smile, but pleasant goosebumps ran up her arm. 'Anyway, follow the web. I need to follow it all the way back to London. That's the goal, the prize at the heart of the web. Get back to my mum before it's too late. And now I've got a way to save her, Irene.'

Irene took a deep breath. 'You've got me.'

'Yes. I've got you. With your knack for healing, I think we've got a chance.'

Irene found herself thinking that she wanted to go with him, that she'd believe him if he told her to jump out of this plane without a parachute and that everything would somehow work out for the best. *He must be so worried . . . but he hides it so well*. 'What about after?'

'After?'

'After London? You told Noemi you'd go to Japan, to her secret school or wherever she thinks you need to go. Doesn't that sound absurd?'

Drake shrugged. 'I think we're going to have to head there first, but I'll make them take me on to London from there. So long as you and Tristan want me around, I'm sticking with you two. That's a promise. But if she can really give us somewhere away from the Alliance . . . somewhere *safe*? Somewhere I can relax and figure out this crystal nonsense. Irene, that sounds too good to pass up.'

Irene agreed.

Chapter Ten

Skeleton Man Has a Plan

'We're about ten minutes outside of Niagara,' a female voice chimed in the cabin. Drake guessed it belonged to the other pilot, some woman named Grace. 'About to begin our descent. No chatter on the ground to indicate the Alliance know we're up here.'

Drake finished a bag of crisps and watched the end of some old sitcom from the turn of the century with Irene and Tristan. He licked the salt from his lips and took his seat again at the back as they made their descent. The lights on the ground grew closer, bands of twinkling streetlamps and houses, running like arteries across the land.

Niagara Falls, he thought. *Never thought I'd be seeing that.* He couldn't shake the irksome feeling that London kept getting further away, as Japan – kilometre by kilometre – grew closer. *It's not a prison*, he reminded himself. *At least, Noemi says as much. But once they have you, will they be so eager to let you go?*

'Will they be able to stop me . . . ?'

He leant over in his chair and stared at the top of Noemi's head, her smooth dark hair trailing over one shoulder in a loose ponytail. He wanted to trust her, he really did, but for all he knew they were about to land at an Alliance military base. That seemed a touch far-fetched, but he'd put nothing past Lucien Whitmore. Not even a cute, magical, sometimes invisible, ninja girl.

'Something coming up alongside us,' Toby said through the intercom. 'It looks like a . . . oh shit – it's an Alliance Seahawk!'

Drake pressed his face against the window and saw the chopper keeping level with the plane as they descended to only a few hundred feet above the ground. They must have still been shooting through the air at hundreds of kilometres an hour. Skeleton Man, that wasted creature with pale skin, leant out of the chopper and grinned at Drake. He should have been blown away, swept into the jet stream, but the trails of air seemed to *bend* around him, as if he were protected by an invisible shield. It looked surreal – and horrifying.

Bastard stole my cool shield move, Drake thought.

Skeleton Man's hand shone with a sphere of rippling yellow energy.

'Oh dear,' Drake muttered, half a second before a beam of raw light exploded from the chopper and shot into the plane. '*Hold on!*'

The entire cockpit of the plane – and the two pilots – disintegrated in a flash of heat and blinding energy. The rest of the cabin was left exposed to the elements, cool air, and wisps of low cloud. Drake heard Irene scream, and his eyes bulged as what remained of the plane fell forward into a spiral, the force pressing him back into his seat. Through the hole where the cockpit had been, lights spun dizzyingly round and round.

Drake gripped the seat in front of him. Raw fear squirmed in his gut. The front few metres of the plane, including half the kitchen, had been sheered away as cleanly as if piano wire had been pulled through an apple. The plane was going to crash.

No . . .

'No!'

Fierce fire burnt down Drake's arm and *incinerated* the leather glove concealing his crystal hand. Glittering blue and white sparks burst from his fingers, twisting into tentacles of power that shot through the plane. The swirling energy coalesced as it left the plane. His stomach doing backflips, Drake watched, amazed, as a shining crystal *bird* emerged from within the furnace of power. With a great screech – as of a hawk or an eagle – the bird grew until it eclipsed the view of the ground. A massive wingspan steadied the bird and sharp claws dug into the ruined fuselage of the falling plane. *Well, better than a damn spider.* Crystal talons punched through the casing of the aircraft as if it were nothing more than a tin of soup.

Close to the ground now, Drake saw a roaring torrent of white water cascading over a cliff face fifty metres above the river in the gorge below. *Niagara Falls!*

With another screech, the crystal bird *wrenched* the plane upwards, and Drake's head spun as they cleared the top of the falls. Freezing spray stung his skin like tiny pebbles. The talons of the bird cut clean through the roof, and the crystal creature lost its grip on the broken and battered fuselage. Still carrying a fair bit of speed, the plane dropped into the river that fed the monumental falls.

Cold water surged into the cabin as Drake was thrown forward from the impact, his seat belt digging painfully into his waist. The abrupt stop disorientated him for a moment, but only a moment. He unclipped his belt and fell into the aisle, cool water already a quarter of a metre deep and rising as the lights in the cabin flickered on and off.

Of Noemi and Takeo he couldn't see a thing, but Drake headed towards the front of the plane for Irene and Tristan. He found Tristan treading water, swimming against the influx from the front of the plane, the backpack slung over his shoulder as he made his escape out into the river. Irene was still in her seat!

A mask of blood covered her face, and her head lolled against her shoulder. Drake pulled himself into Tristan's chair and grasped Irene's shoulders. '*Irene!*'

The water had risen to seat level now, and Drake splashed Irene's face with a cold handful. Some of the blood washed away, quickly replaced from a deep, nasty gash over her left eye, but she coughed and gasped from the cold.

Drake breathed a heavy sigh of relief as she looked around, disorientated and confused.

Irene saw him, smiled, and then grasped the side of her head in pain. 'What . . . Will?'

'I conjured some sort of crystal bird,' he said. 'Big old bird that caught us before we crashed. All magical and what not. Buggered if I know how. Hang on.'

Drake unclasped her seat belt as the water surged over the leather seats and they started to float. The cabin was under a metre of water now, and what remained of the kitchen plunged towards the bottom of the river. It looked as if Tristan had made it out. In the poor light, Drake didn't know if Noemi and Takeo had done the same, but their seats were empty. He looped his arm under Irene's and pulled her against the flood.

The fuselage struck the bottom of the river, and a rush of bubbles from the rear of the aircraft surged forward, shooting him and Irene out of the plane and into the river proper. He kept a firm grasp around Irene as the current swept them back along the length of the plane.

The falls! Drake's heart seized with fear. He'd have no chance to help Noemi or Takeo if they were still in the plane. He and Irene were about to plummet to their deaths.

The current forced them along the surface, and Drake gasped air as the weight of his crystal arm – a weight he didn't feel in the limb itself – tried to pull him back under. Irene grabbed the scruff of his collar and kept him afloat. Swept along the river, Drake heard the falls roaring somewhere ahead in the darkness.

'Will!' Irene called. 'Look!'

She began paddling, large strokes with her free arm, and Drake saw they were close to the shoreline – a series of rocky outcrops and dry land. Irene's strokes pulled them closer, riding the current, until Drake's feet scraped along the bottom of the river as the depth disappeared.

Drake and Irene pulled each other into the shore, gasping and soaked. Warm drops of Irene's blood struck the back of Drake's good hand as they clawed over the rocks, tearing their clothes and nicking their skin.

'The others . . .' Irene managed. She squeezed her eyes together in pain and touched the side of her head. 'Is it bad?'

'You're bleeding,' Drake said, shivering. 'Can you heal –'

'Guys!' Tristan called. He ran along the shoreline to them, up and over the rocks, looking as cold as Drake felt. 'Are you OK? I got swept out, I-I couldn't –'

'What the hell happened?' Irene asked. 'The front of the plane just . . . disappeared. Those poor pilots.'

'We were attacked,' Drake said, as the whirring blades of a chopper cut through the air. 'Three guesses who by . . .'

The Alliance helicopter, sleek and black against a cloudy sky, flew up over Niagara Falls, biting through mist and spray. A wide searchlight on its underside soon picked up the three bedraggled figures on the rocky shore.

'What do we do?' Tristan asked.

Drake got to his feet and glared up at the chopper. 'We're not running from this one,' he said. 'They want this fight so bad, they're going to get it.'

'My head hurts . . .' Tears cut tracks through the blood on Irene's cheeks. Tristan knelt down next to her as Drake stepped away.

'Look after her,' he told Tristan and stuck his middle finger up at the pilot of the chopper. He made sure the searchlight had a good look at his face as he led the chopper away from his friends, further down the shoreline towards the edge of the falls. *Come on, you bastards.*

Drake moved his crystal hand in slow circles. Spears of pure, sharp crystal – long icicles of hard glass an inch thick – formed in the air below his spinning hand. He raised his arm, and the spears moved above his head, floating on the air. Four spears, sparkling blue, spun around his head in a fierce halo.

He let whoever was on the chopper get a good look at the cruel crystal and then hurled his arm forward, as if throwing a javelin. The spears shot through the air and buried themselves in the guts of the chopper. One caught the spinning blades and exploded in a burst of blue fire. The chopper swerved as the pilot tried to recover, and twisted metal rained down over the falls.

Two down in one day, Drake thought grimly.

As the chopper spiralled out of control over the gorge fed by the falls, a figure appeared on the edge of the cabin space and *leapt* from the cabin straight towards Drake.

The figure landed on his haunches, crouched like a tiger ready to strike, on the small spit of shoreline above the falls. Drake stumbled back, heading over a series of partially submerged rocks that ran along the edge of the cascade. The surge of foam and the roar of hundreds of thousands of litres of water cascading into the gorge was near deafening. The power in the falls shook Drake to his bones.

He came to the last plateau of wet stone – nowhere to run but over the edge of the falls – and turned back to face the man who had jumped from the chopper.

'What's the matter, Drake?' Skeleton Man snarled. 'Don't you recognise me?'

He stood only a handful of metres away, his elongated arms and legs of pale, wasted flesh hanging like dead branches. When he and Drake had faced off a few hours ago, it had been at some distance. At the time Drake had thought some trick of the light had given the man the appearance of black eyes. But no . . . as close as they were now, Drake saw he had not been tricked by the light. Skeleton Man blinked, and crimson stars flared within the depths of his demonic eyes.

'Should I recognise you?' Drake asked.

'Oh, we're old friends.' Skeleton Man's voice was like rusty nails scraped against a chalkboard. He lunged, thin arms extended, and nothing but mad fire in his eyes.

Drake took a step back – the heel of his boot stood on open air above the falls – and instinctively raised his crystal arm. Skeleton Man came to an abrupt stop, caught by an invisible shield of power, his wasted outreached hands a few centimetres away from Drake's throat. His fingernails were sharp splinters the colour of old driftwood.

Skeleton Man gnashed yellow teeth against split lips as he struggled against the unseen barrier keeping them apart. Drake felt him *pushing* against the shield, clawing forward millimetre by millimetre. He tensed his crystal arm and threw all the strength he could muster – imposing his will on the awesome power that had seeped into his mind on the *Titan* – against Skeleton Man.

And it wasn't enough.

Skeleton Man's fingernails drew thin lines of blood along Drake's neck. He grasped Drake's throat and pulled them both over the edge of the falls with a cry of mad triumph.

Drake kicked away from Skeleton Man's clawing grip, drawing a thin scratch down his face. The falls battered him like a ragdoll and forced him farther away from the monster.

Drake fell, and there was nothing he could do about it.

This is it . . . I won't survive this. Drake didn't want to die. His mind flashed to Irene, bleeding and scared up on the shoreline. *I'm so sorry.* And then he thought of his mother all alone in London, never knowing what had happened. He'd promised her he was coming home.

The churning waters at the base of the falls grew bigger and bigger, and Drake closed his eyes against the impact.

He had time to take a deep breath and –

The fall came to a stop in a blaze of bright light and an echoing screech. Something grasped Drake's crystal arm, and he was pulled *along* the falls, through mists and freezing rain, held in the talons of a glowing blue eagle. The bird that he had conjured, somehow, during the plane crash had him in its grasp. The shining wings rang with the high chime of glass against glass and soon Drake soared above the falls again. Without needing to be told, the eagle carried him back over to the rocky shore and deposited him near his friends.

As he landed, the glowing magic or whatever the hell it was of the bird dispersed into a thousand falling sparks that seemed to get sucked into his crystal arm. A fly buzzed around his ear, and he swatted it away.

'*Irene*!' Drake shouted. Noemi and Takeo, just as drenched from the crash into the river as the rest of them, stood next to Tristan.

'Will,' Tristan said. 'Your eyes –'

'Stand back!' Takeo roared, and he drew his pistol from the holster at his waist. 'He's taken by the madness!'

Noemi unsheathed her katana and set herself between Drake and his friends. Drake scoffed, flicked his hand, and knocked her aside, as if he'd pushed her on the back. In a single movement she danced with the blow, spinning on one foot as gracefully as a leaf on the wind, and brought her blade to bear against his throat.

'What are you doing?' Drake asked, feeling cool steel against his skin. Irene eyed him as if seeing a monster.

'Your eyes, William Drake,' Noemi said, 'are as red as blood.'

Over the worry he felt for his friends, Drake heard a buzzing in his ears, which increased in volume and rattled around his head like . . . *Like the laughter of that creature from my dream*.

Overwhelming fatigue washed over Drake, and he fell to his knees, gripping the sides of his head. 'Make it stop . . .' he muttered. In the dark crystal of his arm, he saw his eyes reflected back at him. Two points of crimson light, laughing at the world. '*Make it stop!*'

An inferno quashed his thoughts in waterfalls of blinding pain – flowing faster than the Niagara River – and he fell on his back. What had Noemi told him would prevent this? *Balance* . . . Drake whimpered and gazed up at the night sky, strewn with grey clouds like enormous cathedrals lit with ethereal moonlight, as his thoughts descended into bands of red fire.

Irene managed to sit up as Drake fell, one hand pressed to the wound on her head gushing blood into her eye, and tried to crawl over to him.

'Irene,' Tristan said, loud enough to fight the thunderous falls. 'You're bleeding a lot. Just – just stay still . . .'

Irene cursed and felt the familiar bubble of power flowing through her arms. She didn't concentrate on what she was doing, and a surge of energy from the palm against her forehead knocked her back like a blow from a hammer. She saw stars – more stars – and felt the wound stitching itself back together, fusing the skin above her left eye and pulling at her eyebrow.

The power sent the world spinning again, but through her right eye – the one not slick with blood – she saw Noemi approach Drake. He was writhing on the ground, mad light flickering within his eyes. She hoped that meant he was fighting the madness. Noemi knelt next to him.

'Takeo, hold his shoulders,' she said.

'Don't hurt him!' Irene managed to blurt out. The ache pounding behind her eyes nearly blinded her. She tried to sit up again and couldn't manage it. 'Don't you dare! Tristan, don't let them –'

Noemi cast Irene a quick glance as Takeo held Drake down, stopping his thrashing. A line of blue light crossed her lips, as if she'd applied electric blue lipstick. The Japanese girl leant in close next to Drake and whispered in his ear.

After a long moment Drake seemed to relax. Noemi put her face over his and kissed him with her glowing blue lips. Drake bucked, as if he'd been zapped with one of those batons carried by the guards on the Rig, and the red light in his eyes flickered and died. He sighed in relief, and Noemi fell back, smiling.

She kissed him.

Irene felt some of her strength returning. She grasped Tristan's arm and pulled herself up into a sitting position. 'What did you do?'

Noemi stood and gave Drake space. Her face was pinched in pain and she held her stomach as she rose. Drake coughed and sat up.

Irene felt such relief when she saw his eyes. Brown and normal, if a little bloodshot. She moved in close next to him.

'Are you OK?' he rasped.

'Am *I* OK?' Irene swatted his knee with a hand covered in blood. 'You stupid idiot! You went over the falls and . . . and . . . I need to wash my hands.'

Irene crawled over to the water's edge and dipped her hands in the fast current, washing away the blood. She still felt a touch dizzy, but at least the world had stopped tumbling around. She leant close to the water, splashed her face, and cleaned her hair of blood as best she could. In doing so, she felt a bump above her left eye – where her wound had been. Irene thought for a moment that it was a scab on the wound, but it didn't hurt when she rubbed at it. She had no chance of seeing her reflection in the dark, swift-moving water, but it felt as if a line of scar tissue crossed her forehead, through her eyebrow and down to the corner of her eye.

What happened? Did I . . . did I heal it wrong?

'Irene?' Drake asked. 'What's the matter?'

'Nothing,' she said quickly. She brushed her wet hair down over the left side of her face, to hide the damage until she could get a proper look at it herself. 'I'm fine.'

'We need to move,' Tristan said as Irene turned away from the water and back to her companions. 'What now?'

Takeo and Noemi exchanged a troubled look, and the large boy stroked his chin. 'We need transport,' he said. 'Come – we must get away from here and find a vehicle.'

Drake struggled to his feet, and Irene got her shoulder under his arm to help him up.

'What about that . . . that *thing*?' she asked, running her hand over her hair and making sure the lumpy scar tissue above her eye stayed hidden. *Surely it's not that bad . . .* 'The creature that pulled you over the falls?'

'Skeleton Man,' Drake said, slapping his cheek a few times. He looked so tired. 'He said we were old friends. But I think I'd remember that face.'

Chapter Eleven

On the Road Again

By the time Drake and his companions had headed upriver a bit, wading across shallow parts of the Niagara and crossing onto the proper shoreline and into the town of Buffalo, emergency services and all kinds of busy vehicles, helicopters, and news vans had descended on the site of what had become a multiple aircraft crash.

Sodden from the river and trying to look inconspicuous – not so simple when one member of the group carried a sword and another a gun – Drake's group stuck to the road running parallel to the river. Noemi walked with a limp, but Takeo and Tristan had emerged from the crash relatively unscathed. The surge of water had swept Noemi and Takeo from the aircraft as soon as they had unclipped their belts.

Now that the adrenaline from the crash and the ensuing fight had worn off, Drake was shivering from the cold and from the terrifying thrill of going over the falls. Buffalo was a few hundred miles from Newfoundland and Labrador. No snow had fallen, but the night air still had a fierce bite to it. He needed time to hang one of those fiery orbs before the cold turned nasty and his toes started falling off.

'Hang on,' Drake said. 'We're not in Canada any more, are we?'

Irene shook her head and pointed back towards the falls with her thumb. They stood on a small, grassy hill overlooking the river on one side, with the town on the other. 'We crashed in the United States. I guess we're illegal immigrants or something at the moment.'

'Not the worst crime on our list,' Tristan said.

'Damned if that list isn't getting a bit long, though.' Drake shook his head. 'We need to get out of this cold.'

'We need a car,' Takeo said.

Irene sighed. 'Warm showers and a change of clothes before anything else, surely.'

'Hot chocolate,' Tristan chimed in. 'A whole barrel of it.'

'We can't stop moving,' Drake said, in a tone that brooked no argument. 'Not even for hot chocolate. How are we going to get a car?'

Takeo cracked his knuckles and pointed down a quiet suburban street at the bottom of their hill. Old oak trees thick with green leaves lined the street, and the only sign of life was a man whistling a tune and walking a golden retriever. 'I have an affinity with machinery,' he said.

'What? You can use your power to start an engine? Is that your talent, like Noemi's invisibility?' Tristan asked.

Takeo looked at him askance. 'No, little man. My uncles in Japan are mechanics, of a kind. I will see to the vehicle.'

'We got a bag full of money here,' Tristan said. 'And don't you ninja folk have, like, credit cards shaped like throwing stars or something to access all that wealth and resources you were talking about earlier? We could just buy a car from the classifieds. Or rent one.'

'It's getting late,' Irene said. 'Where would we do that? And we're in America now. I don't know how well Canadian dollars spend here. Maybe this close to the border . . .'

'I . . . good points,' Tristan conceded. 'All in favour of stealing a car then?' He raised his hand.

Follow the web. Drake sighed and did the same.

Irene stood alone and shivered, her hair draped over her face. Drake wanted to put his arm around her and pull her close. He didn't think she would appreciate that.

Noemi clasped Takeo's shoulder. She almost had to stand on her tiptoes to reach his cheek and give him a small kiss. 'Be careful. We'll meet you on the corner just down the road, by that house with the white fence.'

Takeo nodded and swept down the hill, hiding in the shadows and moving with a great deal of stealth for someone so large.

Drake watched him go and sighed again, hoping he didn't steal some little old lady's car. 'One more for the list,' he muttered.

'Do you think the fall killed that skeleton thing?' Tristan whispered.

Drake watched Tristan, feeling uncertain. Something in his tone seemed off.

Tristan's teeth chattered in the cold air. 'The fall would have killed him, yeah.' He sounded like he was trying to convince himself.

* * *

Drake and his friends – and Noemi – were waiting behind the trees on the other side of the street from the house with the white fence when Takeo pulled up in a silver hatchback. They piled into the car and Drake was glad to be out of the cold. The engine rattled, and the driver's side window had been suspiciously shattered, but the car was moving.

'Older vehicle,' Takeo said. 'Twenty-twelve model. Less security. No Alliance wireless tracking.'

Irene huddled into the passenger seat for warmth. Drake, Noemi and Tristan were squeezed into the back – Drake in the middle, Tristan on his left and Noemi on his right. She had unclipped her katana and rested the blade across her lap. The end of the sheath rested over Drake's legs.

'Heating, please. Full blast!' Irene fiddled with some dials on the dashboard, and a burst of cool air that quickly turned hot flowed through the vents.

'Can you wind your window up, Takeo?' Drake asked. The giant boy, squished into his seat, gave him a withering look over his shoulder. 'Jokes, my friend. I got, like, seven of 'em.'

Funny guy, aren't you? We should get you a spot in the common room on Saturday nights, the voice of Marcus Brand whispered in the back of his mind. Drake flinched and ran his tongue over the spot in his mouth where he'd lost a tooth, from what he'd suffered at Brand's hands. That beating had finally given Drake the resolve he had needed to follow the web and make his escape.

Takeo kept a safe distance from the other cars on the road, and after about five minutes, the heat from the vents was enough to let Drake relax. They all sat in uncomfortable damp clothing and silence. Tristan was fiddling with his phone, which seemed to have taken a bit of water damage. He cursed and slapped the device against his palm. The drone was stuffed in the backpack at his feet, amidst the revolver, several thousand dollars of Canadian currency stuck together from the dunking in the river, and the strange blue portal crystal.

No one questioned where Takeo was taking them. For now it was just good to be away from the water.

'What was that bird thing?' Irene asked. 'It was made of the crystal, wasn't it? How did you do that, Will?'

'I've no idea,' Drake said. 'Honestly, I'm tired of saying that, but it just *happened*. Take a look at this, though.' He pulled up the sleeve covering his crystal arm and showed them all a sphere embedded above his wrist. No bigger than a marble, it shone with a calm, ethereal radiance. 'That's the eagle,' he said. 'Don't ask me how I know that, but I do. It's a part of me – I think, if I concentrate, it could come back out.'

'Not in the car, please,' Tristan said.

'That light in your arm . . . you summoned a guardian,' Noemi breathed, awed. 'Guardians are so rare that they have become legend, but they are mentioned in the storied histories of the Path of Yūgen. Our ancestors, great wielders of the power, were said to command the loyalty of such creatures.'

'You make it sound like the damn thing is alive,' Tristan whispered.

Drake gave him a serious look and shook his head. 'How do we know it's not?'

Noemi giggled – one of the few things she'd done, Drake thought, that made her seem her age. 'You are destined for greatness, William Drake.'

Drake tilted his head and gave her a stern look. 'I'm destined to be an example of what happens to the idiots that stand up to the Alliance.' That bastard Skeleton Man had certainly managed to survive. *We'll see him again . . .* 'How did they find us?' Drake asked. 'Skeleton Man derailed our train, crashed our plane, and caused me a great deal of pain. Is it . . . could he be doing it the same way you did, Noemi? However the hell you did it? You said that those who knew how to look could find me half a world away.'

'I couldn't say for certain.' Noemi grimaced and stroked the hilt of her katana. 'It is possible.'

'It's also possible that the exposure to Crystal-X,' Tristan said, 'lets him glimpse the future.'

Drake pondered that. 'Seems a bit too absurd, even given everything else that's going on.'

'You've been doing it, mate.'

'Michael . . .' Irene warned.

'What? He has been. Earlier . . . Christ, it was only earlier today. Earlier you answered a question Irene didn't even ask outside that bank. You didn't even know you were doing it.'

Drake frowned and glanced between his two friends. 'I did?'

Irene hesitated and then nodded, a curtain of her auburn hair hiding half her face as she looked over her shoulder into the back.

'Blimey.' Drake chuckled nervously. 'Kind of hope it's the first option then, eh? If the Alliance can see the future . . .' *Then there's nowhere we can hide.*

'Seers are a rare breed,' Noemi said.

'As rare as legendary guardian parrots?' Drake quipped.

She ignored him. 'And often their visions are open to vast interpretation.'

Takeo pulled onto the highway outside Buffalo and joined sparse traffic – a few trucks and caravans, given that it was heading towards midnight. A reflective green road sign that they zoomed past at a hundred kilometres an hour claimed it was 372 miles to New York.

The Big Apple.

'We're not far from New York City,' Takeo said. 'Haven maintains several safe apartments within the bounds of Manhattan we can use until we can figure out our next move. Perhaps call for reinforcements.'

'New York.' Drake chuckled and rubbed at his forehead. 'That's a poor joke, right? As much as I want to see the Statue of Liberty and eat pizza, that city is Alliance headquarters.'

'And the last place they'd expect us to run,' Noemi said. 'We could hide within the shadow of the beast.'

'Not if the beast has super-duper magic powers that can sense me wherever I am.' Drake pointed out. 'Or can see the future. Or perhaps just has a good old-fashioned network of spy cameras.'

'What else would you have us do then, William Drake?' Noemi asked.

'I don't know. Do you have, like, another jet?'

Tristan laughed, but there wasn't much humour in it.

'Not that we could access in a reasonable time frame,' Noemi said. 'And given how the last journey ended – the loss of Grace and Toby – we need to rethink our means of escape to Japan.'

'Well if it's escape you want,' Tristan rolled his eyes and waved dismissively in Drake's direction, 'you've come to the right guy.'

Chapter Twelve

Scar Tissue

Sometime after midnight, as the miles ticked idly by and Tristan dozed against Drake's shoulder, snoring softly, Takeo pulled into a twenty-four-hour service station to put some fuel in the car.

Drake had been fighting sleep himself – what little sleep he seemed capable of managing, these days – afraid of what he might see in his dreams, but as the car came to a slow stop and Takeo's door opened and closed, his eyes snapped open out of a dull doze, and he was alert again. He nudged Tristan over onto the window and turned in time to see Irene exit the car, sniffing, and stumble away from the station front lot with her shoulders slumped.

Noemi watched her go with that eternally serene look on her face. She turned to Drake and gave him a knowing glance.

'I'll go and see what's wrong, then,' he said, nudging her knee. 'Can you let me out?'

Drake's clothes had dried a bit from the crash into the river, but they were still uncomfortably damp in places. He shook his arms and rolled his head around to wake himself up, not that he could fall asleep. He felt wearied and bruised.

He caught up with Irene sitting on a swing in one of those sets of plastic play equipment found at rest stops on long highways around the world, almost as if they were planted and grew from the earth. Somewhere for the kids to play while Dad fuelled up and Mum went and got coffee to keep them going for the next hundred miles. Irene swung gently, the creak of the rusty chains echoing all the way across the small deserted service station. A pool of light from the road cast the playground almost silver.

'Hey, sweet thing,' Drake said. 'What d'you know?'

'Please go away, Will,' Irene whispered, her face hidden by her hair. She sniffed and wiped some tears from her cheeks with the back of her hand. 'I want to be alone.'

'And I want to play on the swings.' Drake sat on the swing next to Irene and kicked his legs, getting a bit of lazy swinging going. 'So what's on your mind?'

'Nothing.'

'Yeah, me too. Not a care in the world.'

Irene chuckled through her tears, and Drake planted his feet on the ground. Without leaving the swing, he pushed himself towards her, grabbed the chain on her swing, and pulled her close. She didn't fight him as he gently brushed the hair back from her face and tilted her chin up into the light from the streetlamps.

'Oh, Irene,' Drake whispered. 'Look what they've done to you.'

Irene saw the look on Drake's face and pushed him away. The chains creaked as his swing bumped them back together. Drake pushed himself aside into awkward figure-of-eights.

'I messed up,' she said. 'You don't have to look at me like that!'

Drake got his swing under control. 'Like what?'

Irene shook her head and got up. She hugged her arms around herself and fought back more tears. Irene wandered down towards where the highway crossed a small bridge, over a still river. Her wet sneakers squeaked on stone steps covered in dry and crunchy leaves. She didn't care if Drake followed her.

She was tired of running and being afraid and having to deal with the walking trouble magnet that was William Drake.

That's not fair –

Irene silenced her inner voice and sat herself down on a damp wooden bench overlooking the water. With the streetlights from the highway above shining down on the tiny river, she could see her reflection in the surface of the still water. The awful scar ran from above her eyebrow down into the corner of her left eye. It was red and bumpy, raised from her skin and, thanks to her healing, looked as if she'd had it for years. Irene thought it made her eye look droopy.

A few minutes passed before Drake came and sat down next to her.

'What took you so long?' she muttered.

'Stopped to play on the monkey bars.' He nudged her with his elbow. 'Seriously, just giving you a minute. It's not that bad, you know.'

She glared at him and brushed her hair down over the side of her face. 'It's hideous.'

'It's cool.'

'You're hideous!'

'I'm cool.'

Irene bit back a retort, even as he shuffled closer to her on the bench. She noticed he'd sat so that his real arm, not the crystal one, was next to her. *Here I am, worrying about a scar, and his entire body is being changed.*

'It's silly, I know,' she said quietly. 'But, even after everything, I've always thought I'd somehow go back to school, you know? College, even, in a few years. I'm only sixteen, but . . . but this is just another way I'll never fit in.'

Drake chuckled.

She fought more tears. 'Why are you *laughing*?'

'Because fitting in is for chumps, Irene.' He frowned. 'Sorry. I don't like that word. *Chumps*. What the hell does it mean? Doesn't matter. Why would you want to fit in?'

'Oh, sure, it's OK for you!' she said. 'You're Will Drake. You don't worry about things, you just . . . you . . .'

'Yeah, because going mad and turning to crystal isn't something to worry about?' Drake tapped her shoulder. 'I worry about my mum, about what's happening to me. Irene, I worry about you – about what you think of me.'

Irene blinked. 'What I think of you?'

He shrugged. 'I've done things,' he said. 'Some not-so-nice things to people. Mostly to not-so-nice people, I know, but that doesn't make it any better. And this crystal stuff is messing with me. I don't know what's happening, but I'm working on this balance thing that Noemi told –'

'What about Noemi?' Irene asked, hating the edge of jealousy in her voice.

'Noemi? What about Noemi?' Drake's brow furrowed. 'Huh?'

'Do you worry what she thinks of you? Well? You must have seen how she looks at you, like . . . like you're the greatest thing she's ever seen. You're "destined" for greatness. *Ooh.*'

Drake laughed. 'Irene, really? Noemi? She only wants me for my superpowers. And . . .'

'And what?'

'And, well, she's not you.' Drake released a long breath and rubbed at his eyelids with the palm of his real hand. 'She wasn't there in that elevator under the Rig, healing me when I fell, or there on the helipad when that crane snapped my leg in half. She wasn't there slipping Tristan pills that kept me breathing after Brand knocked the teeth from my skull. She wasn't on the Rig. What we have – friendship or . . . or whatever – can't be trumped by a pretty girl who looks at me like I'm Superman or something.'

Irene glared. 'You think she's pretty?'

Drake snorted and threw his arm around her, pulling her in close on that cold, lonely bench below an empty highway a long, long way from home. She rested her head in the nook below his shoulder and listened to his heartbeat.

After a long minute like that, Irene pushed off his chest and leant forward to look at her reflection in the lake again. She pulled her hair back behind her ear and revealed the bumpy scar tissue over her eye. She sighed. 'Well, no one could mistake me for pretty . . .'

Drake stood, took her hand in his, and pulled her up so they were face to face. She refused to meet his eyes. 'If that's a mistake, Irene Finlay, then I've been making it for a while now.'

He kissed her forehead, the tip of her nose, and then hesitated, his breath warm against her cool skin.

'Chump,' she whispered. Irene yanked the tassels on his stupid hat to pull his lips down against hers.

'We were just about to come looking for you two,' Tristan said. He was leaning against the car, which was parked up in one of the bays alongside the fuel station's forecourt. The drone hovered inside the car, and Tristan held one of the smart phones, obviously repaired. 'All OK?'

Noemi and Takeo stood nearby as Drake and Irene cast each other a quick look.

Irene sighed and brushed her hair back from her face. 'Something went wrong with the healing,' she said. 'And now I have this.'

Tristan was staring at Drake almost as if he were a stranger.

'What?' Drake asked. *He can't know that we kissed.* Drake looked again at the drone in the car, the phone in Tristan's hand, and thought that maybe he could know. *Surely he didn't . . .*

'Nothing,' Tristan said quickly. 'It's not that bad, Irene. It'll probably fade over time.'

Noemi inspected the scar, running her crystal fingers over Irene's forehead. 'A sloppy job,' she said, as Irene swatted her hand away.

'But, given your training, admirable under the conditions.' Noemi rolled up the sleeve of her blouse and revealed a mess of scar tissue on her elbow. 'Training accident. We are defined by our past, Irene. By scars that can be seen and even more so by scars that run deeper. Better the former than the latter, yes?'

Irene shrugged. 'I'm not so sure.'

'So what's the plan?' Drake asked. 'I'm not a fan of the New York idea.'

'I spoke to our people using Tristan's phone,' Takeo said. 'One of our safe houses near Central Park will be prepped for our arrival. Travel time to the city should be about four hours, barring any unforeseen circumstances.'

Noemi stared at Drake, and he shrugged. 'I've got nothing, Noemi. New York it is. I guess if we can make it there, we can make it anywhere.'

Chapter Thirteen

Overlooking the Park

After the Rig and the relative emptiness of St. John's and Niagara, Drake found the hustle and bustle of New York City almost overwhelming. He sat on the steps of the New York Public Library, an old building with stone pillars guarded by statues of proud lions, in the heart of Manhattan Island on the corner of Fifth Avenue and 42nd Street. A crowd of about a hundred billion people all in a hurry – scurrying through the ordered grids of streets, avenues and lanes that made up the island – paid Drake absolutely no mind.

Almost good to be ignored, he thought. *Lost in a sea of faces . . .* Once more he marvelled at the fact that only a few weeks ago he'd been a prisoner on the Rig, in the middle of the Arctic Ocean. He wouldn't call everything that had happened since escaping particularly good fortune, but he was still alive, still had a chance at reaching London and his mother, and felt pretty good for the most part – when planes weren't crashing around his ears and giant crystal eagles weren't bursting from his palms. *Bad with the good.*

Drake's small group of friends and new allies had driven through the night with only one or two rest stops, as Takeo shared driving duties with Noemi and Drake ate the greasiest food the highway had to offer, to get to the city for just after eight in the morning. Given the number of people looking for Drake, Takeo and Noemi had thought it best he hide out in the open – in the sea of faces – while they traded the stolen car for something more subtle in a less crowded part of town. Given that Irene's blouse was stained and clumps of her hair were matted with blood, she had stayed with them, as they went to exchange cars. Tristan sat next to Drake on the stone steps of the library, playing with his phone. In his ragged jumper, torn jeans, and scruffy old hat, Drake imagined he looked quite homeless.

Drake pulled his hat low over his forehead and made sure his sunglasses from that op shop in St. John's – *What was that sales girl's name?* – were firmly in place. Out here in a city of millions, would the Alliance dare attack? Hell, if Drake were to stand up right now and create a fiery pillar of electric blue crystal in the middle of the road, would the Alliance be able to stop the truth from coming out?

His crystal arm twitched with anticipation, daring him to unleash the power – a power he still didn't understand.

'How many cameras do you think we're on right now?' he asked Tristan.

Tristan grunted. 'Hundreds. Thousands. It doesn't matter. We're on the grid now.'

'How long before they spot us?'

'They already have.' Tristan held up his phone and showed Drake a screen buzzing and bursting with conflicting red, yellow and orange blurs. 'Those are the signals I can find. There'll be more I've missed. We're already marked. It's just going to take some human analyst time to sift through all the marked data and confirm what the cameras already know.' He sighed.

'World we live in, eh?'

'There is nowhere we can run to, you know. Coming to New York was as good as anywhere, I suppose. But they'll still get us in the end.'

Drake considered and then shook his head. An idea had been forming, along the drive to New York, a way to stay a step ahead of the Alliance. *If I can't hide, if I can only run until I drop or they drop me, then I need to outsmart them.* Drake pulled out his phone, a little the worse for wear, and wrote down his idea on the notebook app. *Better than saying it out loud . . . too many chances to be overheard.*

'Take a look at this and then delete it,' Drake said, handing Tristan his phone.

Drake watched Tristan's brow furrow, his eyes narrow, and then a look of worried realisation spread across his face.

'That's insane. It'll never work . . . well, probably never.' Tristan deleted the note and handed the phone back. 'Will, that's clever. But so much could go wrong. Are you sure about this?'

'We're trapped, mate, and this is the only way I can see that even gives us a shot. Like you said, they already know where we are. There's no running this time. New York just became our latest prison. I got you out of the last one, so trust me on this one.'

Tristan nodded slowly and fell silent for a long moment. 'I don't want to die, you know, or end up back in some Alliance jail. Will, what are we doing here?'

123

Drake wasn't so sure he knew, himself. For someone who didn't trust quickly, he had taken to Noemi and Takeo and what they offered a little too easily. Perhaps that was because what they offered was the only option on the table. If not for Noemi's intervention, Drake and his friends would have been icicles in the forests of Newfoundland and Labrador that morning, instead of within spitting distance of hundreds of delicious pizza slices.

'We're finding a way to escape,' he said finally. 'Business as usual, eh? I never asked, but you're coming to Japan, right?'

Tristan shrugged. 'If Irene is going, I'm going, too. I really like her.'

'Yeah, she's great.'

'*More* than like her, Will.'

Drake said nothing, thinking about the kiss he and Irene had shared back at that stop on the highway. Tristan knew about the kiss, Drake was sure of it, and he was letting Drake know that he knew.

Tristan loved Irene – had fallen in love with her on the Rig.

'Well . . .' Drake squeezed his shoulder. 'Time for all that later, after we've escaped.'

'Silly me, I thought we already had.' Tristan gestured with his phone and the hundreds of conflicting signals turned the screen a bright, pulsing red. 'Yeah, I thought we already had. But you're not wrong, this is the real prison, isn't it? Nowhere to run, nowhere to hide. Hell, we could sneak around the Rig more freely than we can around this city.'

'Have you had any chance to make sense of all those readings you recorded from that portal?' Drake said, edging the conversation away from darker topics.

Tristan shrugged. 'It's strange, but I think the drone's instruments measured the frequency of your power, or whatever. It's all numbers but when you analyse it in a data app, turn it into graphs and spreadsheets, there is a pattern. I don't know what that pattern means, but it's there. It spiked when you and Skeleton Man made that portal. It went haywire when that spider stumbled through it.'

'So, do you think I could recreate . . .' He trailed away.

A silver sedan pulled up at the intersection, and a tinted window lowered to reveal Takeo in the driver's seat. Noemi sat opposite him, and Drake glimpsed Irene in the back. He and Tristan piled into the car.

'Any problems?' Drake asked.

'Of course not,' Takeo said. 'The stolen vehicle will be cleaned, repaired, and left somewhere the authorities can find it, so they can return it to its owner. Haven always pays its debts. They'll get their car back in better condition than we found it. This vehicle will suffice to ferry us around the city.'

'So where we headed?' Drake asked.

'Central Park,' Noemi said. 'Haven has provided a penthouse overlooking the park until we can arrange safe passage and proper transport to Japan. I think you'll find it quite to your liking.'

After living in a shoebox with Tristan for the better part of half a year, Drake was willing to agree, sight unseen.

The penthouse was on the east side of Central Park, Park Avenue, and Drake struggled to recall ever seeing something so luxurious in his life. The view of New York alone . . .

seventeen floors above the city, he stood gazing out of the window. It overlooked Central Park and Fifth Avenue down towards the Empire State Building. The clear skies bathed the city in sunlight, and far below hundreds of yellow taxis and other vehicles drove the streets, oblivious to the fact that the infamous terrorist William Drake watched from above.

Drake chuckled. *I'm never going to have a normal life again.* 'Better than no life,' he muttered.

The four-bedroom, three-bathroom apartment covered the entire top floor of the building, with an open balcony, complete with a small garden and spa. They would be more than comfortable – spoilt, even. The open plan, the red brick walls, hardwood floors, impressive library and large wood-burning fireplace reminded Drake of some of the buildings in London. That old London aesthetic was offset a touch by all the modern appliances and conveniences – computers, televisions, two glass refrigerators bookending a steel island stove in the kitchen, and a great deal more.

'Can you believe this place?' Irene asked. She had curled up inside a large red spinning chair shaped like an egg, her legs tucked up underneath her. She glanced at the city, still wearing her bloodstained blouse – *What else does she have to wear?* – and seemed to be speaking as much to herself as to Drake. 'Wonder what my mum's doing today.'

'You could call her,' Drake suggested.

Irene didn't look at him as she shook her head. 'She hates me for what I did to my stepfath— to Thomas.'

Dropped a car on him . . . bastard deserved it. Drake wanted to say something comforting and reassuring but came up empty.

126

Noemi returned from inspecting the rest of the apartment with Takeo and Tristan. 'OK. This place is secure. Master Tristan has assured me of no electronic interference. What I need from you two now is for you to write down your clothing sizes. Takeo is going to go shopping.'

Drake rolled his neck and swung the tassels from his hat back over his shoulders. 'What's wrong with my clothes?'

'Well, apart from the fact you've been on the run for two weeks and are in need of a shower . . .' Noemi gestured from his boots to his hat. 'You look homeless, William Drake.'

Drake had to admit the constant abuse had stretched his woollen jumper out of shape. The cuffs were burnt and frayed, and his jeans – already torn when he'd bought them – had descended from serviceable to shabby.

'Wouldn't hurt to have a shower and a change of clothes, I suppose.' Drake took the notepad from Takeo, jotted down his belt size and a request for a few medium-sized shirts, and handed the pad to Irene. 'So how long do you think we'll be here?'

'A day or two. Three, at the most,' Noemi said. 'Despite the fact that we're in the heart of the Alliance's empire, the relative size of this city and the sheer number of people that live here works in our favour. Our people will negotiate with the Alliance, see if we can achieve safe passage. Other assets are moving into place, as well, should things turn nasty.'

Drake snorted. 'Whitmore wants me dead. That's not going to work.'

Noemi offered him a small smile. 'We have a few bargaining chips of our own, William Drake. Perhaps the Alliance, Lucien

Whitmore, will see their value. Our people will meet at their headquarters in the next day or so. Consider this apartment neutral territory until the negotiations are complete.'

'Yeah, I got a glimpse of the Alliance headquarters building from the window,' Drake said. 'You think I can go and file a customer complaint about the level of service I've been receiving?'

Tristan laughed. 'I'm sure they'd give it the attention it deserves.'

'I'm sure they'd shoot you on sight,' Noemi said.

'What are we going to do here for two or three days?' Irene asked.

Takeo took the notepad back from her and crossed his arms. 'You'll find plenty to entertain yourselves with. We need to minimise our presence as much as possible until we intend to leave, which means staying off the streets.'

Drake agreed. He was actually looking forward to a bit of a rest. Hot shower, change of clothes, sleep for a year. The idea of sleep turned his thoughts bitter. Days of fatigue weighed on his shoulders, but the best he could hope for would be a troubled doze. The Crystal-X wasn't letting him sleep. Worse, when he was allowed a few minutes, the nightmares seemed far too real. *Still, two out of three ain't bad. Hot shower and clothes.*

'Right then,' he said. 'Thank you, Noemi, and thank you, Takeo, for bringing us here. You're risking a lot, and I appreciate it. That said, I'm about to go and raid the fridge, but first I'd like to know how you're planning on getting us out of New York when the time comes – if we're allowed to leave safely.'

'We'll most likely arrange passage through the harbour and out to sea,' Takeo said. 'Once we're in international waters and away from the Alliance, we can change vessels and cross the ocean to Europe.'

'What? On a boat?' Tristan asked.

'Better than another plane . . .' Irene muttered and brushed her hair down her face, making sure it covered her scar.

Drake pulled his hat from his head and ran a hand through his hair. 'How long will that take?'

'Direct crossing can be done in six days,' Takeo said. 'Probably closer to eight.'

'A week at sea.' Drake thought of the endless water surrounding the Rig and sighed. 'I knew if we ever saw the open water again it would be too soon.'

But he had to suppress a shiver of excitement. Anywhere in Europe put him closer to London than he'd been in over a year.

Chapter Fourteen

Magic Training

Given the struggles of the past few weeks – the escape from the Rig, the better part of two weeks on the run, the derailed train, the crashed plane, and the constant worry that an Alliance attack chopper was about to shoot him in the back – Drake found it a touch hard to relax in the penthouse apartment.

He tried watching TV, he tried reading a book, he tried working out a bit in the small gym in the western corner of the apartment, but nothing could shake the nagging itch between his shoulders that the Alliance was nipping at his heels.

That's because they are, Drake, nattered a voice in his head that sounded a lot like Marcus Brand. Brand before he had been killed by the fire and Crystal-X in the hold of the *Titan*. *They already know you're in the city. Only a matter of time before you're running for your life again. Haven can't help you.*

Drake made himself a ham sandwich for lunch, because despite the well-stocked fridge, there was no blackberry jam for a jam sandwich. A grievous oversight, in his opinion, but he would forgive Haven just the once, given their current circumstances were a damn sight better than Canadian icefields.

The first morning Drake and his friends spent in that apartment – after Takeo returned with whole wardrobes of clothing suitable for all climates and circumstances, and after they had each spent a good hour under the hot water blasting from the chrome showerhead, washing away grime and more than a little blood – Tristan seemed to be the only one of them who could put himself at ease. He had set up shop with his drone and phones, and he'd plugged himself into the bank of computer terminals built into the far wall of the apartment, off the grand foyer. He was researching the data from the drone, which had collected all manner of interesting points about Drake's power. Drake took one look at the screens of scrolling numbers, felt a headache brewing, and left Tristan to it.

Irene seemed better for a shower and change of clothes, but she had quietly settled into a large beanbag in the library, a thick book on her lap and a posture that said pretty clearly 'Do Not Disturb'.

It took Drake almost half the day to realise he was *bored* and waiting for something disastrous to happen. Unable to sleep, unable to settle, he stood staring out of the window overlooking the city, his hands stuffed into the pockets of a new pair of jeans, thinking about his sleep troubles. *It was a dream, but it felt more like a memory. A memory of something that hasn't happened yet . . . ?*

Those thoughts were also giving him a headache, icing on the cake of his boredom, so when Noemi emerged from her room, barefoot and wearing a blue dress with a simple pair of black leggings – and no damned sword – Drake leapt at the chance to ask her a few of the questions that had been preying on his mind.

'Let's sit out on the balcony,' Noemi suggested. 'It's a nice day out there.'

The square terrace overlooked a few smaller buildings and uptown along the edge of Central Park. The day was warm – warmer than Canada and Niagara had been, at any rate – and there was no wind. Drake watched a game of baseball being played on one of the fields in the park far below, as Noemi unrolled an outdoor mat on a raised decking next to a set of perfectly good sun chairs, in the shade of two large potted ferns. She sat on the mat and crossed her legs.

Drake shrugged and sat down opposite her, almost falling back from the weight of his crystal arm as he struggled to cross his legs in a similar fashion. *This damn thing* . . . his arm didn't hurt from the transformation, so Drake tried not to think too much about his predicament, which he knew was about as smart as hoping a suspicious lump would go away by ignoring it, but he was willing to bet no doctor had seen his particular affliction before. *So how can I help you today, Mr. Drake? Well, Doc, I absorbed a shit-tonne of radioactive alien juice, and now my arm has hardened into pure crystal. You got a cream for that?* 'Probably not covered under Alliance Medicare anyway . . .' he muttered.

'You are concerned about what's happening to you,' Noemi said.

Drake held up his arm of dark crystal, visible thanks to his short-sleeved T-shirt. 'This is a bit of a concern to me, yeah.'

'Has the crystal progressed any further across your chest?'

Drake pressed his good hand to his chest. 'Not that I can tell. Still got veins of the stuff running towards my heart.'

'And how do you feel? Give me the first word that comes to mind.'

'Powerful,' Drake said. 'Yeah, like I could lift a train with my bare hands or . . . or tear apart an oil rig.'

Noemi bit her lip, and Drake caught a flash of worry slip through her mask of calm. She held him with her emerald green eyes, as if trying to read his mind. *What's to say she can't?* Drake kept his thoughts clear and away from how he liked her shape in that blue dress, particularly the curve of olive skin from her shoulder down her chest and towards her . . . he shook his head.

Noemi grinned. 'How do you make things happen with your power, then?'

'What do you mean?'

'You have done some fairly miraculous things in just the short time we've been acquainted. And all without the professional training and guidance students of the Path are given at Haven. I want to know how you make your gift work.'

'So far I've just wanted stuff to happen, and it has,' Drake said. He frowned and shook his head. 'Actually, no, it's more like the Crystal-X –'

'Yūgen,' Noemi corrected gently. 'If you're to follow the Path, then perception matters. Do not associate your gift with the mundane name the Alliance has given to something so incredible. Crystal-X is a brand. Yūgen is a unique way of seeing the world.'

Drake shrugged. 'Yeah, OK. Well, so far it's been more like the Yūgen has been doing what I want before I even know I

133

want it. Like the shields and that eagle guardian or whatever the hell it was.' He stared at the small white sphere glowing in the crystal of his wrist. 'It's anticipating what I want, like it knows what to do before I do.'

Noemi nodded. 'There are scholars and followers of the Path at Haven that could explain this a hundred times better than I, but what you're doing is letting the power master you – instead of the other way around. It's dangerous and will, if you don't take control, drive you mad.'

Drake rubbed at his forehead with his good hand and chuckled. 'It's keeping me awake. I've slept all of five minutes in about four days.'

'Those at Haven who . . . fail to assert control over their gift often suffer from insomnia. The descent usually takes months. However, given the amount of Yūgen you absorbed, William Drake, we may not have that long.'

'Already too late, you think?'

Noemi shook her head fiercely. 'Absolutely not. I'll have you on the right path, balanced and at peace, before the madness can claim you. I didn't come all this way and lose two friends just to have you burn yourself away.'

Drake felt a sliver of guilt that he hadn't spared much thought to Toby or Grace, Noemi's pilots, since they'd been obliterated by the Skeleton Man. Two people had died for him, to help him escape. He didn't want to think on it, just like he didn't want to think too much about his arm, or Doctor Lambros, or Aaron and the fire at Cedarwood, or his mother . . .

'I understand this is a lot to deal with,' Noemi said. 'Especially given your status as a fugitive.'

'The Alliance have got half the world after my head,' he said. 'Calling me a terrorist and making my mother worry. I swear, Noemi, if I could wipe them all out with a wave of my hand . . .' Dozens of sparks rushed down the length of his crystal arm, and Drake clenched his fist, putting a tight rein on his temper. 'Heh. Now I sound like the colour they're trying to paint me.'

'Fear,' Noemi said. 'The great manipulator. The Alliance are old hands at this game, and none more so than Lucien Whitmore. Fear and faith, two sides of the same coin that the powerful use to manipulate the weak. A patient manipulation.'

Drake considered and found he agreed. 'All this just for me.'

Noemi chuckled. 'You broke free of their chains, figuratively and literally, William Drake. You became something that the great giant itself has to fear. A player instead of a pawn. Not only have you embarrassed them, undermined their vital reputation, but you are walking proof of the true nature of the Alliance. If you live long enough, if you *survive* – well, anything is possible. You can drag the fearmongers into the light and show the world their cowardice.'

Drake grunted. 'I'm not the hero you want. At best, I'm, like, a self-employed freedom fighter, working my own hours. If Haven is looking for someone to fight the good fight and fly their banner against the Alliance . . . that's not me. I don't want that. I just want to get back to London.'

'Which is why, whether you want it or not, the chance to make a difference has fallen to you, William Drake.'

Drake scowled. 'Don't twist things around like that. You're trying to get me to believe I'm some sort of *good* guy, or something. I'm not, Noemi. After what I did in London to land in my first Alliance prison . . . I kinda deserved it. I put a police officer in the hospital. He was just doing his job, and I . . . not on purpose, but it was my fault – I cracked his skull.'

Noemi remained silent, staring into Drake's eyes.

'The hell of it is, though,' Drake said, 'I'd do it again if it meant my mum got the medicine. I'm sorry it happened, but I'd . . . I'd do it again. Even knowing the copper was going to get hurt, because family comes first. It was only ever me and my mum when I was growing up. Family comes first. Yeah. But I bet that policeman has a family, too.'

'You acted after all other avenues had been closed to you – by the Alliance – and people got hurt. This does not make you a bad person.'

'What else could I have done?' Drake asked, slamming his fist into the decking. 'It was important.'

'You owe the lawman you hurt a debt, William Drake. To him and his family.' Noemi nodded. 'Yes, one day you will have to settle your debt, earn his forgiveness and forgive yourself. Society demanded you pay this debt in the Alliance juvenile prisons, but in matters of guilt and forgiveness, the justice system has descended into corruption and cruelty. Ever since the governments of the world bent the knee to the Alliance . . . profit has replaced justice.'

'The corporation is the giant,' Drake said. 'When you say I made the giant afraid, you don't mean just people like Lucien Whitmore and Warden Storm, you're talking about the corporation itself – as if it were alive.'

Noemi shrugged. 'Isn't it? Over the last few generations, we let the giant grow – we gave control to a handful of faceless

136

men – and we're only just starting to see the amount of suffering the Alliance will cause before it is toppled. It is too late to avoid the fight to come. You, and people like you, will drag the Shadow War screaming into the light. The corporation watches us, William Drake. It listens. It touches our lives, and we offer tribute to it through paying taxes, through buying the materialistic garbage spewing from its mouth. We feed it, and it hates us. We protect it, and it strips away our freedoms.'

'It's a cancer,' Drake muttered, more than familiar with that particular disease. Cancer was the sickness eating his mother from the inside. 'Sucking the life from everything we love.'

'Yes, and cancer is alive, is it not? A malignant type of life. The Alliance is the cruelty and avarice inherent in all humanity. A seething pile of cancerous cells that have spread across the planet. Very soon, it will be too late to stop.'

The global network controlled by the Alliance was massive, incomprehensible in size. He couldn't think of one thing the Alliance didn't control in some way, shape, or form. The list of what it didn't have power over could have been written on the back of his hand in large letters. *Too late to stop.* 'So what's the solution then?'

'We have to show the world just how sick it is,' Noemi said. 'Drag the cowards kicking and screaming from their cruel towers.'

'And that's what you believe? That's what all your people in Haven believe?'

'If the Alliance is the cancer, William Drake, then Haven is the cure.'

'Tell me more about Haven, then.'

An honest smile spread across Noemi's face. 'Haven is wonderful. A secluded valley, nestled between snow-capped mountains and dotted with forests and winding rivers, old cave systems and secret paths. Buildings over two thousand years old, markets and libraries, centres for learning and study. Home to hundreds of people and families, Haven is the last bastion of privacy in the world.'

Drake let out a slow breath and scratched at the back of his neck. 'Sounds cool. Like something out of a fairy tale.'

'Haven has had centuries of Yūgen users walking through her fields and her hills, her glades and glens. Some of that intent, that power, has seeped into the earth. It is a blessed place.'

For the next few hours, as the sun slowly dipped between the long canyons of New York City and the weather turned December cold, Drake worked on a series of training exercises devised by Noemi that were supposed to help him take true control of the power in his body.

'Think of Yūgen like a muscle,' she told him. 'It is not – Yūgen is an intangible force in our minds – but perception of the force matters. So think of it as a muscle that must be exercised every day.'

'How do you exercise an intangible muscle?' Drake realised the answer on his own. 'By using it.'

'Yes.'

He practised calling his power into his hand, creating little flickering balls of light in his palm – smaller versions of the orbs that had kept him from freezing to death in Newfoundland and Labrador – and making them hover in the air, as if he were carrying a small sun. At first he could only get a few sparks of blue light to dance within the crystal of his arm, but after concentrating for a long moment, in the right mindset – *balance* – he found he had some control over whether the fire appeared or not.

'That was interesting.' He clenched his fist, snuffing out the orb. 'It didn't want to happen, at first. When I practised in the forest, learnt tricks like fireballs and spikes of hard crystal, I always had to force it.'

'So what did you do?'

'I concentrated on making it happen, sort of tapping into the ocean of power in my head . . . it's almost like a sixth sense, isn't it?'

Noemi tilted her head. 'How so?'

'I mean, activating the power, it's like . . . like, I know how to breathe, right? We all do. Breathe air in, breathe it out, but the muscles or whatever that make that happen, that let me breathe in and out – I don't know how they work, but I can still make them work.' Drake considered and then nodded. 'Yeah, and Crystal-X – sorry, Yūgen – it feels the same. I don't know how it works, but I can breathe it in and out.'

'And you can strengthen the muscle through understanding,' Noemi said. 'Very good.'

Drake grinned.

'Now make two spheres of fire, please, the size of grapes, and have them dance between your fingers.'

Drake's grin faded, and he mumbled to himself under his breath. Concentrating on his breathing, he raised his palm towards the sky – *breathe in* – and a torrent of blue sparks rushed down his arm – *breathe out* – and fell from his hand, like water boiling over the rim of a pan. Hot sparks splashed against the mat and burnt through to the decking, igniting a small but fierce blaze in the wood.

Noemi snapped her crystal fingers, and the flames flickered and died, leaving nothing but black scorch marks in the wood and the reek of burning rubber on the air.

'How did you do that?' Drake asked, as the lights in his arm faded again – all save the marble of light from the eagle.

'Long practice,' she said.

'What else can you do?'

Noemi shook her head. 'That question is considered impolite, William Drake. At Haven, one's abilities are closely guarded secrets. We are all taught basic skills, of course, but the talents we develop in secret, wandering our own Path . . . you might as well have asked to see me naked.' She relaxed and smiled. 'However, you had no way of knowing that.'

'Well, now I do.'

'Now you do.'

'Sorry,' he said. 'But I don't know how I do any of the things I do. Irene can heal, as well as kind of morph her arm and make it thinner. It's how she managed to slip the tracker off her wrist back on the Rig. I haven't seen her do anything else, but I've been just making it up as I go along. Could I do what Irene does, you think? Or make myself invisible, like you did when we first met?'

Noemi tapped her crystal fingers together, producing a dull chime, and the air around her shimmered, like heat rising from the road on a summer's day. She vanished. Drake's vision went a touch fuzzy until he blinked a few times, but Noemi didn't reappear.

'Ha!' he said, genuinely surprised. 'That's amazing. Are you still there?'

'Can you not sense me?' Her voice came from empty air and, even though he'd expected it, startled Drake.

Drake stared at the spot where she had been sitting – *where she's still sitting* – and concentrated. He squinted, trying to see through whatever quirk of power that had made her disappear, and thought he glimpsed a vague outline. *I felt her back in the forest, but now* . . .

He reached out to make sure she hadn't moved and brushed her foot on the mat. A wild shiver rushed through him. 'Oh, that's weird. Touching something that doesn't look like it's there.'

The air shimmered again, and Noemi reappeared. She hadn't moved an inch. 'The gift manifests itself in a number of ways. Some have talents towards disguise. Some find an affinity towards healing, battle enchantments, or myriad other skills.'

'So what's my skill, then?' Drake tapped his crystal fingers against his thumb. 'I'm good at, like, shooting energy bolts.'

'William Drake,' Noemi said. 'Nothing you have done has been skilful. That's what I've tried to explain from the start. What you have been doing is akin to standing in a lightning storm waving a metal rod. You are using Yūgen in a raw, untempered form. You're standing in a pool of gasoline, in the dark, and think lighting a match is the solution to your problem. This is what you need to control before it burns you away. Focus, discipline and understanding of the balance are the only things I know that can help you succeed.'

'Breathe in, breathe out,' Drake said. 'OK, I can work on that.'

Chapter Fifteen

Falling With Style

Dinner the first night in the apartment was New York City pizza from a place called Lombardi's. Drake helped himself to a slice topped with sausage, bacon and chilli flakes and, after his first bite, decided then and there he was never going to leave New York. It was approaching ten o'clock when they finished dinner, the table a mess of pizza boxes and soda cans. Both Irene and Tristan shuffled off to bed. Irene, Takeo and Noemi each had a room to themselves, while Drake was sharing with Tristan – in much more opulent conditions than they had been sharing on the Rig. Unable to sleep, he watched ten minutes of an old Spider-Man movie and found himself zoning out. At eleven o'clock, Takeo disappeared to bed, while Noemi stayed up on watch. They were going to split the guard between them, sleeping alternate shifts. At midnight, still wide awake, Drake began to think it was going to be a long night.

He went out on the balcony and practised his breathing, shivering a touch in the early-morning air. New York still hustled and bustled far below. The city that never slept seemed fitting to Drake, given his inability to rest, but although he wanted to head out and explore, he knew the Alliance would be on him fast, if they weren't already. The apartment was defensible against threats from below, but had the Alliance already tracked them here? Had the smart cameras patched together their roundabout trip from the library down on Fifth Avenue? If he was trapped here, then couldn't the Alliance just keep an eye on him from afar? *Neutral territory*, Noemi had said.

Again, a prison didn't always have to be cold concrete and steel bars. So long as he was hunted, he would never be free.

Drake practised his breathing and worried what tomorrow – given the hour, later that day – might bring.

The morning brought cornflakes for breakfast and the better part of five days awake, give or take an hour's worth of napping. Drake sat at the dining table next to the kitchen with Tristan. Noemi was sleeping after her shift standing watch. Takeo sat in the lounge, one loaded weapon at his side, and another disassembled for cleaning on the coffee table.

Even after the long night, Drake felt not even close to tired. More weary, as if he'd put in a hard but satisfying day's work – and then been told to do it all over again, and smile this time.

At what point do I have to worry this is killing me? he wondered. *Cornflakes taste different in America. Or maybe it's the milk.*

If Drake concentrated a little harder on how he was feeling, he could sense his body working overtime – pulling double, triple, quadruple shifts to keep up with the crystal transformation and long days without proper rest. *I'd bloody sleep if I could*. Working Tubes, clearing out the water pipes and worse, on the Rig had run him ragged for months, but at least he'd slept well after the work.

Irene had mumbled a sleepy good morning and brewed herself a cup of tea, and now sat out on the terrace, staring at the city. Drake finished his cornflakes and stepped out to see her. He slid the glass door closed behind him and stretched in the cool morning air. Clear skies suggested it was going to be a nice day.

'You've been quiet,' he said.

'Just been thinking.' Two sun chairs faced the spires of New York, overlooking Fifth Avenue, but Irene shuffled over and patted the space next to her, inviting Drake to share just the one.

Drake sat down, and she grasped his hand. 'Thinking?' he asked.

'About what I want to be when I grow up.'

'I'm going to work on a blackberry farm,' Drake said.

Irene giggled. 'Yeah, I remember that conversation from the Rig. Do they even have blackberry farms?'

'Of course they do,' Drake said, but he wasn't certain. He and his mother had picked them wild. 'Where do you think the jam comes from?'

'Don't they just mix Ribena with strawberries?'

'How dare you, Irene Finlay.' Drake tried to let go of her hand, but she held on tight. 'Actually, now that I think about it, I know for a fact there are blackberry farms. I went to one on a school trip in Sussex. It was next to this little river, and I pushed Harry Robb into the water because he threw a blackberry at Michelle White, who I fancied, and hit her in the eye. Saw a fox, too.' Drake nodded. 'Or were they raspberries . . . ?'

144

Irene laughed again and swatted his chest. 'How's the arm?'

'Made of crystal and magical birds,' Drake said, casting aside that topic. 'So what did you decide you wanted to be when you grow up?'

Irene shook her head. 'Doesn't matter, does it? We're either going to be on the run forever or tossed in a shallow grave.'

'Blimey, that's morbid. I'm not going to let that happen, Irene.'

'No? Why not?'

'Because I can't wait to tell my mates back in London about the hot redhead I snogged. A year older than me, too. They won't believe it unless you're there, very much alive and not on the run.'

Irene fought a smile, and Drake wanted to brush back the hair hiding half her face, but he didn't think that would go over well, especially if he did it with his crystal arm, so he did nothing.

'Still trying to get me to come to London, are you?' she asked with a kind smile. 'So subtle, Will.'

'Just tell me what you're going to be when you grow up, already.'

'I've been thinking about studying, actually.'

'Yeah?' Drake squeezed her fingers. 'Studying what?'

'You.'

'A degree in Will Drake?' He laughed. 'Take all of five minutes to complete. He broke things and *out* of things. The end.'

'Seriously,' Irene said. 'Think about it. How much longer is the Alliance going to be able to keep the Crystal-X a secret? On the Rig it was contained, nothing could get in or out, but now that you're free and making a lot of noise . . . it's only a matter of time, and the world's going to want to know all about it.'

'I'll be famous,' Drake said, rolling his eyes. 'Instead of just plain old infamous and wanted for murder.'

Irene smiled warmly. 'The truth will come out, and when it does, I want to say I was there all along. I'm going to get a notebook and keep notes on you.'

'You should talk to Tristan – he's trying to decipher all that info the drone collected. But you're assuming a lot, you know. That the Alliance won't get away with all this, that I won't die or go mad from the crystal, that the world will even care.'

Irene blinked. 'Of course they'll care.'

'From what Noemi's said, Haven has been playing with the Crystal – with Yūgen – for centuries. You'd think in that time, something would have leaked out, wouldn't you? I think people ignore or pretend not to see what frightens them.'

Irene brushed the hair back from her left eye and exposed her scar. 'Is that why you didn't tell us about your arm?'

Drake forced a chuckle. 'It scares me a little, yeah.'

Irene stared at the glowing sphere embedded in Drake's wrist. 'Can I touch it?'

Drake hesitated and then rested his crystal arm on his lap. The arm itself didn't feel heavy at all when he lifted it, but the weight on his legs was considerable. Irene touched his obsidian forearm with the tips of her fingers – gently at first, and then pressing hard enough to shift his arm.

'Can you feel that?' she asked.

Drake shook his head.

She tickled his arm, running her fingers from his elbow down to his wrist. 'Oh, it's warm near the light. Did you feel any of that?'

'I didn't.'

'I saw you make fire come out of your other hand,' Irene said. 'Why didn't that one turn to crystal?'

'One of the thousands of questions I wish I knew the answer to.'

Irene sighed. 'What does Noemi say?'

'Not to stray too close to the dark side of the Force.' Drake tapped his crystal fingers against his knee. 'I dunno. She talks almost in riddles. "Balance" this and "balance" that. Some of it makes sense. The rest just sounds like a lot of vague crap.'

'Is it helping, do you think?'

Drake took a deep breath and exhaled slowly. 'Maybe. I haven't gone mad yet, Irene.' He jerked his thumb towards the edge of the balcony. 'You see that monkey in a clown costume doing cartwheels on the railing too, right?'

She laughed and cuddled against his side, pulling his good arm around her shoulders. 'Tell me a story, Will.'

Drake considered, then shook his head. 'Sorry, can't think of anything. Not sure where to start . . .'

Irene *tsk*ed. 'So tell me how it ends then.'

He grinned. 'Infamously.'

Tristan joined them in the morning light about half an hour later, as Drake and Irene sat giggling, swapping stories from their time before the Rig. He carried a laptop and the backpack, which contained the stolen Alliance drone, the last of the Canadian cash, the blue portal crystal, and Warden Storm's heavy revolver.

'Hey, mate,' Drake said. He shuffled away from Irene, just a bit, as they had been leaning against one another. 'What's the word?'

Tristan glanced between them for a long moment, his eyes unreadable, then sat on the spare sun chair. 'I think I figured something out,' he said. 'About that portal, from the drone data. I wanted to test it.' He opened the backpack and the drone flew out, hovering just at head height. Tristan tapped a few keys on the laptop and the drone flew in a lazy circle.

'What's that then?' Irene asked.

'I've keyed the drone to you, Drake. It'll follow you. Can you . . .' He hesitated. 'Can you do something magical? Like, make one of those fire orbs that kept us alive in the forest?'

Drake shrugged, eyed the apartments and buildings further down and along the length of Central Park, and shrugged again. 'Something small, eh?'

'Sure, I just want to confirm the readings with the drone.'

Drake stood and stepped away from his friends. He rubbed his hands together, crystal against flesh, and took a deep breath. Blue sparks shivered down his arm, splitting around the marble of light in his wrist, and jumped from his fingertips in tiny arcs of lightning that blurred from bright blue to wicked red. He used his real hand to catch those arcs, creating a web of lightning strikes between his palms. The power coalesced into a sphere as the drone watched from above, taking it all in.

'That's good,' Tristan said, watching his laptop screen. 'If I've got this right, then you're using about . . . two and a quarter units of energy to do that.'

'Units of energy?' Irene asked.

Tristan nodded. 'I don't have a name for whatever it really is,' he said. 'Crystal-X, Yūgen, whatever the light and power *actually* is. But I figured out the pattern, and can monitor Will's power usage. Sort of. Kind of . . . maybe.'

Drake pushed a bit more power down his arm, barely scraping the surface of the impossible source in his body, and the sphere shone brighter, flared hotter. It was about the size of a tennis ball. 'How about that?'

'Yeah, good.' Tristan bit his tongue and glared at the figures on his screen. 'About five units, give or take a drop. Heh. This is so cool.'

Drake asked the question that had been on his mind for nearly two days. 'So how many units did it take to pull that spider thing through the portal back at the train?'

Tristan nodded. 'That's where I was going with this, yeah. Wherever that portal led, it took you exactly two hundred and ten units to make it happen.'

Drake took a deep breath and exhaled slowly. 'It didn't have anything to do with my energy colliding with Skeleton Man's?'

'I can't say,' Tristan said. 'But the bolt you threw at him and the soldiers was sizzling at about a hundred energy units before it collided. When the two bolts hit the energy doubled, just over, and created that portal into crystal spider hell.' He paused. 'And the readings I got from *that* were . . . scary.'

'I could do it again,' Drake said. 'Couldn't I? If I concentrated, figured out how to hit that energy level, I could open a way through again.'

'This crystal,' Tristan said, and removed the spike of blue crystal, shining softly, from the backpack, 'is only one piece of the puzzle. We need the other one, the red one Skeleton Man took, to test it properly. I'm fairly sure they're keys.' He met Drake's eyes and gave him a significant look. 'What you wrote on your phone, on the library steps . . . as far as I can tell you're right about what it means.'

'What are you talking about?' Irene asked, as Tristan put the crystal back in the pack.

Drake let out a low whistle. 'I've been scheming,' he said. 'About opening that portal again. About . . . escaping.'

Irene grimaced. 'Why would you *want* to open that thing again? One monster wasn't enough?'

'What if it's my talent?' Drake said. 'Noemi has her invisibility, you've got your healing, and so far all I've done is set things on fire. What if this . . . whatever we're calling it, portal magic, is my best trick?' *What if I could figure out how to open one to London?* A shiver of excitement rushed through him. *Or what if it only opens on wherever that spider came from?*

Drake let the sphere of energy dissipate.

Tristan stood and, steeling himself, met Drake's gaze. His mouth formed a thin, grim line and he exhaled slowly. 'You guys want something to eat? Because the Alliance are on their way to pick me up. I called them. Worked out a deal. I don't want to be running the rest of my life – getting shot at and falling out of the sky.'

150

'You *what*?' Irene gasped. 'Michael, was that a joke – ?'

'What did you do?' Drake asked slowly, as the drone still followed him in wide circles above his head.

Irene felt the world slip from under her feet, tilt forty-five degrees, and her heart leapt into her throat. A nervous rush made her feel sick. She picked up the backpack full of cash and the revolver, clutching the strap to her chest.

'You know,' Tristan said to Drake as he crossed his arms over his chest, 'you're clever in ways that surprise me all the time.'

'Why did you do it?' Drake asked, casting another look up at the drone. Irene looked up, as well. The blue sky was dazzling, the breeze cool against her suddenly hot skin. 'Did you use that thing?'

'I've run out of use for you, is about the long and the short of it. I'm smart, you know. Like, genius-level smart.' Tristan shrugged a shoulder. 'Smart enough to know how smart I am, yeah? But you are *clever*, Will. And there's an important difference between smart and clever. Sometimes that difference puts you ahead. I hate that. But most of the time it makes you easy to, well, exploit.'

Irene watched Drake's face turn dark, his eyes shining with hard anger. 'What's the difference then?'

'Clever is often kind. Kind, kind, *kind*. Smart doesn't have that ugly weakness.' Tristan nodded. 'That's why smart is better.'

Drake took a deep breath and Irene could almost feel him trying to calm himself. 'Why did you do it?' he asked again. 'Why did you use that damn drone to let the Alliance find us? Find *her*?'

'*I saw you!*' Tristan glared behind his glasses, angry and flushed. He gestured to the drone, no doubt recording and transmitting their conversation back to the Alliance. 'With the drone. I saw you and Irene, Will, at that service station! Didn't take you long to tongue her, did it?'

'You're saying that like we should be ashamed or something.' Drake clenched and unclenched his fists – and took a step back away from Tristan. 'You betrayed us to the Alliance because me and Irene *kissed*?'

'No. I betrayed *you* to the Alliance because hanging around with *you* is going to get *us* killed! I want you away from her! You're the problem. You're the . . . damn problem. I did the right thing. You're not well, Will, and – shit, look at you! You're not even *human* any more. You're putting us all in danger.'

Drake blinked and shook his head. 'You jealous asshole.'

Tristan smirked. 'It's not like that.'

'I think it's exactly like that.'

'Michael,' Irene said. Her thoughts raced, her mind a tangled mess of disbelief. 'You can't possibly think I would agree to this, that I'd want to go with you'

He gave her such a look of longing and pity that Irene almost slapped him. 'It's not like that,' he muttered. 'I hope you'll understand soon. But no, I don't expect you to come with me. I'm going, though. They're sending someone to come and get me.'

Drake grimaced as blue light shivered down his arm, against his will.

'You're not going to hurt me, Will.' Tristan sneered. 'You're not even close to mad, yet. For whatever reason – and you

152

have so many not to be – you're too clever. You're too much of a *good* guy.'

'You're sure about that, are you? Got me figured out, do you?'

Tristan shrugged. 'Difference between me and you, Will, is that I kind of belonged in prison. Maybe not the Rig, given what was happening there, but I definitely *deserved* to be locked up, according to the law – I killed twelve people.'

Twelve . . . Irene covered her mouth

'You told me it was *eight*.'

'Well, sure.' He grinned and clapped his hands together. 'That they know about.'

A shiver ran down Irene's spine. One dark, lonely night on the Rig, Tristan had confided the truth of his crimes to her in the old control room they had used as a secret meeting place after hours. He had hacked and severed the power supply to his home city, Perth, and one of the hospital's emergency power systems had failed to come on. He'd been responsible for the deaths of those patients.

'You also told me it was an accident,' she said. 'What you did to that hospital. What are you saying now?'

'That I'm not clever. I'm smart. And that I'm not a good guy, Will. I'm selfish, often cruel, out for myself. You have to be, these days, to get ahead with the Alliance. Otherwise they'll crush you. Lock you away and turn you into shark food. I can't help it, you know? I played you to get me off the Rig, because you were my best shot, and when I saw that you were trying to take something I wanted, I told the Alliance where to come and find you to get you out of the way. To protect myself, more than anything, but also to get you away from Irene. They offered me a job, even, to work out those portal crystals.' He laughed as if that were the best joke he'd ever heard. 'It's a bit of a relief, you know, being honest with you. I had to pretend to be your friend every day when we were stuck in that cell.'

'You think we're going to forgive you for this?' Drake asked. 'That we'll understand?'

Tristan pushed his glasses up the bridge of his nose – an act that had seemed innocent before but now was full of derision. He sighed. 'No, I guess not, but the Alliance can't be beaten, so I'm going to cut my losses. I'm free, thanks to you, but you're too dangerous to hang with. Things keep breaking around you.' He looked to the drone and then to Irene. 'And I'll find another hot redhead with daddy issues.'

Tears pricked at Irene's eyes and, from the look on Drake's face, she worried he was only a step from throwing Tristan over the balcony and into Central Park. *A flaming blue meteorite of a bastard*, she thought.

Drake sighed and ran a hand back through his hair. 'You saved my life on the Rig. You got the trackers off, stopped Alan Grey from gutting me like a fish . . . who the hell are you?'

'Like I said, I needed you then. I don't now. I don't have to pretend to be your friend.'

A familiar sound, of rotating blades, echoed down the street and Drake snapped his head over to the edge of the terrace, away from Tristan. He stood just on the threshold of the balcony, in the doorway back into the apartment.

The chopper distinguished itself above the general noise of the city as it flew up from hiding in the canyon of the street below and buffeted the terrace with gusts of air. Skeleton Man stood in the hold of the chopper, wearing a wide grin and a harness. He jumped from the hold, attached to a thick black cord, and landed on the terrace. A faceless guard, masked and armed, leapt from the hold alongside him, attached to a similar rope.

In the space of about two desperate seconds, Skeleton Man wrapped his long, thin arms around Irene, who screamed and clutched the backpack to her chest. The cord of rope yanked him back up and off the balcony into the air. The cord spooled back into the hold, whipping Skeleton Man and Irene – who struggled in his grasp – towards the hovering chopper.

The masked guard grabbed Tristan, only a split second behind Skeleton Man, and reeled his rope back in. Both Tristan and Irene had been whisked towards the chopper.

'*Oh no you don't!*' Drake ran across the terrace and hurled himself over the glass barrier, high above the city, and out into the open air, his arms outstretched and reaching for Irene. His fingers brushed the heel of her sneaker as she was lifted out of reach, and snapped away into the hold of the chopper.

Drake's momentum carried him forward, and he grabbed the landing strut of the chopper as it pulled away from the balcony. Unexpected fire burst from his crystal arm and melted the strut around his fingers, leaving him dangling by his good hand. Drake restrained the flames and pulled his elbows over the metal skids, clinging on as hard as he could, as the chopper flew away from the apartment and headed down Fifth Avenue, skirting the edge of Central Park.

'Give her back!' Drake roared. A wild fury forced his heart into his throat. *This wasn't the plan!* He didn't care that he was dangling a hundred metres above the city, that one slip would mean death. He wanted Irene back before Skeleton Man could hurt her.

The chopper flew downtown, moving swiftly through the city, over thick crowds of people and gridlocked traffic, alongside apartment buildings and the mighty skyscrapers. The nose of the chopper tilted up and above the tallest buildings on Manhattan Island as Drake tried to pull himself up over the skids and into the hold. He tried to swing his legs around the skid, but the force from the blades and the wind kept him dangling by his arms – barely.

Skeleton Man appeared on the edge of the hold and watched Drake struggle. He took a seat with an easy grin, riffling through the backpack Irene had been holding, and winked down at Drake with an eye of dull red coal. Loose banknotes, Canadian greens and reds, fluttered from the backpack and fell on the city below.

'Drake!' Skeleton Man said, and his voice seemed to reverberate through Drake's head, above the sound of the rotors. 'No one invited you to this party. Shit, son, you're like a bad penny.'

He slammed his boot into Drake's nose, and Drake felt something snap. Pain blossomed behind his eyes, but he held on as hot blood gushed down his face. Drops swept away in the wind, following the cash. *Something in his voice . . .*

Drake pulled his head back and caught sight of a mark on Skeleton Man's pale, bony arm that sent his mind reeling. A faded and stretched tattoo of twin swords crossed over a wreath

156

under a silver crown. *C-F 13* was etched under the tattoo in blurred, burnt letters.

C-F . . . Crystal Force! The militarised special forces of the Alliance. C-F 13.

Oh, oh shit.

'You're dead!' Drake gasped, and his grip on the power wavered. 'You *burned*, Brand!'

Officer Marcus Brand, former prison guard on the Rig, frowned and drew Warden Storm's heavy revolver from the bottom of the backpack. He stared at the weapon, a slack look on his face, as if he'd never seen a gun before. And then he pointed it between Drake's eyes. 'Let go,' he said.

'Give her back, Brand,' Drake growled, his voice a dull roar above the wind and the rotors. Irene struggled behind Brand with another Alliance soldier, who was trying to restrain her in the hold. She met Drake's eyes briefly and kept fighting.

Brand's eyes flared red, twitched, and he tilted his head as if listening to something only he could hear. 'Huh. Someone wants to talk to you, Drake. Best not to keep her waiting. Remember to be polite and give her my best.' Brand licked his lips, shrugged and pulled the trigger.

A spinning marble of hot lead took Drake above his left eye. He felt a fierce burn shoot back across his ear, a bone-shattering cold. Someone screamed.

He fell.

Irene screamed as an arc of crimson droplets burst from Will's forehead, and he fell away from the chopper. Tristan clutched his phone to his chest and stared, wide-eyed and shocked.

Irene's heart leapt into her throat and a desperate shiver ran through her body as Will disappeared, like old leaves caught in the wind. She stopped struggling against the masked Alliance goon that held her arms behind her back. She stopped breathing.

He's OK, he's OK, he's OK . . .

The Skeleton Man – Marcus Brand – had shot Drake in the head.

Brand stood and stared at her. His face, thin skin stretched over an elongated skull and yellow teeth, looked confused.

'Thought he'd let go,' the masked guard said. 'Whitmore ain't gonna like this.'

Brand grinned. A hideous, stretched travesty of a grin. 'Oh, I think we'll be OK.'

Irene found her voice and her fury. 'You killed him!'

She tore her arms from the soldier's hands and lunged at Brand, clawing at his throat, his eyes, his ruined face. As if swatting a fly, he slammed the butt of Storm's revolver into her jaw. She spun back into the soldier's grip and slumped into his arms, dazed.

Will Drake was dead.

Will Drake was pretty sure he'd died and gone to heaven.

He sat at his mother's old, worn table in their home in London. An entire plate of buttery toast rested on the table, next to a pot of homemade blackberry jam, well within arm's reach. For some reason, the whole set-up seemed impossible.

Drake helped himself to a piece of toast. He scraped some jam onto the bread with a knife held in his left hand. He stared at that hand, at his skin, and wondered why he expected to see dark glass.

A dull ache above his eye plagued him.

He worried, just for a moment, that someone had gone and shot him in the head. But that was absurd.

Drake's toast tasted like coming home. The clock on the wall told him it was eight in the morning. He had to be at school in half an hour, but he had a nagging feeling that he'd missed a fair chunk of schooling in the last year and a half.

Cool London half-light streamed in through the small windows above the sink. The remnants of last night's dinner, spaghetti and meatballs, rested on the rack next to the sink. Drake had been going to wash the plates, as Mum didn't have the strength these days, but he'd played old-school video games with Gaz late last night. He hoped she hadn't seen the mess.

Strewn on the kitchen counter were a pharmacy's worth of medicine bottles – twenty-two in total, to be taken twice a day. The only medicine the Alliance healthcare system would give someone with a pre-existing condition.

Pills to let the sick die slowly in a hazy shroud of not-quite-felt suffering.

Anger swirled in Drake's gut. If he could just get some of the good drugs, the Detrolazyne, his mother would have a chance. As it stood, he would be burying her in a few months, Nanna Vera's arm around his shoulders. Illness left a taste lingering in the air that was most likely the source of his headache.

Drake smeared another piece of toast in a good quarter-inch of blackberry jam and chomped down on his breakfast. The flood of taste from the jam almost brought him to tears.

I'm gonna skip today. Stay home with Mum, do a few jobs around the house. He coughed some crumbs from his throat.

Go and check out the Alliance warehouse district again and see if I can find the medicine she needs.

A sharp stab of pain above his eyes made him wince. He saw a flash of burning buildings – a policeman falling and hitting his head on a concrete kerb – and the pain burrowed deeper, as if someone had driven a metal spike through his forehead.

Drake blinked, and his mother sat across from him at the table, wearing a floral summer dress and smiling at him. Her eyes were full of life – vitality. It had been so long since he'd seen her looking well that for a moment, he failed to recognise her, but her short brunette hair, her brown eyes and warm smile were all too familiar.

She held a mug of coffee in her hands. Steam rose in lazy circles before her face. 'Everything OK, Will?' she asked. 'Do you need a headache pill?'

Drake glanced to the counter. The dozens of medicine bottles had been removed. The dishes had disappeared. Some time had passed. He frowned and pushed his plate of toast away. The pot of jam had been replenished, the surface of the spread undisturbed. 'What's . . . all this then?'

'Did you enjoy your breakfast?' She sipped her coffee, and her eyes seemed to catch the light and sparkle like blue crystal. 'I could make you some bacon and eggs, if you like. Streaky bacon?'

'I don't think I should . . . should be here.' The pain above his eye felt a lot less like a headache and more like a bullet to the brain. He saw a flash of New York City sunlight, the blades of a chopper rotating against the thin clouds, a pretty redhead, and one bastard of a wasted, living skeleton.

He remembered.

'You're not my mother,' Drake said. 'You're not human.'

The creature wearing his mother's face smiled, but it didn't touch her eyes – which now shone a dull crimson. Behind that smile Drake thought he saw something else, something . . . a flash of surprise.

'Well, that was unexpectedly quick of you. You may struggle to sort your thoughts out for a moment, Will. I'm knitting the damage back together swiftly, but this is the only way we can speak.' She placed her mug down on the table hard enough to slosh coffee against the wood. 'Far too early in the game for you to retire, William Drake.'

'Who are you?' Drake held a hand against his forehead. What seemed like litres of blood seeped between his fingers, down his face, and pooled onto the table. He could feel a metal parasite burrowing into his skull. A hot marble fired from an ugly silver revolver. 'Brand . . . shot me. Brand's alive!'

'My toys, fighting amongst themselves.' The creature waggled her finger back and forth. 'You have far too much work to do, William – you and Marcus Brand both – before I'll let you die.'

'Let's pretend for a moment I have no idea just what the hell is going on . . .'

'You've been drafted, my son, to fight the good fight. I've gifted you with my radiance so we can turn this world into a paradise. An Eden, if I can use the local vernacular. It sure is a long walk back there, William, but you've got the resolve to see us through.'

'OK. Sure. But a skeleton asshole just shot me in the head.' *He has Irene.* 'And I'm not entirely sure I'm alive. Is this . . . am I dead?'

'Close enough, but we're joined at the hip, so to speak. My blood is your blood.' The creature laughed, and its cheeks split, revealing dark crystal speckled with electric blue light. 'A minor inconvenience. You're not playing in the real world any more. Here there be monsters and magic and *resets*. But, until things change, this is the only way we can talk – on the borders of consciousness. Eat your breakfast, while I fix that pesky bullet to the brain.'

Drake's plate was overflowing with blood from his head. 'What are you?'

'For all that matters, William Drake, I am your god. And you do not get to die before you've presented me with the proper tribute.'

'And what would that be?' Drake asked through gritted teeth.

The creature that looked like his mother grinned. It rose from the chair and walked around the table until it stood next to Drake. It leant down until they were eye to eye. Drake could smell his mother's perfume, lilac and jasmine.

'I need you to break me out of prison, William Drake.'

The creature pressed its lips against Drake's forehead, against the bullet wound, and sizzling hot pain blinded Drake to all else. His mind reeled. He fell back through a haze of pounding red light and left the blackberry jam behind.

Sunlight burst through the red, the kitchen disappeared, and a fast wind whistled past his ears high above New York City.

Still reaching for the chopper, Drake spun in the air, stared absurdly at Tristan's Alliance drone still following him all the way from the apartment, and then got a good look at the street rushing up to meet him at about a million miles an hour.

The memory of his mother's kitchen and the creature was fresh in his mind, and it felt as if someone had pressed a branding iron against his forehead, but he was – somehow, impossibly – alive.

And falling.

Come on, magic angel wings. Or that bloody eagle! I'll take the eagle!

Nothing, magic or otherwise, appeared to slow his descent, and Drake laughed as he fell alongside the Empire State Building in a spin. A fountain of blue sparks burst from his arm, wild power, useless and hot. The street, so far below and yet getting closer, would kill him just as swiftly as the bullet to the head should have. Alive but not for long. Dead twice in the same swift minute.

Drake shouted and clapped his hands together.

His crystal arm erupted with cords of thick blue light. The light became liquid crystal and swam through the air in a hundred different directions. Tentacles, snakes of living light, slammed into the buildings of New York City. Drake was wrenched upward, as if he'd deployed a parachute.

The splashes of light surged back over against the skyscrapers, both above and below Drake, like a set of waves about to crash against the shore. The waves clutched onto the sides of the buildings, great pillars of blue light gripping the glass and concrete, hardening from liquid light to solid, and formed a slide of smooth, almost ice-like crystal.

The light caught him, no more than a dozen metres above the street, and he was swept along, the slide carrying most of the speed from his fall. The chopper had disappeared from sight.

Drake slid along the crystal, wild memories of the Slip 'N Slide at East London Leisure running through his mind as Fifth Avenue blurred past his head. The light ran ahead of him in loops and curves, and Drake began to wash off a bit more speed. The ride made him dizzy, but he couldn't help but marvel at what was happening. He spun in a loop and glimpsed the drone still following his progress, swift and sure.

One turn threw him from the slide, along the length of glass windows that formed the wall of some office complex. He caught amazed looks from the men and women inside and flashed them a grin before the light caught him at his back again and curved down towards the street.

Five seconds later, Drake slid over a rise in the crystal and slowed. The rise gave way to a final spiralling slide of hardened blue light and he stumbled forward, his feet hitting the sidewalk, and almost fell flat on his face amid a crowd of surprised onlookers.

'Whoa, kid!' said a young man in baggy jeans and a cap, standing on the corner of Fifth Avenue and 42nd Street, according to the sign and the library across the street. 'Dude, that was straight up Spider-Man!'

Drake steadied himself and swallowed hard, checking his body for cuts or broken bones. What felt like a bumpy line of scar tissue above his left eye was all that remained of Brand's shot to the head. His crystal arm was on display for the whole world to see, but apart from a few developing bruises, he seemed to be in one piece. He'd seen the public library out of the corner of his eye. He confirmed where he was – *Right back to the start* – and took a deep, nervous breath that turned into wild laughter.

He looked back down Fifth Avenue just in time to see his network of crystal waves and web-like slides shatter into bright light. A million sparks fell like snow. They landed harmlessly on the street, on cars, and on New Yorkers, who shook them off, some laughing, before the sparks faded away.

'What's up with that arm, man?' the guy on the corner asked.

Irene.

'Looks cool.' He laughed. 'Hey, you want to buy a wallet? Real leather, man.'

The Alliance have her . . . again. Tristan, you little idiot.

'No, thanks. I don't need a wallet. I need to kill Marcus Brand.'

'You in a movie or something, with that arm? Special effects, man. Lights all up and down town. You sound like you're not from around here.'

Drake took and a deep breath and exhaled with all the patience he could muster. His forehead burned and his bones ached. He'd lost Irene to a monstrous madman who had shot him in the head, and a creature from another world was wearing his mother's face.

He licked his lips, tasted blackberry jam, and needed to take a moment on the kerb. The drone hovered just above his shoulder, attracting a few curious glances, before abruptly hovering away, downtown and after Tristan on the chopper.

A few minutes later, Takeo and Noemi pulled up beside him in the silver sedan, and Drake cursed before getting into the car.

Chapter Sixteen

Dinner with the President

The helicopter landed on the roof of a skyscraper that dominated the cityscape of downtown Manhattan. The tall spire of a building was constructed of dark metal, with windows of thick, tinted glass the colour of polished sapphires. A cool breeze stung Irene's jaw, which she was sure was broken, as she was offloaded from the chopper by the masked soldiers, who shoved her along behind what was left of Marcus Brand.

He killed Will.

'Irene . . .' Tristan said. She glared at him through her tears and he fell silent. He was ushered aside by the masked guard.

Irene was pulled under her arms, her feet dragging across the helipad. A shock so numbing it dulled the pain in her jaw had sent her head spinning. Off in the distance, out in the harbour, she saw the Statue of Liberty and dozens of boats floating around the landmark. Such a sight seemed far too normal. The world wasn't normal. The world was arctic prisons, glowing crystal, murder, chaos, heartache, betrayal, and the world was full of monsters who would laugh as they shot kids in the head.

Irene was led over to a set of metal doors. Brand thumbed a button next to the doors. They slid open on smooth rails, revealing an opulent elevator with stained wooden walls and a rich velvet carpet. Irene felt a warm burst of air from within the car, and she began to cry – from stress, sadness, anger, she didn't know.

'Welcome to Alliance HQ,' Brand said. 'Get in.'

The doors slid closed, leaving Tristan with the chopper pilot on the roof.

Irene was taken to a room a few floors below the roof. The soldiers opened the room with a swipe card, shoved her into the corner suite, and slammed the door behind her. Irene couldn't see a lock. She tried the handle and it didn't budge.

Locked away again.

The room was nicer than the cells on the Rig, but it felt far more dangerous. Large windows made up two of the walls, overlooking the streets of New York towards Central Park and the apartment she had been hiding in not half an hour ago. A single bed and cabinet made up most of the room, across from a couch and television. A small kitchenette with a kettle and mini-fridge connected to a washroom.

Irene stepped into the washroom and looked at herself in the mirror. Her jaw felt as if someone had filled her mouth with sharp nails, or she'd been stung by a nest of angry wasps. Every movement and breath sent sharp bolts of agony shooting through her skull and down her back.

The wind had swept her hair out of her face and revealed the patch of scar tissue over her eye. Irene's lips quivered as she fought more tears, tried not to think of Will Drake, and gently cupped her chin with her hand. She hesitated a moment before summoning the gentle crystal power, worried it could go wrong again, but once the cool light touched her skin, the pain in her jaw faded away.

Irene sighed and slowly rotated her jaw clockwise. She tapped her teeth together and squeezed her cheeks. The pain was gone, and her jaw was healed. A tear escaped her eye and ran down to her lips, salty and bitter.

'Remarkable,' said a voice from just outside the washroom.

Irene jumped. She hadn't heard anyone enter the room, and yet standing in the doorway was a face she knew all too well. He wore his trademark reflective sunglasses, hiding his eyes below a smooth and shiny mane of silver hair, and grinned with teeth white enough to blind. Irene struggled to recall a day where she hadn't seen this man splashed across TV, magazines, newspapers, and the internet.

'You're . . .'

'Yes.' Lucien Whitmore smoothed the front of his dark suit, worn with a black shirt and midnight blue tie, before clasping his hands behind his back. 'A pleasure, Miss Finlay.'

Irene swallowed and held a hand to her throat, uncertain and afraid. 'If you want me to help you get Drake, it's too late . . . not that I'd help anyway.'

Whitmore stepped back from the doorway and gestured with his hand for Irene to leave the washroom. Irene caught the scent of his cologne – a strong scent that reminded her of oak and snowfall – as she moved across the room, keeping her distance from him and placing the couch between them.

'I am here to help you, Irene – ah, forgive me, may I call you Irene?' Whitmore chuckled and ran a hand back through his silver hair. 'To bring you in from the cold, so to speak. You must be tired, given the events of the last week.'

'I'm not tired,' she said. 'I'm angry and . . . and Brand shot Will in the head! Brand killed him!'

'Ah yes, unpleasant business, that,' Whitmore said. 'When Marcus emerged from underneath the ruins of the Rig, mutated and . . . powerful . . . I almost had him put down. Keep a rabid dog on too short a leash, and he'll bite you eventually, I suppose.'

'Then why didn't you?' Irene muttered and brushed her hair down over her ugly scar. 'He's a murderer.'

'The world is full of murderers,' Whitmore said. 'Keeping my prisons full and profitable. I didn't destroy Marcus Brand, my dear, because his madness serves a purpose – it is directed solely towards one young man.'

'Towards Will.'

'Yes. Will. William Drake. A name that has come across my desk more than once in the past eighteen months, given his fondness for escape. A useful skill – one that, in any other circumstance, I'd put to work.' Whitmore stared out of the window for a moment before turning back to Irene. 'What is he like? Tell me about William Drake. I have only heard from his enemies, I wish to hear from his friend.'

'What do you care now?' Irene screamed, and her voice cracked. 'He's gone . . .'

'Sit down, Irene Finlay.'

'I'd rather stand.'

Whitmore shrugged. 'Do as you like, but do not waste my time. Every second of my day is worth twelve hundred dollars – that's thirty-five billion a year. So understand I do not spend that time frivolously or on people that cannot offer me something of value.'

Irene hesitated, sensing a threat in his words, and sat gingerly on the edge of the couch next to the window, still keeping about half the room between her and Whitmore.

Whitmore smiled. 'Wonderful. Now, I'm going to ask you to attend a party of mine tonight, Irene, and before you say no or . . . perhaps something even less polite, hear me out. Attending this party will help young Mr. Drake, and afterwards, you have my word that you are free to go.'

'You're not listening. I can't help him. Your man shot him in the head and he fell!'

'And a week ago, the fall alone would have killed him as surely as it would kill you or me, but the game has changed, hasn't it? William Drake is *more* than human now. Do you honestly think, given all that he's done so far, that something so crude as a bullet could stop him?'

Irene felt a rush of something she didn't dare accept as hope. 'You weren't there. I saw him fall –'

'You've also seen him fly.'

Irene bit her lip, crossed her arms, and stared out at the city. *How am I going to get out of here?*

Whitmore's pocket started ringing. He pulled out his phone and smirked. 'Excuse me. I need to take this.' He held the phone to his ear. 'You owe me two helicopters, Mr. Drake,' Lucien Whitmore said. 'And an oil rig.'

Chapter Seventeen

Scarred Kisses

Back in the apartment, Drake brushed past his allies and locked himself in the washroom. He avoided looking at himself in the mirror, splashed his face with cold water, and fell back onto the rim of the bathtub with a weary sigh. 'Irene . . .'

'William Drake.' Noemi knocked on the door. 'Speak to me. What happened? Where are Miss Finlay and Mr. Tristan?'

'Just give me a minute. I was shot in the head.'

'You . . . no, I –'

He could feel Noemi hesitate for a moment, and then her footsteps disappeared down the hallway. Drake squeezed the rim of the bath with his crystal hand and the marble cracked under the strength in his limb. A handful of fractured stone and dust fell to the floor.

He stood up and looked in the damn mirror.

Above his left eye, touching his eyebrow, was a crooked scar in the shape of a kiss, as if the creature wearing his mother's face had also been wearing dark lipstick.

'Well.' He swallowed. 'How about that for a kick in the teeth?'

The scar looked like an old burn, soft and almost shiny. He ran the fingers of his good hand over the smooth tissue and suppressed a shudder of revulsion. Brand had shot him dead, well and truly, and whatever was under the Rig – alien or not – had brought him back from the brink using the power in the crystal.

The bastard took Irene and killed me. He shook with anger. *At least they'll think I'm dead now.*

'No. No, they won't.' Drake slammed his crystal hand into the mirror. The glass shattered, as did the wooden frame and a good chunk of brick behind it. *They won't think I'm dead after the light show down Fifth Avenue.*

'Irene will think I'm dead. I should be dead.' Drake didn't know how he felt about that just yet, so he decided not to dwell on it. *I wish I'd never been sent to the Rig.* 'Time for . . . peanut butter candy.'

Time to roll the dice, follow the web and hope this pays off.

Drake let himself out of the washroom and traipsed down the hallway to the kitchen. He tore open a bag of peanut butter candy bits and tossed a handful into his mouth. Takeo and Noemi were deep in quiet conversation out on the balcony. She shook her head as he cut his hand down through the air. Arguing, then.

Tristan's bank of computer terminals were still humming away along the far wall. Drake felt ill; his body shook with stress or fatigue, or the clawing fingers of madness, he didn't know. He threw the bag of candy aside. Down the hallway, a heavy knock came from the apartment door. Someone was out in the corridor.

The balcony door slid open, letting in a cool breeze and the sounds of far-below traffic, and Noemi and Takeo let themselves back in to the apartment.

Noemi's eyes flicked from Drake to the scattered peanut butter candy, and back to Drake. 'What is going on here?'

Drake leant against the countertop and shook his head. 'Tristan . . . Michael sold us out to the Alliance.'

'Why would he do this?' Noemi's hand rested on the hilt of her sword.

There was another knock at the door, a touch more insistent than before.

'I'll see to that,' Takeo grumbled. 'You,' – he pointed at Drake – 'do not move.'

'I do not understand,' Noemi said as Takeo disappeared down the hallway.

Drake could only shake his head. So much was on the line now. So much that could go devastatingly wrong.

Takeo returned a minute later, carrying a large white box wrapped in thin strips of sheer purple lace. He put it down on the island in the kitchen. A card on the box, in fancy cursive script, read:

William Drake

'That was an Alliance courier at the door,' Takeo said. 'I made him open the box to ensure it wasn't an explosive. The contents appear to be for you, Mr. Drake.'

Drake gave him a glance and picked up the card. On the reverse side, he found an invitation for an Alliance-funded event in the city that evening.

Dear Mr. William Drake and Miss Irene Finlay,

You are cordially invited
to attend the presentation
of the Whitmore Meteorite to the
American Museum of Natural History.

The Alliance Relief Fund
will be gladly accepting donations
for the Peruvian earthquake disaster.

Time: 7:30PM
Attire: Black Tie

With kind regards,
Lucien Whitmore & family

Drake read the card again, just to make sure he wasn't dreaming. He placed it on the counter and opened the box. Inside he found a black suit that, even to his untrained eye, looked worth more than his home back in London.

What game are you playing, Whitmore? He met Noemi's gaze. *She's not going to like this.*

'It's an invite to some presentation tonight at the . . . Museum of Natural History.' Drake paused. 'Lucien Whitmore is hosting, and I think Irene is going to be there. I think he took Irene to make sure I would be there.'

'You are not seriously going,' Noemi said, as Drake shrugged out of his shirt in his bedroom. She sounded uncertain, incredulous. *Young.* He didn't doubt the fancy tuxedo would fit him just fine. 'William Drake, Haven has arranged transport out of this city and across to Europe, but we must leave *now*. The Alliance knows us, knows we are here. The net is closing, and we are no longer protected by Haven's negotiations. The Alliance want you dead far more than we thought. So I say again – you are not going to meet Lucien Whitmore.'

Drake grinned. She was giving him an order? 'Can you stop me?' he asked, as politely as he could. 'Your skills and sword against my raw power? Who'd win that fight, you think, when I can Spider-Man my way through this town?' He loosened the tie and slipped it over his head, against his collar, and tightened it back up. 'I'm glad this came already knotted. Never had much need to wear one before.'

'Lucien Whitmore is baiting you. He's spent considerable effort and resources to recapture you these last few weeks, and now that he knows you're here, under his thumb, he's set the trap with honey.'

Drake chuckled. 'Irene is as sweet as honey, yeah. Damn it all, but she is.'

'You think she'll be at this party?' Noemi threw up her hands. 'She'll have already disappeared into one of the pits the Alliance call prisons.'

175

'Then I'll find that pit and break her out. Kind of my thing. But, yes, I think she'll be there. And I've got something Whitmore wants, I guess.' Drake stared at his hands. 'I've absorbed way more of his Crystal-X than anyone, and I'm still kind of normal. Don't you see what he's doing? He can't capture me with force, so he's tempting me with something I want. I don't think he wants me dead, not really.'

'Tempting you with Irene Finlay?' Noemi threw up her hands in frustration.

Drake held up the invitation. 'This was addressed to both of us. "Mr. William Drake and Miss Irene Finlay". Whitmore's taunting me. She'll be my date for the evening, I guess. But do you see what I'm doing, Noemi?' Drake scoffed – at himself and the absurdity of the situation. 'I'm choosing Irene over getting home. I've been working towards getting back to London for so long . . . since long before the Rig. And now this is more important. Just for tonight, perhaps, until Irene is safe, but I'm choosing not to leave her behind.' He fought a snarl. 'And back on that train in Canada, Whitmore as much as said he's dangling a sword above my mother's head . . . time we spoke face to face, me and him, and cleared the air, because this can't go on.'

'William Drake,' Noemi said. 'I must advise against this. What you are, what you could be in the war to come –'

'If you're about to say my life is more important than Irene's because I drank a whole bottle of the crystal Kool-Aid you lot set so much stock by – then stop.' Drake straightened his bow tie in the mirror and, reluctantly, removed his woolly hat. 'I like you, Noemi, you're cool, so don't make me hate you.'

'Once they have you, they won't let you go.'

He snorted a rough chuckle. 'They haven't been able to hold me so far, and that was before I had flamethrowers for arms.' Drake sighed. 'I know they won't let me go, but I've been thinking about the balance. You've been trying to make me understand it since we met, not that long ago. Basically what the balance boils down to is perception, yeah? Perception. How I see myself in the world, what I'm willing to do, and what I know, deep down inside, is the right thing. The balance isn't good or evil. You tried to tell me that back on the plane. It's just what I can live with. What I can accept as . . . acceptable. That's what stops the Crystal-X from driving me mad. Doing the right thing as I believe – heh, and perceive – it to be right. So long as I'm fighting for something worth fighting for, then I've got a balance – a reason not to be selfish. It comes down to this: I couldn't live with myself if I abandoned Irene. It would drive me mad as sure as if I killed her myself.'

Noemi opened and closed her mouth a few times and then settled on a sad smile. 'Thank you for reminding me of the balance,' she said. 'My instructors in Haven would have me whipped bloody, if they heard me arguing against your Path just now. You are right, of course, but that doesn't mean you have to go alone. I can follow you under a veil, completely unseen, and watch your back.'

Drake considered that and then shook his head. 'No, no tricks tonight. Thank you for the offer, but no.'

'You shouldn't go alone –'

'This one's on me, Noemi. You want me to come to Japan, then you give me your word you won't follow me.' *And ruin the plan.* 'You can be nearby, if you want, but not in that museum.'

Noemi glared and, after a long moment, gave a curt nod.

Takeo let himself into Drake's room. 'Michael Tristan did not leave any surveillance equipment,' he said with a rough grunt. 'He took nothing but his few belongings and that drone.'

Drake nodded. *Best of luck, you little idiot.* 'You know, it was never going to be the Alliance or the crystal powers that came between us. It was always going to be her. Should have seen it coming.'

He pulled out his phone – the phone that Tristan had given him – and dialled his mother.

Lucien Whitmore picked up on the first ring.

'You owe me two helicopters, Mr. Drake,' the King of the Alliance said. 'And an oil rig. I'm willing to let the absurd amount of Crystal-X you absorbed slide – a drink on the house, so to speak – but I can't abide you on the loose with such stolen power. Once a thief, yes?'

'You owe me one Canadian girl, red hair, cute as a button,' Drake replied, a dangerous edge to his voice. 'And, what, were you just sitting by the phone, waiting for me to call?'

Whitmore chuckled. 'Any and all calls originating from the continent of North America to your home in London, or to the families of Miss Finlay and Mr. Tristan, are redirected to my personal cell.'

'Well, Mikey Tristan sold us down the river, so you can strike him from my close friends list.'

'How far gone are you, Mr. Drake? Would you kill Mr. Tristan, if given the chance?' Whitmore chuckled. 'I offered Mr. Tristan sanctuary in exchange for his assistance. And I didn't want to have to take Miss Finlay, you understand. Indeed, I consider that a debt to be repaid. But please know she is unharmed – well, save a broken jaw upon her arrival, courtesy of Marcus Brand, but she has healed that with her remarkable talent.'

Drake almost crushed the phone in his grip. 'He broke her jaw?'

'She was hysterical. Screaming that you were dead. Brand shot you in the head, or so I'm told.'

'He did. I got over it.'

Whitmore grunted. 'I dislike using what Brand has become, but I believe he is the only creature on this good earth capable of getting results when it comes to you.'

Noemi stood at Drake's shoulder. She moved to meet his gaze and looked worried.

He gave her a wink. 'Kind of my fault, really,' he said to Whitmore. 'I let him burn on that tanker full of Crystal-X.'

'William, I don't want to imprison you. I don't even want to stop you. There's a greater threat, isn't there? I want you to join me. We must discuss a matter of importance.'

Drake let that hang in the air for a moment. He licked his lips. 'Will there be blackberry jam at this function of yours tonight?'

'I'm looking forward to meeting you, Mr. Drake. Face to face.'

Drake hung up on Lucien Whitmore and tossed his phone onto the bed. 'Don't know what you got against that guy,' he said to Noemi and Takeo, as he removed his tie and undid the top button on his fine collared shirt. His woolly tassel hat, speckled with only a bit of blood, fit far better than the tie anyway. 'I'm going to a party in half a suit and this hat. Here's what I want you two to do.'

179

Chapter Eighteen

Mini Cheeseburgers and Sniper Rifles

Irene picked at imaginary strands on the flawless cerulean blue dress Whitmore had arranged for the evening. The dress was strapless, and a personal stylist had spent an hour on her hair and makeup. The white heels on her feet were expensive and added two inches to her height. Irene had protested all of it, but she hadn't been alone in the room when the dress and stylist had arrived. She had made a very unlikely friend. As they travelled uptown in a luxurious limousine, Irene sat with her ankles crossed and body turned away from the president of the Alliance, who wore an immaculate tuxedo, on the opposite side of the car. An escort of half a dozen other vehicles and NYPD cars cleared traffic and blocked side streets, and the limousine seemed to get all the green lights without fail.

'Where are we going?' Irene asked. She didn't turn her head to direct her question towards Whitmore, across the aisle. Even if she had, she would have only seen her own reflection in his sunglasses – which he even wore at night, it seemed.

'To see the dinosaurs!' squeaked an excitable young girl on Whitmore's left.

While the Alliance had prepared Irene for the evening, she'd had company – Amy Whitmore, the daughter of the man who had imprisoned her, hunted her and had her kidnapped by a monster. She couldn't have been more than six or seven years old, and had spent the whole evening bubbling with excitement about the party.

But she kept remembering Will's voice on the phone. *He's alive. Somehow, he's alive. Unless this is all a trick.* Given what had happened on the Rig, she would put nothing past Lucien Whitmore.

Whitmore grinned at his daughter and patted her shoulder. He held a tablet computer on his knee, through which he seemed to be commanding the entire Alliance Systems network. Or playing Scrabble. Irene wasn't sure which, and she didn't care.

'We're going to the Natural History Museum,' he said. 'I'm sorry I didn't mention that earlier. I'm hosting a charity ball this evening for the victims of that earthquake in Peru a few weeks ago. A tragedy, as you know.'

'Actually I was locked up on the Rig a few weeks ago, worried the warden or his goons were going to kill me and my friends, so no, no I don't bloody know.'

'Please, Irene, choose your words more carefully with my daughter in the car.'

Irene pursed her lips, glanced at the little girl, and her resolve wavered. She nodded and turned back to the window, watching the bustling streets of New York pass her by. 'You're only being nice to me for Will,' she said. 'I'm . . . bait.'

'Yes, you are, but believe me when I say I can help Mr. Drake far more than those fools at Haven. My resources are unlimited. The best medical and scientific minds in the world are at my disposal. On the run, he will burn out and die – and perhaps hurt a lot of people doing so. Back under our care, Mr. Drake has a chance to harness his impressive talents for the greater good. And we are much in need of that greater good this evening.'

'What greater good? The Alliance's?'

Whitmore straightened his bow tie and then stroked his daughter's blonde hair, which was tied in loose knots with colourful ribbons. 'There's a war coming, Irene. And we must be ready.'

'You won't be able to make him fight for you. He *hates* the Alliance.'

'When he sees what I have to offer, he'll make the only reasonable choice available to him.'

Irene shook her head. 'You don't understand him at all, Mr. Whitmore. You've threatened his friends and, worse, his mother. He loves his mother.'

'I've ensured Ms. Drake has received nothing but the best medical care –'

'You're holding a knife to her throat, and Will knows it.' Irene fought a desperate chuckle and failed. *Could he really still be alive?* She decided that to hope was better than to give in to the crushing despair. 'Whatever you think is going to happen tonight, I guarantee you that Drake is going to find a way to escape.'

Whitmore grinned. 'I sincerely doubt that.'

* * *

The cool New York air tasted nothing like the wet, ancient air of London against Drake's lips, but dangerous and charged – as if anything could and would happen. A dark, moonless night had settled over the city, the stars obscured behind grey clouds. He tried to feel at ease, but the Alliance would already be watching him, dozens of cameras zoomed in on his position. Takeo and Noemi had dropped him off in the silver sedan in front of the Natural History Museum and had circled around the block, close but not too close, just a phone call away.

A day ago I was on the run, and just two weeks before that on the Rig . . . now it's fancy parties. The sidewalk and steps in front of the museum were abuzz with people dressed in expensive suits and evening dresses. Laughter, polite conversation, and a table with champagne set against the old pillars of the museum made the night seem wholesome.

Drake felt out of place even with his suit jacket shrugged over his shirt and a slim glove to conceal his crystal hand. The tasselled hat, at least, set him apart from the crowd. He didn't want to be here – didn't belong here. He was just a kid from London, liked to play a bit of football, liked to steal kisses with Mary Mallory behind the bike sheds after school, maybe take her to the chippy for a student special with mushy peas and curry if he had a few spare quid.

With a weary sense of trepidation he climbed the steps, presented his invitation to a stern-looking man in a tuxedo who frowned at his hat, and entered the impressive foyer of the Natural History Museum. A heavy fatigue had settled in Drake's bones. In the past few hours, the lack of sleep and collection of injuries garnered over the days on the run had straddled his shoulders like a death shroud. He caught himself almost wanting to curl up on his bunk, back on the Rig. At least there he had been left well enough alone – crawling through waste pipes and playing some mean rigball during the day, but alone at night.

I died today, he thought, as he marvelled at the wide open space of the museum foyer. Skeletons of long-dead dinosaurs drew the eye to the centre of the room. The neck of one of the creatures ended in a screaming jaw, high above the marble floors. Tables of finger food and sparkling glasses had been set up between the displays of fossilised bones. A jazz quartet performed some light background music as people, dressed in their best, mingled and laughed.

William Drake stared at the crowds of the rich and the beautiful, the young and the old, and wondered if anyone would recognise him from the nightly news.

'Mr. Drake? William Drake?' A woman in a sparkling emerald green evening gown approached him. She wore her dark brown hair tied loosely at the back and two curled strands framed her face. She stared at Drake from behind a pair of wire-framed glasses, her eyes like grey stone. 'I'm Danielle DeMarco. Personal assistant to Mr. Whitmore. He asked me to welcome you to the museum. He'd like to see you shortly. Is there anything I can do for you until then?'

'I know you,' Drake said. 'You were with Whitmore under the Rig. You saw what they were doing down there. Who they – you – *killed*. For shame, Danielle DeMarco. Oh, for shame.'

'Perhaps I can get you something to drink?' she asked with a smile, revealing twin rows of perfect white teeth. 'Or take your . . . hat?'

'I'll bring this museum crashing down around our heads before I let you take my hat. Don't think I won't.' He was pleased to see a glimmer of uncertainty flash across her eyes. 'Now. Where is Irene Finlay?'

'Entertaining young Amy, I believe.' Danielle DeMarco composed herself and found a fresh grin. 'Let's go and see if we can't track her down. She's not entirely convinced you're alive.' Whitmore's assistant looped her arm under Drake's and led him further into the museum, away from the grand entrance and across the foyer.

Weaving through marble pillars, around old display cases of fossilised bones and new tables of delicious food, Drake started counting the number of guards in the room. Old habits died hard, if they ever died at all. Drake had been counting Alliance guards for nearly two years. Even dressed as they were in expensive suits, Drake knew the bearing of Alliance soldiers – how they held themselves and how they walked, how their eyes scanned the room. He counted at least a dozen such men, spaced across the foyer. He didn't doubt there would be more, and that they were there for him. He could feel eyes on his back, burning like cigarettes pressed against his skin.

'I did die today,' Drake said idly. His thoughts strayed to the creature that had worn his mother's face. The *alien* made of living crystal that was imprisoned beneath the Rig in a reef of pulsating blue light. *It's a prison beneath a prison . . . and it needs me to escape.* Somehow it had reached him, across distance and time, to save his life. *But it isn't my friend.*

'Perhaps better for you if you had,' DeMarco said. 'Not very wise, Will, to antagonise President Whitmore.'

Drake snorted. 'Aren't you just a loyal little thing? I'm very displeased with your behaviour, Miss DeMarco. You and your boss will be sorry for what you've done before *I'm* done.'

A shiver ran down Drake's crystal arm and a cascade of blue sparks spilled from under the cuff of his jacket and over the edge of his glove. Whitmore's assistant flinched, her grip tightening on his real arm, and her smile became more than a touch forced.

'Will –'

'Don't want people knowing about my magic tricks, huh?' Drake picked up a flute of champagne from the tray of a passing waiter and held it gently in his gloved hand. He met Danielle DeMarco's eyes and squeezed the glass.

The flute shattered and shards of glass, along with champagne, hit the marble floors. Nearby eyes turned to Drake and DeMarco.

'Oops,' he said. 'Look at all the attention I have. Ladies and gentlemen!' Drake took a mock bow. 'For my next trick –'

Danielle DeMarco pulled him away and Drake let himself be pulled. The woman looked furious, behind her smile that was more of a snarl, and eyes of hard flint. 'You idiot boy,' she whispered. 'Listen to me closely, Mr. Drake – there are soldiers from Crystal Force up on the balconies. Several of them have high-powered rifles aimed directly at your heart. They are instructed to *shoot you dead* if you stray.'

'Yeah, one of those Crystal Force bastards already shot me today. In the head. It tickled somewhat. And check out the cool scar.' Drake uncurled his arm from DeMarco's and shoved her aside. 'I see my date over there. You can bugger off.'

DeMarco reached for him again and caught the shoulder of his jacket. Drake paused, clenched his fists, and opened his mouth.

'You may be able to survive being shot, Mr. Drake,' DeMarco whispered. 'But can Irene Finlay?'

'Touch her ever again,' Drake felt an absurd giggle rising in his throat, 'and the glove comes off. I mean it.'

DeMarco pursed her lips into a thin line and nodded once. 'Five minutes. And I'll collect you for your meeting with President Whitmore.'

Drake shrugged her arm from his shoulder and stepped through the crowd towards a long table draped in a dark velvet cloth. Standing at that table, looking good in blue, Irene held hands with a girl who looked no older than six or seven.

'Good evening, Irene,' Drake said, in what he hoped was a charming and suave voice. 'Drake. Will Drake.'

Irene staggered a step back, bumping into the table, and then lunged forward and threw her arms around him in a hug that nearly sent Drake tumbling to the ground. He laughed, a genuine laugh of surprise, and placed his good hand around the small of Irene's back.

'I didn't believe them!' she said. 'I mean, Whitmore, he said you'd survived but . . . there's a scar above your eye! How did that happen? Will, what the hell were you thinking *jumping* onto the chopper after me?' Irene pulled away and swatted him on his chest. Tears swam in her eyes and fought her smile. She was stuck between relieved and furious.

'Well, you know me, right?' He struggled to find a grin. 'And I met something, something powerful, that gave me a kiss on the forehead.' Drake exhaled slowly and shook his head. 'Irene, you look . . .'

She stepped back and smoothed her dress down. 'Oh, like what you see, do you?'

Drake smirked. 'No. I was going to say you look awful and I liked you better in the Rig jumpsuit. Far more flattering.'

Irene swatted him again – harder this time, more of a slap – then leant in and gave him a quick kiss. 'So you came here to rescue me? Took your time. I was getting bored.'

Drake tasted strawberry on his lips. 'No, I came here for the free food.'

A cadre of Alliance guards stood by the large doors that led back out of the museum, eyeing Drake firmly. Their stance, and the bulges under their jackets, suggested they were armed and not about to let him go. *Armed with something larger than a pistol.* Drake hesitated, contemplated forcing his way through in a barrage of crystal fire, but he foresaw a lot of collateral damage. Irene squeezed his forearm and Drake relaxed.

'Excuse me,' said the little girl next to Irene. She tugged on Irene's wrist. 'Can we dance again?' she asked. 'Who's that?'

Irene smiled down at the little girl. 'Amy,' she said. 'This is my friend Will.'

Amy blinked. 'Are you married together?'

Drake coughed but Irene kept her kind smile. 'No, no. But me and Will can't dance right now. We have to go, actually. Don't we, Will?'

'Afraid so,' Drake said, keeping an eye on the guards. He didn't like that Amy had become a shield between him and them. 'Why don't you go find your parents and we'll dance again soon, OK?'

Amy thought about that and then nodded. She dashed off with a quick laugh, hair floating around her head like an aura, and the ribbons on her dress caught in her wake.

'Cute kid,' Drake said.

'That's Lucien Whitmore's daughter. Come on, we have to go – let's find another door.'

'I'm supposed to be meeting with Whitmore,' Drake said. 'Kind of want to hear what he's got to say.'

Irene spun on him. 'Are you *mad*?' She winced. 'I mean, sorry . . .'

Drake tapped his forehead and the kiss-shaped scar brushing his eyebrow. 'Not yet, but I'm working on it.'

'I've spoken to him,' Irene said, as Drake helped himself to something that looked like a mini cheeseburger on a toothpick. 'He's . . . he's not *kind*, Will. He felt awful.'

'Felt awful?' The mini cheeseburgers were good. Drake grabbed a handful.

'Well, he was polite and didn't hurt me, but it's like he had no soul. He was *cold*. I never even saw his eyes behind those sunglasses he always wears.'

Drake nodded. 'There's more going on here than we know, you know. Either I am mad, Irene, or there's an alien demon thing trying to break out of a crystal prison beneath the Rig. I want to know what Whitmore knows. And I don't think he can stop me – I don't think he *wants* to stop me, to be honest.'

Irene frowned. 'What do you mean?'

'Well, I've been thinking about it. How quickly did the Alliance find us in St. John's, or on that train, or over Niagara Falls? Very quickly, is the answer, once we emerged from the forest. They were on us the whole time. Probably never really lost us. As soon as we started heading to New York the soldiers and helicopters left us alone. Whitmore wanted us here, wanted *me* here. He had Brand nab you in that helicopter to force me to this museum.' Drake sighed. 'Is Tristan here?'

Can I tell her more? What if they're listening?

'No, I haven't seen him since the helicopter.'

Drake shrugged a shoulder. 'He told Whitmore where we were staying. Apparently they offered him a job and everything. Little rat was . . . well . . . a little rat.'

Irene shook her head fiercely. 'I still can't believe it.'

'You were there. He admitted it. Because of him they kidnapped you, I got shot, and now we're forced to eat half a dozen of these mini cheeseburgers at this fancy party.'

'What are you going do to him?' Irene asked quietly. 'If you see him again.'

Drake met her gaze. 'Kindly ask him to leave.' His lips were set in a grim line but his eyes *laughed*. 'The Alliance have left their front door unlocked again.'

Irene looked confused and then surprised. Her mouth settled into a similar grim line.

'Michael . . .' she said softly. 'I can't believe it.'

'He wasn't as helpless as he made it seem on the Rig. Wasn't a nice guy, either.' Drake hesitated.

'Will, we have to find him –'

190

'Forgive me for the interruption,' Danielle DeMarco said. 'But President Whitmore will see you now. Follow me.'

'Irene's coming, as well.' Drake glanced up, through the dinosaur fossils, and scanned the dark, secluded balconies full of soldiers and rifles. He couldn't see them, but he did believe Whitmore's assistant – they were up there.

'So be it.' DeMarco turned and walked through the crowds, smiling and greeting guests in their fine suits and dresses, and led Drake and Irene – hand in hand – to meet the President of the Alliance.

Chapter Nineteen

The Shadow War

Irene squeezed Drake's hand as he led her up a set of stone stairs, following the woman with the ugly sneer. They left the party down below in the expansive foyer and walked up to the third floor. Wide oil paintings of men on old wooden ships adorned the walls, between cabinets of Native American tools and clothing. The long-necked dinosaur fossil reached the third floor. A large, grinning skull of flat teeth and hollow eye sockets surveyed the party.

Irene followed the fossil's gaze, into a sea of black suits and colourful dresses, and caught sight of little Amy Whitmore weaving in between the guests on the dance floor. *She's a nice girl . . . who has no idea what kind of monster she has for a father.*

'Are . . . our other friends OK?' Irene asked, whispering close to Drake's ear. She didn't know either Noemi or Takeo well, but they had both struggled to keep them alive so far. And their pilots, Grace and Toby, had died getting them out of Canada.

He nodded slightly. 'Parked nearby. Worst comes to worst we can duck out of a fire exit and head into the park.'

'I advise you to be polite, Mr. Drake,' DeMarco said, her high heels clicking against the stone floors. 'President Whitmore does not suffer fools gladly.'

'Then how'd you get your job?' Drake asked and Irene hid her smile.

DeMarco glared at him and then rapped gently on a set of dark wooden doors with her knuckles. After a moment, she leant against the wood and the door slid open over a deep red carpet. The room beyond was lit well, with a window overlooking the foyer and the party. A large meeting table took up most of the space, with screens built into the surface and raised slightly towards the high-backed leather chairs, six in total. The crest of the Alliance spun slowly on each of the screens. A second door with an ornate golden handle led deeper into the museum. Another window on the opposite wall showed a nice view of Central Park and some of the skyscrapers down towards Times Square.

It was in front of this window that Lucien Whitmore stood, staring at the city, his hands clasped behind his back.

'Mr. Drake and Miss Finlay, sir,' Danielle DeMarco said and then stepped quietly from the room, pulling the door closed behind her.

Drake's grip on Irene's hand tensed as the man with the silver hair, his eyes hidden behind those trademark reflective lenses, turned slowly and offered them both a smile that, on anyone else, might have been charming. On Whitmore it looked like a half-smile of contempt.

'Hello, Mr. Drake,' Whitmore said. 'Quite a day you've had. Tell me, what did the creature show you?'

'I haven't the foggiest what you could mean, mate,' Drake said, although the way he said it – a deadpan yet dangerous edge to his voice – made Irene think he knew exactly what Whitmore meant.

Whitmore nodded to himself and picked up a glass of sparkling water from the table. He took a sip and gestured to the chairs. 'Please sit – we have much to discuss, and little time in which to do so. Tonight many things will be decided.'

Irene and Drake shared a look, of trepidation, and he pulled a chair out for her. She sat and he took the next one along, closer to Whitmore.

'What the hell are you doing letting Marcus Brand run loose?' Drake asked. 'He's the one that gave me this, you know.' Drake tapped his strange scar. 'Bullet to the head. Whatever you want from me, I should be dead, and it was his fault.'

'Marcus Brand has been disciplined for disobeying my commands. You were to be left alive and unharmed.'

'I've been shooting down helicopters all week. Helicopters filled with your soldiers and your guns. Alive and unharmed is a bit of stretch, don't you think?'

Whitmore grinned and raised his hands, palms outward. 'You are here, are you not? And you will listen to what I have to say.'

Irene saw Drake struggling with his anger, and no doubt with the power residing in his crystal arm. His gloved hand clutched the arm of the chair hard enough to tear the fine leather.

'I'll listen, I guess, but if I don't like what I hear you can't stop me from leaving.'

'As I assured Miss Finlay earlier this evening, all I ask is that you listen. I've an offer for you, William, a chance to do some good in this world – clear your name, so to speak, and help a lot of people. Your mother included.'

Wrong move, Irene thought. *You shouldn't have mentioned his mother.*

Drake sat up straighter in his chair. 'I'll say this just once – face to face. *Lucien*,' and Drake spat the name, 'you go near my mother and I'll kill you.' Fierce warmth bled from Drake, from his crystal arm. He was barely in control.

Tingles ran through Irene, and the tiny hairs on the back of her neck shivered. She wasn't sitting next to a person, she was sitting next to a bottle of caged lightning. A bottle that was falling from the sky, unable to be caught or stopped, and when it hit the ground . . . the force of that lightning would be unleashed. She shivered again. Lucien Whitmore might have been the president of Alliance Systems, might have commanded the respect and fear of governments and militaries all over the world, but the moment Drake had absorbed the Crystal-X Whitmore's power began to crumble.

And Whitmore knows that. Does Will?

'I have ensured your mother receives nothing but the finest care for her condition. My personal doctors report she is in good health, responding well to the leukaemia treatment and a course of Detrolazyne-V. She asks after you often.'

Irene wanted to say something, anything, to calm Drake. But she also thought that perhaps right now he didn't need calming. That the angrier he was the more likely they'd make it out of the museum alive.

'Whatever good you've done, or think you're doing,' Drake said quietly, 'doesn't – can't – make up for what you did under the Rig. The kids that died. And what Brand did to Doctor Acacia Lambros . . . I found her body, Whitmore, stuffed into an old crate to be fed to the sharks. Murderers, the both of you.'

'You are not entirely without sin, Mr. Drake.' Whitmore stroked his chin. 'Allow me to show you something.'

Irene seemed forgotten between the two of them. She touched the back of Drake's hand, half expecting an electric shock, but he didn't look at her. If Whitmore had been made of ice then Drake's intense glare would have melted him in his chair. Whitmore's expression was carefully controlled: *calm*, she thought. She couldn't see his eyes, but a tiny frown line between his eyebrows made her think Drake's words bothered the Alliance's president more than he was letting on.

Whitmore tapped the screen on the table in front of him and the Alliance logo on the screens before Drake and Irene changed.

'Oh my,' Irene breathed. 'Is that – ?'

'Footage taken at sunset today, yes, indeed,' Whitmore said. 'As you can see, your escape has caused more damage than you could possibly have imagined.'

'The hell . . .' Drake took a deep breath and exhaled slowly. 'That's the Rig.'

On the screen, an Alliance drone circled the four remaining platforms of the Rig from above – at least a few hundred metres or so. Much of the oil-rig prison was covered in sharp spires and twisting loops of dark crystal – the colour of midnight, of Drake's arm. Mixed within the entanglements, and strung

196

across the platforms, were bands of glowing clear crystal which pulsed blue every few seconds.

'Our drones have been circling the facility since you forced an evacuation and escaped.' If Whitmore was bothered by Drake's escape, his voice didn't reflect it. 'As you can see, the fall of the eastern platform and the explosion of Crystal-X within the hold of the *Titan* seems to have . . . exacerbated the growth of the underwater reef.'

Irene leant forward in her chair and stared wide-eyed at the screen. 'It's grown that much in two weeks?'

'Oh, it's worse than that, Miss Finlay. For apart from what you see above the surface, tendrils of thick crystal have grown for hundreds of miles *beneath* the water.' He clapped his hands together and looked at Drake. 'Congratulations, Mr. Drake, you've awoken a very old, very cruel god.'

Drake stared at the screen and felt true fear squirming around in his gut. 'Oh, sure,' he said, letting his mouth run again, 'because I was the one drilling holes into the crystal, wasn't I? You should have left the damn stuff down there.'

'The creature is building,' Whitmore said. 'Whatever you awoke beneath those dark waters, creature or alien, is building that structure around the Rig. That is about as close as the drones can get before they simply stop working.'

'What about . . . ?' Irene said. 'There's no one still on there, is there?'

'Warden Jonathan Storm is unaccounted for,' Whitmore said. 'After he dropped you off in St. John's and flew back to the Rig, he refused to evacuate with the helicopters that collected the rest of the staff and inmates from their life rafts. As far as we know, he's still on the platform. Most likely perished, at this point.'

Drake spared about a second's thought for Storm and couldn't help himself from thinking the world was better off without the man. 'You said it was growing under the water, as well?'

Whitmore nodded.

'Growing where?'

'Thick tentacles from the underwater reef and that abomination you see claiming my prison have travelled hundreds of miles in a matter of days. Shipping lanes have been closed as the crystal cut through the hulls of three tankers like they were tissue paper. Worse, the tentacles shifted course to destroy those ships. At its current rate of growth, and it's only got faster, it will be on our shores . . .' Whitmore paused and glanced at his watch. '. . . in an hour and twelve minutes.'

'Whoa, what?' Drake leant back and looked at Irene. 'It'll hit land? What land?'

'This land, Mr. Drake.' Whitmore chuckled but there was no humour in his voice. 'The crystal is coming here.' He gestured behind him, out at the city. 'Why do you think I have guided you here? To New York City this evening? The fight is tonight, Mr. Drake. The creature in the Crystal-X is coming and you are the only one capable of fighting it. Michael Tristan has assured me, in exchange for a pardon on his sentence, that you can open a portal using the crystals that were created in the incident with the train. He is working on them now, collating the data. You and Marcus Brand will step through that portal together; you will join Crystal Force, and take the fight to these creatures.'

Drake didn't need to think too hard about that. 'No, thank you. I won't work with you or Brand.' Drake glanced at Irene from the corner of his eye. 'I'm not your pawn, Whitmore.'

'I am asking you to be my ally!' Whitmore shook his head and straightened his tie. 'You are free to leave here tonight, Mr. Drake,' he said. 'As I promised. And I will take your dismissal of my offer as final and consider you an enemy – much like those fools in Japan – and use much less . . . *decent* means to persuade you to my cause. Either way, that portal will open.'

'I'm not taking sides,' Drake said. 'I just want to go home.' *But I can't leave New York if it's about to be attacked.* He sighed. *But what can I do?*

Whitmore scoffed and ran a hand back through his silver hair. 'Home? You can never go home again. Like it or not, the amount of Crystal-X you absorbed and your ability to stave off the madness puts you on the frontlines. You have the power – the *responsibility* – to fight.'

'I'm not fighting your wars – against crystal aliens or Haven!'

Whitmore gave Drake a withering look. 'There's something more at stake here. You've seen it, haven't you? The world to come if the entity sealed away at the bottom of the Arctic Ocean has its way? You've seen it in your dreams. The devastation.' He licked his lips and scowled, as if his words had a foul taste. 'Crystal spires marring the land, ash and dust on the wind under a ruined, crimson sky.'

'How can you . . .' Drake shook his head. 'Take off your glasses. Show me your eyes.'

Whitmore's grin looked like a wolf about to feed. 'War is coming, Drake, and you will be called into service one way or another. We cannot allow the Degradation to happen. The fate of the world depends upon you.'

Degradation? The word sounded ugly and cruel.

'This is the true Shadow War, no matter what those cultists from Haven may have told you.' Whitmore took off his glasses and rubbed at his eyelids. 'And a significant amount of light is about to be cast on the shadow. You are the only soldier I have that has absorbed enough of the Crystal-X to make a difference tonight.'

Whitmore looked up and removed his hands from his face. Irene gasped but Drake merely grunted at the colour of the man's eyes. His left eye shone faintly blue, deep within his pupil, and his right carried a twinkle of dark red.

Balance, Drake thought. *He's balanced between madness and whatever the blue means. Sanity? No . . . clarity. The Path.*

'Noemi called you the Betrayer,' Drake said, piecing together things he should have already been told. He barked a rough laugh. 'Oh, man, you were at Haven, weren't you? When you were a kid. You bobbed for a magic apple.'

'Very astute, Mr. Drake. For a thief and a thug, you are quite perceptive.' Whitmore replaced his glasses and sighed. 'Forgive me. That was impolite. I was once a student of Haven, yes, my family's wealth and influence guaranteed that, but no longer. They couldn't see what was coming, what my father found beneath the Rig. Betrayer? I abandoned those fools and their precious Path for the greater good of humanity. They are not warriors, but mere scholars.'

'That greater good has got a lot of people killed, you know. You put a price tag on things that should be basic human rights,' Drake said. 'Healthcare, justice . . . you're asking me to choose sides, to choose your side – but I've waded through the shit and blood on the Rig, Mr. President. I've seen what happens to people on your side.' He stood and kicked his chair back against the wall. 'Irene, we should go.'

'Mr. Drake, I am asking you to become a member of Crystal Force tonight. To lead a specialist unit alongside Marcus Brand. Consider that the creature may be targeting New York because it *knew* you would be here. Glimpses of the future are more than possible, as you well know. Without the resources and command structure of the Alliance, Bluebird will hunt you down alone – no matter how fast you run.'

'Bluebird?' Irene asked.

'That's what Crystal Force have designated this threat. Operation Bluebird.'

Drake pictured the creature he'd glimpsed hiding under his mother's skin and suppressed a shudder. 'Bluebird is too kind,' he said. 'It's uglier than that. And I don't want your job.'

Whitmore replaced his sunglasses and gave a curt nod. 'So be it. You may leave the museum, as I promised, but I won't allow you to leave the city. Rousing Bluebird was partly your doing, Drake, and you'll suffer the consequences of that with the rest of us.'

Drake sighed and nodded once. 'Suppose I will. See you later, Lucien.'

Drake took Irene's hand as they swept out of the room, leaving the president of the Alliance to his thoughts, and stepped quickly past Danielle DeMarco and her patented scowl, along the corridor back towards the party. They took the stone steps two at a time, almost dancing down to the ground floor. The sounds of merriment and the click of shoes against the marble foyer seemed at odds with what Drake had just learnt.

'So what do we do?' Irene asked. 'And don't say something smart like "let's go get pizza and make out", Will.'

Drake snapped his fingers. 'Heh. You know me too well, Finlay. No, I . . . I'm not sure. Let me think for a minute.'

'Follow the web?'

Drake smiled. 'Follow the web.' He gave her a quick kiss, missed her mouth, and got some upper lip action. 'Follow the damn web.'

The party was in full swing, people dancing and drinking and eating little plates of finger food, as Drake, a wanted terrorist if the news was to be believed, moved among them – with a good half a dozen balconies overhead that might have contained a good half a dozen highly trained special forces soldiers with a good half a dozen high-powered rifles pointed at him and Irene.

The ornate doors out onto the street had been closed, save for a sliding glass door that was manned by a collection of Alliance goons. One of them grinned and gave Drake a quick salute.

He clenched his crystal fist and was sorely tempted to melt a path on through, see the guards scatter, but the suspected guns above made him hesitate.

'We should head out to that fire escape now, yeah,' Irene said.

'What, you don't trust Whitmore to keep his word and let us leave?'

'Come on, let's head further into the museum and find an exit that way.'

Drake had to agree it was the best option, short of creating a crystal-blue panic, so he let himself be led. Irene weaved through the crowd, making her dress look good, and led them around the massive dinosaur fossil and around a velvet rope blocking access deeper into the museum. The corridor was dimly lit, but deserted, and ended in a left turn, a right turn and a narrow set of carpeted stairs.

A screen on the wall said the *Journey to the Stars* exhibit was to the left and the *Cretaceous Period* could be found down the corridor to the right.

He and Irene shared a look, shrugged, and took the right turn.

The corridor led them to a large chamber with high vaulted ceilings above an incredible display of dinosaur bones. Several pedestals held complete skeletons of long-dead beasts. Inside glass cases were holographic images of what the creatures had looked like millions of years ago, in a world of erupting volcanoes and cloudy skies. Speakers on the walls played sounds that reminded Drake of the rainforest.

In the heart of the vast chamber stood a massive and vicious fossil – Drake's favourite since he was four – the *Tyrannosaurus rex*.

Marcus Brand, the Skeleton Man, rested at ease against the central pedestal beneath the *Tyrannosaurus*. He gave Drake a ragged wave and shot him a toothy, feral grin.

'Hey, Drake, still kickin'?' Brand asked and pressed his hand against the tail of the T-Rex. 'You meet the new boss? She gave you a kiss, huh?'

'You're not working for Whitmore any longer, are you?' Drake clenched his fists. 'What is it you want from me?'

'Whitmore thinks he can stop what's to come.' Brand laughed. 'Look at me, Drake – look at what we did to each other! There's no stopping Bluebird.'

'You could, you know, *not* help it, though.'

Brand shrugged a shoulder. 'Hey, look what I can do.'

A fetid yellow light bled from under Brand's hand and slithered across the immense fossil like a river of honey. The light hardened against the old bones, coating the T-Rex from fanged jaw to clawed foot in a hard shell of amber.

'Cool,' Drake said, stepping in front of Irene. He wanted to kill Brand – to put him down. 'You can make toffee apples. Whoop-de –'

The T-Rex roared and its massive head swung through the air. Red fire flared within the depths of its empty eye sockets, which seemed to glare at Drake with a bitter, hateful intelligence.

Drake whipped out his phone and speed-dialled Noemi. She answered halfway through the first ring.

'Dinosaurs,' he said.

'*Excuse me?*'

'Will . . .' Irene grasped his arm.

The T-Rex broke away from its pedestal and took a step, its first in sixty-five million years, onto the hardwood floors. The museum shook. A decade of dust in the arched rafters of the high ceilings fell like snow.

Irene pulled Drake away and they turned to run – back towards the party.

'*William Drake?*' Noemi's voice was urgent.

'Yeah, Brand is here and he made dinosaurs. Noemi, please tell me you're waiting outside with a car . . . and a rocket launcher.'

'*RUN, DRAKE!*' Marcus Brand's laughter echoed up into the cathedral-like ceiling. '*RUN!*'

Drake ran.

Chapter Twenty

Cretaceous Park

Irene squeezed Drake's hand hard enough to hurt as they ran back the way they had come, towards the party, as the dinosaur chasing them down roared again, rattling windows and knocking paintings from the walls.

She leant down as they reached the split in the corridor and slipped the straps of her heels from around her ankles. With no real thought, Drake took a turn back towards the foyer and, barefoot, Irene kept pace. The museum shook again and a tremendous *boom* of concrete striking marble reverberated ahead of them and rattled Drake's bones.

Drake and Irene separated at the velvet barrier in the foyer and, his heart pounding in his chest, he cursed. If that thing had followed them then he'd led it to a crowded room full of innocent people. And Alliance guards. *Oh . . . damn, they're innocent enough.* Another unholy roar echoed down the corridor. 'Of course it's following us . . .'

He looked over at Irene just as she slammed her fist into the fire alarm on the wall. A shrill siren echoed across the foyer and brought the party to an abrupt end. Without any heat or smoke to set them off, the sprinklers along the corridor didn't start to rain, but sprinklers were not going to stop the beast anyway.

Irene offered Drake a wicked grin as the party began to clear out. He returned her grin and then watched as a bullet tore through her right arm, entering from behind, and spurting an arc of crimson droplets through the air that struck Drake's face. A taste he was all too familiar with – hot, coppery blood – hit his lips. Irene cried out and spun before falling back, cradling her arm. The bullet had gone straight through, from high above, and buried itself in the marble at Drake's feet.

He took a step forward, just one, before his crystal arm flared to life and a beam of intense light burst from his hand. The glove he wore was incinerated, like the previous pair bought what felt like years ago in Canada. He created a band of fire in the air, a whip of pure flame, and sent it swirling around him and Irene, hiding them from sight. The power appeared so swiftly that Drake wasn't sure it was entirely his own doing. *Instincts kicking in*, he thought. *Or I'm letting it control me. Noemi said using it like this was bad.*

'Will . . .' Irene said through gritted teeth as he knelt next to her within the cocoon of fire. Blood gushed down her arm, staining her dress. 'Ouch. Very ouch.'

'Heal it, Irene. We've got to go.'

Drake looked through the breaks in the fire in time to see the T-Rex swing its massive head around the split in the corridor and bellow an ancient, extinct roar. He felt more than saw the rush of people in the party start to make a swift exit – spurred

207

on now not only by the fire alarm, but also by a collective scream that rose on the air, answered by another roar from the reanimated dinosaur.

He checked on Irene, who nodded, and clasped her hand over the bullet wound. Blue light danced beneath her skin and a warm glow ignited her blood from within. Satisfied she could take care of herself, Drake turned to the monster at the far end of the corridor, the amber-coated fossil, as it tore apart the museum to reach him.

Power, he thought. *Lots of bloody energy units.*

Thrusting his crystal arm forward sent bands of burning white flame rushing towards the T-Rex. The amber coating the fossil absorbed the flame, rippling like dark water struck by a pebble, and the beast lowered its head. Drake *felt* the glare from the empty eye sockets and doubled his efforts. He poured more power down his arm and out of his hand, throwing his other arm into the mix. The obsidian crystal arm swam with thousands of blue sparks, with what the Alliance called Crystal-X and Noemi called Yūgen. His good arm, flesh and bone, burnt white beneath his skin.

Drake collected the power in his palms, the heat of the energy once again singeing his cuffs but leaving his skin unburnt. As the beast lumbered towards him, digging deep furrows in the floor with its claws and tearing displays from the walls with its bulk, Drake opened his hands as if in supplication.

A concentrated beam of light and fire, as thick as a soccer ball, erupted from his palms. He was forced back a step, two, and on to one knee as his arms jerked against the absurd column of hot flame. The beam glanced off the walls and left blackened scorch marks, a trail of ash and smoke. With the power still flowing down his arms, the beam struck the T-Rex halfway down the corridor and blew a hole in its chest. The amber coating shattered and the crystal fire bored through into the fossil.

Drake grinned and moved his open palms, touching just at his wrists, in slow circles. The beam of fire *ate* the T-Rex – a slow spiral reducing the beast to dust and less than dust. He severed the fossilised bones at the neck and the T-Rex's body fell away from its head. The bulk of the creature became lifeless and hit the floor, leaking Brand's amber slop. Drake clapped his hands together and cut off his immense power. He'd set the corridor on fire. Water burst from the sprinklers overhead, tasting the smoke. The monumental head of the T-Rex whirled through the air, striking the marble floors, before coming to a spinning stop at Drake's feet. The jaw stood open, as if snarling, but once again inert. More amber liquid dripped from its fangs.

'How's the arm?' Drake asked. He'd kept the cocoon of fire spinning above their heads in case of more shots from above, sizzling now as drops of water from the sprinklers struck the flame, but he had a feeling the snipers had abandoned their posts.

Irene looked at her bloody palm and then poked her arm. 'Not . . . not even a scar,' she said. 'Better job than last time, eh?'

Most of the party guests had forced their way out onto the street, toppling museum pieces and tables in their hurry to escape. Dozens of shattered champagne flutes and silver trays littered the foyer, mixed with canapés. Even the Alliance guards seemed to have fled outside.

'What do we do now?' Irene asked.

Drake clenched his fist and glared down the corridor. He put his crystal hand on the skull of the T-Rex and knocked it aside. 'Brand is down there. He hurt you. He *killed* me. I'm going to –'

Half a dozen fast-moving creatures, shining in the museum light, shrieked around the corner of the corridor, following in the wake of the T-Rex. They varied in height, from three feet to five, sleek with amber, and even at a distance Drake could see razor-sharp claws attached to each arm and leg.

'Raptors,' Irene said. 'Oh hell, I've seen this movie before.'

The raptors – resurrected by Brand, had to be – caught sight of Drake and shrieked again. The six dinosaurs moved as a pack, leaping over the remains of the T-Rex, and snapped their jaws at him.

Drake contemplated another beam of fire and energy, thought about hitting six moving targets and what would happen if he missed, thought about running, and was still thinking when Irene made the decision for him. She grabbed his hand and together they turned to flee.

Irene made it halfway across the foyer, Drake's hand in hers, before she stepped on a piece of shattered glass. She'd cast aside her heels in order to run, so the glass cut deep into her foot.

Irene screamed and stumbled.

His breath coming in hard gasps, Drake didn't let her fall. He swept her up with his hard, dark crystal limb and Irene threw her arms around his neck. Warm blood dripped down the sole of her foot and left large drops along the marble floors, mixing with spilt champagne. Looking over Drake's shoulder, she saw the raptors burst into the foyer in two groups of three. *A hunting pack.*

'Faster!' she whispered fiercely. 'Will, *faster!*'

Drake grunted and put on a burst of speed. To Irene he smelt of flame and sweat and something charged – like ozone in the air during a thunderstorm. He kicked open the side door leading out onto the street without losing much speed. The night air was cool against Irene's flushed skin. The panicked crowds had spilled out onto the steps of the museum. People fled in all directions, across the road into the park and down Central Park West, disappearing into the city.

'Noemi and Takeo are in that silver car over there,' Drake said quickly. 'Near the taxi line.' He dropped Irene on the steps. 'The dinosaurs are after me, so I'm ditching you here. Pretty dud first date, huh?' He grinned, turned on his heel, and jumped down the steps three at a time.

'Will!' Irene called, her heart hammering and her eyes wide. *You can't just leave!*

The raptors burst through the museum doors, shrieking and shattering glass, and were met with renewed screams from the crowd.

Irene rolled along the stone steps, bruising her ribs, as the partygoers were set upon by the extinct creatures. An older man in a tuxedo, wearing an Alliance earpiece, fell under the assault of one of the raptors. A gun clattered from the holster at his waist – he was an Alliance guard. The beast snapped its amber jaw around the man's neck and bit down – hard. His screams stopped abruptly.

Most of the remaining crowd ran into the road, between parked cars, taxis and buses. Irene had lost Drake somewhere in the chaos – but caught sight of him again on the other side of the street. He met her eyes briefly and held his crystal arm towards the sky. Four balls of white light erupted from his hand, flares in the dark, and exploded twenty metres above the road like silver fireworks. As one, as if they were dogs and Drake had blown a whistle only they could hear, the raptors left the crowd alone and moved towards him.

He grinned again – *idiot!* – and leapt the wall into Central Park.

Scraping across cars and the sidewalk, pushing people to the ground, the raptors gave chase and bounded over the wall and into the park after Drake. Their shrieks were diluted by the noise of the crowd, but an intense light flashed between and silhouetted the trees – Drake was fighting.

He was right . . . they are just after him.

One of the raptors exploded as it jumped over the wall into the park, struck by a bolt of blue energy. The fossil lost all vestiges of life and a rain of smouldering pieces struck the sidewalk.

'Nice shot, Will.' Irene pulled a thick piece of glass from her right foot and held a hand to the wound. The bullet to the arm had been painful – an inch or so to the left and it would have hit her chest – but easy to heal in half a minute. At this point, after months on the Rig and mending Drake every five minutes, fixing her foot was the work of five seconds.

She rose to her feet on shaky legs, sick to her stomach, and intended to give chase after Drake – to help him, if she could. A desperate, quiet sob behind her made her pause and turn.

Hunched just against the wall of the museum, tears running in little rivers down her face and clutching a small, sparkly handbag with a teddy bear poking out of the top as if her life depended on it, was Amy Whitmore.

The girl's terrified eyes latched onto Irene and she held her arms out. 'It ate Joshie!' she said, and cast a quick look at the man who had died on the steps. 'He was my friend.'

Irene bit her lip, heard a distant explosion from the park, and then swept Amy into her arms.

'That silly boy can look after himself,' she said kindly, before her voice – her nerve – broke. 'Us girls need to stick together. Come on, Amy, let's get out of here.'

Another bright idea, Will, Drake thought, throwing himself down a grassy embankment and rolling onto a stone path with a grunt. He spun onto his back and fired a burst of energy into the air, catching one of the raptors just before it could bury its claws in his chest. The creature exploded into a hundred pieces, some of which grazed his cheeks and exposed skin, slicing small, sharp cuts.

Two down . . . four to go.

The shards of old fossil stung but weren't the worst of his concerns at the moment, not by a long shot. Drake stood quickly, stumbled back into a couple of people clutching each other, and offered them a grin and a wink. 'Stroll in the park,' he breathed. 'Raptors, eh? Run that way.'

He ran the other way, his lungs gasping for air, away from the couple. He wasn't worried so much about the raptors attacking anyone else – they had his crystal scent now – but more so having room to use his power to destroy them. One of the amber-coated creatures appeared through the trees off to his left. Drake raised his arm and the familiar, alien light spiralled down his limb and escaped from his hand. A beam of energy cut the raptor in half – as well as the tree behind it, like a hot knife through butter. The old elm fell to the ground in blue flames.

That was a nice tree, Drake thought. *Three down. Three to –*

Something that was either a raptor or a freight train slammed into his side and sent Drake flying through the air. He spun and his crystal arm exploded with light, out of control, and propelled him across the park. Lashings of power struck the stone path and the grass, leaving bands of wicked flame in his wake, as if the earth had been struck with a fiery nine-tailed whip. He landed on his feet twenty metres away and kept running – for all of about three steps before the momentum caught up with his legs and he fell forward onto the hard ground.

With another grunt Drake stood, bruised and bleeding. He'd landed on a cobblestoned bridge built over a pool of dark water. Lanterns of soft orange light lined the bridge and the banks of the pool. But he didn't have long to admire his new surroundings. The raptors had followed his mad, spinning arc through the air and, one in the front and two following the leader, made for the bridge with vicious shrieks. He had about five seconds.

Drake licked his lips and clapped his hands together. His real palm stung against his crystal hand and bounced away as if made of elastic. Between his hands spun a furious sphere of white light, crackling with blue bolts of energy. The sphere grew swiftly, to about the size of a basketball, and just as the raptors reached the bridge Drake pulled his hands away and the basketball exploded with raw heat and pure lightning. He dived over the edge of the bridge, caught the edge of the explosion, which set his clothes and awesome hat on fire, and hit the water as hard as if it were a brick wall.

The pool wasn't too deep, certainly not as deep as the Arctic Ocean had been as it flooded the hold of the *Titan*. Drake struck the bottom and all the air was forced from his lungs. He floated for a handful of seconds, savouring the quiet, the pool lit up by the white and blue fire above, and then created a thin shield of energy as large chunks of the cobblestone bridge splashed into the water and threatened to crush him.

Barely feeling his injuries, or the fatigue he knew his body must be straining under, Drake pushed off the bottom of the pool with his feet and swam back from the fire. His lungs burnt for air and he breached the surface near the far bank, away from the collapsed and burning bridge, and drew a deep breath between fits of giggles.

Of the raptors, nothing remained. He'd vaporised all three in the blast.

'I'm good at this stuff,' he said with a smirk and thinking about Whitmore's job offer – to join Crystal Force.

Drake stood on the bank, dripping from head to toe in clothes scorched by alien fire, bleeding from a dozen nicks and scratches, bruised all along his ribs – a few of which he felt might have been broken – and grinned. *I am crystal force.*

Chapter Twenty-One

Make Feel Nice

It took Drake fifteen minutes to limp back to the apartment overlooking Fifth Avenue and the park. Dozens of police cars swept by the park, sirens blazing. Drake kept his head down as he crossed the street, tried to look as inconspicuous as someone burnt and battered and sporting a crystal limb could look, and found drawing a breath was getting harder and harder.

No longer using his power, the pain from his injuries seeped through his body like water breaking through cracks in a dam. Every breath felt like one of his perhaps-broken-ribs was piercing his lung. He was given a wide berth by the people he stumbled past on the street. He imagined the look on his face was something close to ghastly strain. *I'd avoid me too . . .*

The doorman gave him a nod and said nothing as he reached the apartment building. *Haven must pay him well.* Given the world of crystal power and violence he had stepped into, Drake imagined he wasn't the first bloody and beaten chap the doorman had seen collapse in a Haven safe house. He stepped across the lobby and into an ornate elevator with a golden grille. Drake punched the button for the top floor, their penthouse, and slumped against the wall as the lift took its sweet time. What felt like minutes but was only about fifteen seconds later, he fell forward into the hallway out the front of the opulent apartment and would have once again hit the floor, nose first to break the fall, if not for the pair of strong arms that caught him.

Drake fell into Takeo's chest and the giant man's muscles felt about as firm and as yielding as a mountain. 'Smleth lifander,' he said.

'Your pardon?' Takeo asked, pulling him back up onto his feet.

'I said you smell like lavender,' Drake said, throwing his arm around Takeo's shoulders. 'All fancy like, buddy. That's some nice shower gel. Did you find Irene?'

Takeo hesitated. 'Yes, she is inside with Noemi and . . . a young guest.' He moved down the hallway to the penthouse, almost carrying Drake. 'And you smell like pond water and blood, William Drake. Less than fancy.'

'Hey, I killed seven dinosaurs tonight,' he said, wincing against the pain in his side from ribs that were definitely perhaps broken. 'Well, re-killed. Killed again. Does that make me responsible for the extinction of the dinosaurs? Heh.'

'I know.'

Drake frowned. 'You don't sound too impressed.'

'Oh, I am.'

'How many dinosaurs did you kill tonight?'

'Less than seven,' Takeo conceded.

'Damn right,' Drake muttered and the hallway spun. He gave Takeo a thumbs-up as his eyes rolled into the back of his head.

He blacked out.

When Takeo brought – *dragged* – Drake into the penthouse Irene gave a startled yelp and pulled little Amy Whitmore out of his way, clutching her against her legs. Takeo calmly carried him to the closest bedroom, calling for aid from the living area, where Irene had been arguing discreetly with Noemi over just what to do about the little girl she had pulled from the chaos at the museum.

'We will discuss this development,' Noemi said, nodding towards Amy as her eyes followed Drake intently, 'after you have healed, William Drake.'

'Yeah, whatever,' Irene said, biting her tongue. She knelt down in front of Lucien Whitmore's daughter and struggled to find a smile. 'I need to go and help my friend, Amy. Do you want to play with your doll on the couch and stay right there? I'll just be a few minutes.'

'I think I should go home now,' Amy said. 'Can you call my daddy?'

Irene tried not to let the wild laughter in the back of her throat escape through her teeth. 'I will, yes, in just a minute, OK.'

'Irene Finlay,' Noemi said.

'Yes. Fine.' Irene pushed her loose hair back behind her ears, exposing her face and determined not to be bothered by the ropy scar tissue. She was still barefoot and wearing the blue party dress courtesy of the Alliance, stained dark red down her side from the gunshot wound back in the museum – also courtesy of the Alliance.

She brushed past Noemi and followed Takeo into the bedroom.

He'd placed Drake on the bed and was in the process of unbuttoning his shirt, having already removed his burnt tuxedo jacket. The tassels on his stupid hat had been scorched as well, and the yarn bobble was reduced to a pitiful nub.

'Numerous lacerations to his face and hands,' Takeo said, as urgently as if he were reading a starter menu and couldn't decide between the garlic bread or the bruschetta. 'From the way he's breathing I'd wager at least three broken ribs. Possibly more. Minor burns to his neck. I think he is also running a fever . . .'

Irene crawled onto the bed next to Drake, leaning over him. Her knees rested just against his frightening crystal arm. His eyelids were closed but his eyes darted beneath them, and Irene wondered just what he was seeing. *Has he gone mad?* That thought wouldn't go away, not after what she'd seen of Carl Anderson on the Rig. But no, when he'd left her at the museum he'd been fine – if coaxing half a dozen zombie dinosaurs to chase him into the park could be called 'fine'. As fine as things got around William Drake, anyway. *But how quickly does the madness happen . . . when it happens? Surely not within half an hour.*

'Doesn't matter,' she whispered.

Irene placed a hand gently on his bare chest, over his heart. His skin was hot and wet with perspiration. She had a flashback to crawling down the elevator shaft beneath the Rig.

'Cuts and stuff are easy, but fixing things I can't see on the inside – I'm worried I'll set your heart on fire or something,' she had said. And Drake had laughed. 'Sweetheart, you already have.'

'Was that still less than a month ago?' Irene muttered, as her pale hand against his dark skin shone with blue light. 'Yes, I can believe it was.'

Irene let her power seep into Drake and she *felt* what was wrong with him. The crystal light travelled through his body, knitting bones back together and healing his cuts and bruises. Her power wasn't so much diagnosing what was wrong, as mending bumps in the road. An all-purpose curative. Irene allowed the light to flow through her and heal the damage. She could feel his burns – not the pain – but more as if she were running her hand across a smooth canvas and her fingertips came across an imperfection in the cloth. Her power healed those imperfections.

Drake was bruised, broken, and wounded in a dozen different places, but apart from some nasty breaks in his ribs, it was mostly superficial. Her power touched the edge of something else, something hot and fierce and spinning, and she nearly recoiled. A wave of exhaustion accompanied the nauseating heat and she saw a flash of red eyes above a smile stained crimson on Drake's face. *He's sick*, she thought – her power said. *He's unwell.*

Irene pushed what she suspected was raw insanity aside and had Drake physically mended in under two minutes, as Takeo and Noemi watched on from the side of the bed. They hadn't – she hoped – noticed her fight the recoil.

Drake's eyes stopped darting about beneath his lids as she removed her hand, but a small frown creased his forehead, which made Irene smile. *He's cute when he frowns.* She lay down on the bed next to him, resting on one arm, and gently pressed her thumb to his forehead and rubbed slow circles. She avoided massaging the kiss-shaped burn tissue – how he'd got that scared her more than almost anything else. More than dinosaurs or all the power of the Alliance.

More than the worry he was losing his mind.

'Will he live then?' Takeo asked.

'He's running hot,' Irene said. *And his mind is eating itself.* 'But there's nothing I can do about that. It's the Crystal-X – sorry, the Yūgen – burning inside him.'

'We must remember it is a miracle he survived absorbing that much of the gift at all,' Noemi said softly. 'He is unique in the world. But he uses the power recklessly, too fiercely. I have tried to guide him, but he is wildfire and will burn without regard.' She shook her head. 'I am failing.'

'His use of the power will burn him alive as surely as an engine running without oil,' Takeo said grimly. 'You must help him, Irene.'

'Me?' Irene nodded. *Yes, of course me.*

'Yes,' Noemi said, a strange glint in her eye. 'Of course you. For whatever reason, he will listen to you, Irene.' Her tone sounded neutral, guarded. 'William Drake is loyal to you.'

'Oh, he's fiercely loyal, Noemi, once you've earned his trust.' She gave the Japanese girl a cool smile. 'Earn his trust, *deserve* his trust, and he'll bring entire oil rigs crashing down for you.'

* * *

221

Drake awoke to find himself in bed with Irene.

He took a second to process that, found the circumstances to his liking, and offered her a weary wink. 'Hello, Miss Finlay,' he said. 'How long was I out?'

'Not even ten minutes,' she replied. 'I healed you as best I could, Will.'

'I feel great,' Drake lied. He felt like roadkill. 'A few aches and pains, but nothing a good night's sleep wouldn't fix.'

Drake knew that Irene knew that he hadn't slept more than an hour in the last week. And when he had, his dreams had been of nightmarish crystal landscapes. He took a deep breath and it didn't hurt. His ribs were mended. Irene was a wonder – and the sooner he got her to London, the sooner she could heal his mother.

And then they could get fish and chips.

The last two years of prisons and escapes may actually pay off.

'We don't have a lot of time left, if Whitmore is to be believed,' Irene said. 'Only half an hour before the creature, whatever it is, attacks New York.'

Drake leant up and caught her lips. He kissed her deeply, cupping her cheek with his real hand. 'Thank you,' he said after the kiss and took a deep breath, enjoying the smell of her hair – like strawberries and rainfall.

'You're welcome,' she said, with a pleased smile.

Irene kissed him again and Drake moved his hand to her shoulder, and then down along the curve of her side. He rested his palm on her hip and remembered that he was almost shirtless, and what shirt he did have on was stained bloody and black.

He sighed and sat up on the bed. Irene shifted next to him, shuffling her legs under her and resting her hands in her lap. 'What's wrong?' she asked.

He grinned. 'You mean besides the fact that Brand is still out there and we've got only half an hour before Whitmore said New York is going to be attacked by the crystal beneath the Rig?'

'Yeah, besides that.'

Drake laughed. 'Well besides that, I'd really like to have an hour together, just you and me – maybe some pizza from Lombardi's – without being interrupted by the Alliance, or Haven, or crystal doom and gloom. I kind of want to ask you out for fish and chips, Irene Finlay.'

'Please stop being so cavalier. What are we going to do, Will?'

Irene was afraid. She was strong, but she was afraid. He went to hug her with both arms, thought better of wrapping his crystal monstrosity around her, and stroked her shoulder with his real hand instead.

'Amy Whitmore is in the living room,' she said.

'She . . . huh, what?'

'She was alone at the museum and I just kind of . . . brought her with me. I didn't know what else to do. The man watching her was killed. I was worried there'd be more dinosaurs or Brand would find us or something.'

Drake considered and then nodded. 'So, kidnapping. May as well add it to the ever-growing list of crimes we've committed.'

'I didn't kidnap her!'

'Does her father know?'

'She wants to call him.'

Drake nodded and pulled his battered phone out of his pocket. The screen had cracked and water beads bubbled under the glass. The device was dead. 'Do you have your phone?'

'On the kitchen bench.'

Drake swung his legs off the bed and took a second before standing up. The room didn't spin but his legs felt a little like brittle twigs. 'Let's go and make a call then.'

He stepped out into the hallway and Irene followed at his side. *Ready to catch me if I fall.* That was a nice thought. He found her phone on the marble island bench in the middle of the kitchen and accessed the contacts.

'Who are you calling, William Drake?' Noemi asked, stepping over from the living area to join him in the kitchen.

She was dressed all in black, her katana hanging loose in its sheath at her waist and her dark hair pulled back into a tight ponytail. He glanced past her and saw Takeo on the couch playing with Amy Whitmore. He held a small patchwork doll by the arms and was making it dance in the air. Irene squeezed his arm and walked over to the couch.

'Michael Tristan,' Drake said. 'I'm calling Tristan, because I just can't quit him. He's working with Whitmore, somewhere, feeding him all my secrets. We need to let President Lucien know his daughter is safe.'

Noemi quirked an eyebrow. 'Safe? Around you?'

'Heh. Oh, fair point. But if it were my family or whatever, I'd want to know. Especially after that trick Brand pulled with the dinosaurs.'

'You are assuming Lucien Whitmore has any emotional connection to this child.'

Drake shrugged. 'She wants us to call him. Little girl frightened and lost in a big city after running from evil dinosaurs and she wants her dad – what would you do?'

'Whitmore may use this as an opportunity to seize you.'

'That he may, but I am not so easily seized.' Drake thought about the three times he'd been captured in the past two years after escaping Alliance prisons across the face of the world. 'Well, not so easily any more. Also, he told me we're in trouble.'

Noemi tensed. 'What manner of trouble?'

'The crystal under the Rig? It's been growing since I escaped. And it's coming here. I think whatever is living in it – the creature or alien or whatever – is coming for us. We went and woke it up. Whitmore said the crystal would reach New York tonight.'

'And you believed him?'

'He had some pretty convincing charts and maps and stuff, yeah. I'm easily swayed by pie charts.'

Noemi hesitated and then sighed. 'We must leave the city. But if the population here is exposed to so much Yūgen . . .'

'Kind of thinking the same thing. This could get really nasty. Give me five minutes and I'll show you a pie chart supporting my position.'

'Haven is safe,' Noemi said. 'Whatever darkness has grown under the ocean cannot touch the grounds of Haven. Our borders are protected. If we can make it to Japan, then you can rest.'

Drake clenched his crystal fist and exhaled slowly. 'We have to make it out of New York first,' he said. 'And then hop, skip, and jump across a continent or two. What's the plan?'

'It was going to be a ship,' Noemi said. 'A vessel in the harbour that will take us out to sea. Once we're far enough away, several hundred miles, a long-range helicopter will collect us and fly us over to Europe.' She bit her lip. 'Looks like we are taking the long way round after all, but if it's true the creature under the Rig is approaching, the ocean may prove treacherous.'

'Plane to London, then?' Drake asked.

'We have come this far, so why not?' Noemi hesitated. 'It is your mother, isn't it? Your reason for journeying home.'

Drake nodded.

'Takeo has done his research on you. We had to leave Haven in such a rush, after I sensed you. We knew nothing more than that you were half a world away. And then reports of the terrorist William Drake started to surface, of the chaos on the Rig, and I knew you were the one I had been sent to find.'

'Are you glad you did?'

Noemi tilted her head and grinned. 'Oh yes. From now on I go where you go, Drake.'

'Call me Will – all my friends do.' He pressed his thumb to the name *Michael Tristan* in the phone's contacts and held the device to his ear.

Whitmore answered on the first ring. 'Hello, Mr. Drake.'

'Tristan is with you, then?' *Good*.

'Indeed. I apologise for the unpleasantness at the museum. Have you reconsidered my offer?'

'Is Brand still breathing?'

'Mr. Brand will be reprimanded for his actions.'

Drake scowled. 'You keep saying that. I'm not buying it.'

226

'If not to accept my offer, then what do you want?'

'I've got Amy here,' Drake said.

'Yes, of that I am aware. She left the museum with Miss Finlay. My people tell me you're back in that apartment on Park Avenue.' Whitmore paused. 'Are you threatening me with my daughter's life, Mr. Drake? I warn you now, that is a line you can only cross once.'

'No, no threats. Who the hell do you think I am?'

Whitmore sighed down the line. 'Do you even know yourself any more?'

That made Drake frown. 'I'm asking if you want to come and pick her up. Or we'll drop her off somewhere. We're leaving town.'

'You cannot run from the fight.'

'I've been running for two years. Why stop now?'

Whitmore chuckled. 'Very well. Safe passage from the city in exchange for my daughter? Agreed. Times Square. Ten minutes.' He disconnected the call.

Drake took a deep breath and let it out slowly. He slipped Irene's phone into his pocket and thought through the rough sketch of a plan he'd been making up as he went along these past few days. *This is my chance. Follow the web.*

'What are we to do, Will?' Noemi asked.

Drake blinked and looked up. 'Hmm? Oh. Times Square. We'll drop Amy off there and, with any luck, the Alliance will let us leave town.' *After I take care of one little thing, most likely, if I've read you right at all, Whitmore.*

'I would not trust Lucien Whitmore to keep his word,' Noemi said.

Drake tapped his crystal fingers against the marble bench top, producing a dull chime, and nodded slowly. *Neither would I.* 'Deal's a deal, right? You know he's got colourful eyes. The President of the Alliance was at Haven, once upon a time, wasn't he?'

'Yes, yes he was.'

'You should have told me that before. What can he do with the power?'

Noemi bristled. 'I have told you, that question is impolite at best, offensive at worst.'

'You don't know, do you?'

Noemi shook her head. 'Lucien Whitmore left Haven when I was only a child of four. He . . . made enemies before he left, and assumed control of Alliance Systems not long after his father's death.'

'Some of the oldest and wealthiest families in the world, that's what you said.' Drake chuckled. 'And then his family went and discovered another source of Yūgen, beneath the deep blue, icy arctic sea, and what he must have thought about that . . .'

'The Yūgen beneath the Rig does not act entirely like the gemstones grown in Haven. We believe this is why he was experimenting on the inmates.'

'It also went boom when exposed to the air.'

'Yes, that is interesting.'

'And there's something living in it. Something . . . mean. Something that Whitmore wants to fight.'

Noemi shivered and gripped the hilt of her sword. 'That terrifies me. The creature beneath the sea.'

'Bluebird, they're calling it. What is it, do you think? Honestly.'

She looked at his forehead, her lips a thin, pale line as she examined his kiss-shaped scar. 'Nothing kind.'

Drake nodded and clapped his hands together – gently. 'Best we be somewhere else very soon, then. If Whitmore's right, it could be following me, which means if I leave it may spare the city. Either way, the Alliance have enough resources. We're not needed here. We can get out while they're distracted. And if not . . . well, I can't just leave the city to its fate.' He walked over to the couch, to Takeo and Irene. 'Hey, Amy. We're going to take you to see your dad now. I just need to change out of these stinky clothes.'

'Your hat is funny!' Amy said and giggled.

'Maybe a little bit, yeah,' he said. 'We're getting out of here, you two, so pack a bag. Leaving in two minutes.'

'Are you in charge now?' Takeo asked.

Drake winked. 'Was I ever not? No, we're a team, mate. Team Drake.' He glanced at Noemi. 'We drop Amy off and her father will let us leave the city. We need to hurry. Two minutes and we're out the door.'

Chapter Twenty-Two

Times Square

Irene's healing had taken the edge off Drake's bone-numbing fatigue. He felt charged, alive – ready to kick ass, take names, drink milkshakes, and get the hell out of town. A pervasive heat had settled in his chest, around his heart and near the thin claws of skeletal crystal growing in sharp lines from his shoulder. His forehead pounded, thrummed, on the edge of a migraine. He wasn't sure if it was the madness from the Crystal-X or just how much he was falling for Irene Finlay.

Love and madness are the same thing, he thought, feeling wise beyond his years for a brief second before snorting a rough chuckle. *I don't know what the hell I'm feeling . . . I can't, with all this Crystal-X inside me.*

He and Irene walked to Times Square, holding Amy Whitmore's hands, along 59th Street next to the park. She skipped between them, happy and laughing, as only the very young can be. Noemi and Takeo kept a clear path ahead. A cadre of Alliance soldiers, goons in fine suits, had met them out front of the apartment, and under their 'guard', the NYPD officers around Central Park didn't waylay them. Walking would be quicker than trying to steer the car through the traffic and police checkpoints that had sprung up after the museum incident.

Drake had changed into a clean pair of navy jeans and a black short-sleeved shirt. His crystal limb was on full display and he found that didn't bother him so much. Perhaps his lack of worry should have worried him, how quickly he was becoming used to the obsidian change. The marble of light in his wrist, the guardian eagle, shone softly. He had no idea how to summon the ethereal creature. What remained of his tassel hat kept his head warm – so far the wool had mostly escaped the blue flames, gunfire, helicopter crashes, and reanimated dinosaurs. Irene had also changed out of her party dress, into jeans and a tank top. She wore a light jacket against the frosty bite in the night air. New York was cold. Takeo and Noemi had dressed for a fight. Dark clothes, solid boots, and while Noemi carried her curved sword in its sheath at her waist, Takeo had a pistol holstered under each arm. *But what can he do with Yūgen, I wonder?*

'Do you think Michael will be there?' Irene asked, as they took a left down onto 7th Avenue.

Drake stared down the avenue at the lights of Times Square – something he had never seen before in person, but in a hundred films and TV shows. The throngs of people walking the streets worried him. So far all his encounters with the Alliance had ended in crystal fire. They were about ten minutes away, at a steady clip. Drake met her eyes. 'I'm counting on it.'

231

'My daddy has an ice cream store near here,' Amy said. 'Do you want ice cream, Irene?'

Irene smiled. 'Not right now. What's your favourite flavour?'

Amy shrugged. 'Maybe the pink one. Or the one with cookie bits. Do you want ice cream, Will?'

'I really, really, really . . . really, really, really super do,' Drake said. 'Maybe later, though. Must be past your bedtime by now!'

Amy huffed. 'I'm allowed to stay up and watch Teddy's Adventures!'

'Oh yeah?' Drake smiled wryly. 'What time's that on?'

'After Arthur the Antelope.'

'Ah, of course. It's way past my bedtime.' Drake shuffled around a food cart full of hotdogs and pretzels. His stomach grumbled, he was famished from the amount of power he had used, but he resisted the temptation. A delay could cost him at this point in the game. The webbed path in his mind trembled. So much was on the line, and he was dragging all of his friends into this – hopefully last – confrontation with the Alliance.

I should have told them to run. It's me they want. Irene shouldn't be here, and neither should Noemi and Takeo. Still got a hidden ace to play, though.

Too late to back out. The half a dozen soldiers shadowing them, the half a dozen he could see, would put up a fight.

And little Amy didn't deserve to be caught in the crossfire.

Times Square punched Drake in the face with a thousand bright lights, screens full of corporate advertisements, and dozens of clubs, pubs and department stores. He contemplated raiding the M&M World store for much-needed supplies, but as with the pretzel vendor he decided against what his stomach

232

was telling him. Food would come later, if Lucien Whitmore did what Drake thought he would.

As soon as they entered the heart of Times Square, the shadowy figures in suits dispersed and at least two dozen SUVs with blazing lights and sirens converged from all the available side streets. Alliance guards, soldiers and NYPD officers, all heavily armed, emerged from the vehicles and began to evacuate Times Square between 46th and 47th Streets. Drake watched – he marvelled – keeping hold of Amy Whitmore's hand as the entire space emptied out. Irene shuffled in closer and Noemi and Takeo kept a hand near their weapons.

New Yorkers, tourists, performers, ticket hawkers and food vendors were shuffled out of the area. In the space of less than five minutes, Drake stood with only his handful of allies, and Whitmore's daughter, in the bustling, hustling heart of Manhattan Island. The guards and police had set up a perimeter stretching two blocks, with the public on the other side, and barricaded people in the hotels and restaurants.

Empty of all save a few people, Drake thought Times Square looked bigger, cavernous – where wide streets met and branched away.

Only once the space was clear did a sleek limousine pull into Times Square, driving off the street and onto the pedestrian walkway between 7th Avenue and the skyscrapers. Drake and his group had a set of red and white steps rising at their backs, forming the roof of the TKTS Times Square building. Broadway sales had come to a sudden stop, given the situation. The limousine parked in front of Drake, trapping his group between the car and the stairs and, as Drake felt a rush that he might just pull this off, Lucien Whitmore and Michael Tristan emerged from the luxurious vehicle.

So everybody is here except Brand. Where's he hiding? A shiver ran down Drake's spine. Something was about to happen . . .

The stolen Alliance drone hovered behind Tristan, and he shouldered the backpack Brand had swiped during Irene's abduction from the apartment.

'Daddy!' Amy Whitmore cried and dashed forward. She stumbled and Whitmore caught her under her arms, sweeping her into a quick hug. After a moment, he put her in the limousine and shut the door.

'Thank you,' Whitmore said to Irene. 'For keeping her safe.'

Drake glared at Tristan, and his old cellmate shifted nervously on the spot, gripping the strap on the backpack a little tighter.

'We may leave now, yes?' Takeo said. 'Your word, President Whitmore.'

Whitmore regarded Noemi and Takeo for a long moment. 'Your precious Haven will offer no protection in the war to come.' He dismissed them with a wave and looked at Drake behind his sleek, reflective sunglasses. 'I will honour our arrangement to a degree and allow your friends safe passage. The two from Haven and Miss Finlay. But I simply cannot allow you to leave New York, Mr. Drake.'

Drake laughed. 'Oh look, you're betraying us. I am shocked. Shocked and surprised. Curse you, Whitmore!' He shook his fist at the president of the Alliance.

Whitmore checked his wrist watch and sighed. 'And that is time, ladies and gentlemen. Drake, take the deal – if your friends do not leave now they may not get another chance.'

'Where's Brand?' Drake asked. Another shiver, stronger this time, almost like an electric shock, ran down his back. 'What's . . . ?' He looked at Irene, at Noemi and Takeo, and his heart skipped a few beats.

The air felt tense, as if the entire city was holding its breath. The hustle and bustle of New York, the sights and sounds, grew dull to Drake. The sights and sounds were still there, the slow gyration of ten million people living their lives, of streets packed with food carts and yellow taxis, but all that faded into the background.

Drake crouched down on his haunches and pressed his crystal hand against the concrete. He tilted his head, grimaced, and felt a low, but powerful vibration shudder up his arm and through his body. *That's not the subway*, he thought, a split second before a tremendous, glass-shattering *boom* echoed down the canyons of New York City.

His friends and allies – and his enemies, dressed in their sleek, faceless Alliance armour – all pressed their hands to their ears as the ground shook and white steam burst from the drains and sewers. A heavy pause followed the boom, time for Drake and Tristan to share a quick look, and then the manhole covers exploded from the road and thick tendrils of dark crystal swimming with bruised-purple light burst from underground.

Several dozen tentacles, on all corners of Times Square, broke the surface, shattering the roads and tipping over parked Alliance and NYPD cars. The crystal pillars, each about as thick as an ancient oak tree, clawed along the ground and slithered up the sides of the hotels and other buildings, trapping the people inside.

All of this happened in the space of about three seconds, but in those brief moments a tangled nest of dark crystal enclosed Times Square in an ugly purple wall. Arcs of wicked lightning crackled along the surface of the crystal, striking at the ground and the ring of Alliance goons Whitmore had brought with him. They stumbled back, some burnt and screaming, all of them trapped with Drake and his friends in the heart of the square.

'Well,' Irene said. 'That's ugly.'

The crystal continued to grow, to spew forth from under the ground, and claw its way up the buildings. Something moved within the crystal briar patch, something more than purple light. Drake glimpsed a pair of yellow eyes, then another, and behind those eyes shadowed forms swimming within the dark bands.

Visions of horrendous crystal spiders danced in his head. He didn't need an ability to see the future to know what was about to happen.

'I'm afraid,' Drake whispered, then cleared his throat. 'I'm afraid we're in a spot of bother.'

'*More than you know, Drake!*' a loud, twisted voice echoed across Times Square.

With a weary sort of sigh, Drake turned and followed the red and white stairs of the TKTS building to its top. Marcus Brand, the Skeleton Man, his pasty skin painted with purple light from the walls of crystal, and a sleek rifle slung over his shoulder, waved at him.

'Oh, look, it's this bastard . . .' Drake muttered.

Brand pointed at Drake. 'Now watch what happens next!'

The crystal choking the buildings all around Times Square began to pulse with a dull, deadly light. Vicious cracks splintered up and down the twisted tendrils, like a thin sheet of ice breaking underfoot.

From those cracks burst dozens – hundreds – of crystal monstrosities.

Chapter Twenty-Three

Crystal Force

The creatures born inside the bands of thick, glowing crystal took to the sky and slammed into the ground. Of all shapes and sizes, resembling spiders and cockroaches with thin wings, bugs and insects, they all burst into the world with the familiar chime of glass striking glass.

'To arms!' Whitmore roared. 'Protect the limousine.'

Drake snapped his head back to Brand in time to see the man disappear over the edge of the steps and out of sight, rifle slung over his shoulder and more weaponry holstered at his waist. He took a step forward to follow him, to put an end to the mess, but Takeo grasped his arm.

'We must stay together,' the giant boy said, and his grip on Drake's arm was unbreakable. Blue light swam deep within his eyes. 'We must protect each other.'

Drake hesitated only a moment and then nodded. He turned to Whitmore and Tristan, with Irene and Noemi at his back next to Takeo. 'Well?' he said.

Whitmore pressed a phone against his ear and barked a few commands. The soldiers and police opened fire, blasting the dozens of monsters sweeping along Times Square with bullets that did next to nothing. Gunshots echoed throughout the square, reverberating off the crystal pillars, and tore chunks of dark material from the creatures – but sparkling light swirled to the wounds and healed the damage, fusing the crystal skin back in place.

The hundreds of flying beasts, large cockroaches, spiralled up into the air in one flock. As they reached the height of One Times Square, the tower, the crystal cockroaches dispersed across the city, flying out to every point of the compass – and began to descend on New York.

The chiming of crystal limbs on concrete brought Drake's attention back to the ground. A six-legged monstrosity, with a maw of sparkling silver fangs, leapt at them. He raised his palms and fired a burst of raw power – something he wasn't supposed to do, according to Noemi – and shattered the creature beyond repair.

Distant explosions, tyres squealing on unseen roads and high-pitched screams echoed down the avenues and streets of New York City. Drake began firing wildly into groups of the crystal creatures, slaying as many as he could with nothing but pure, hot power – with force enough to crack their impossible hides.

Damned or dead either way, he thought.

Takeo was at his back, and his hands were encased in mittens of silver light. As one of the spiders moved in, Takeo lunged forward and grasped its sharp-angled head in his hands. With a grunt of effort, he twisted and wrenched the head from the spider's body. The crystal monster twitched, legs splaying, and fell to the ground.

'Will!' Irene cried. 'Behind the limo!'

Drake turned in time to see a spider dig its limbs into the trunk of the limousine, shifting the whole car. He raised his arm to destroy it, to protect young Amy, but Lucien Whitmore stepped in the way. The President of the Alliance removed his sunglasses and clapped his hands together. A dull chime, almost below hearing over the noise of the attack – *of the invasion* – reverberated in Drake's head.

A pale mist flowed from Whitmore's hand, snakes of glowing smoke, and enveloped the spider on the limousine. The mist *ate* the crystal, dissolved the monster, reducing its bulk to vicious spasms, which rolled from the car. Whitmore opened the rear door and retrieved Amy, holding her to his chest and shielding her face.

He turned and ran past Drake, giving him a desperate look with eyes glowing blue and red, to the front of the vehicle. Once there he raised his hand and a surge of fresh mist fell in a wide sphere, as if he were encased in a bubble, around him and his daughter. Whitmore disappeared under his shield.

Something pushed Drake in the back, hard, and he fell against the limousine. He turned, furious, to see it was Irene, who leapt back as a leg from one of the spiders swept the space he had been standing just a moment before. That close, Drake saw just how razor-sharp the legs on the monsters were. It dug a clean laceration in the concrete, sweeping for his head.

Takeo grabbed the monster and tore it apart, pushing Drake and Irene closer together.

'Thanks,' he breathed to her with a grin.

Irene smiled. 'No problem –'

Drake's eyes widened and Irene fell silent at the look on his face. Marcus Brand appeared behind her with his wasted arm held towards the sky, a blade of fetid yellow light – *hard light* – three feet long in his grasp. He snarled at Drake and brought the blade swinging down towards Irene's neck.

Noemi met his attack halfway, her sleek, silver katana catching and deflecting the blade before it could cleave Irene's head from her shoulders. Irene ducked, and Tristan pulled her aside.

Brand dispelled his blade and took a large step back. Fresh power flooded his palms and he fired a sphere of hot, rippling energy at Noemi. At that distance, he couldn't miss.

The burst of fiery energy should have fried Noemi on the spot, but she moved fast – faster than Drake had ever seen any one move, and closed in on Brand. The fireball struck the remains of a spider and it exploded into a rain of sharp, crystal shards. Noemi curved around the blast, the trail of her cloak absorbed by the flame, and spun with her sword.

Noemi moved with such balance and grace that Drake felt like he was watching silk fall over curved glass. She danced below Brand's guard and moved in on his left, nicking and slicing at his exposed skin with her blade. She sketched lines in his flesh that bled light, fusing the wounds closed as quickly as she could draw them. The sword wasn't so much a tool as an extension of her arm.

All of this happened in seconds, as Drake tried to circle closer, through the remains of crystal spiders and dodging the strikes of a few more. He glanced at Takeo and saw a ring of decapitated spider corpses encircling him. His eyes were wild and he threw his head back and laughed.

Crazier than me, Drake thought.

Brand grew frustrated with Noemi's deadly elegance – moves that would have killed any other opponent by now – and drew a familiar revolver from the holster at his waist.

Warden Storm's revolver, stolen from the Rig, which Drake had last seen pointed at his skull before Brand had shot him above New York. *Should not have kept that.* Brand pointed the gun at Noemi as she flowed away.

'Dodge this, bitch,' he growled – as Drake closed the gap – and pulled the trigger.

Drake threw his arm forward to shield her, but she simply disappeared. The bullet shot across the square, a wicked snap echoing through the rest of the noise, and struck the front window of the limousine. The bulletproof glass splintered but held.

Noemi reappeared from behind her veil on Brand's left and, with a cry, sliced her katana down from above and severed his hand.

'Yes!' Drake said as Brand's hand fell away, still grasping the revolver.

Brand cursed and stumbled back, clutching his wrist, which sizzled with bubbling white light – what passed for his blood.

Drake moved in to end the fight.

He ducked as he approached, picked up the revolver by its barrel, and slapped Brand across the face with his own severed hand, wrapped around the butt of the gun.

Brand struck back at him with a closed fist and the blow glanced off his jaw. Noemi used the distraction to glide in again, her blade gleaming, and drove the sword through Brand's shoulder, piercing the fused armour and his flesh. Three inches of folded steel emerged out of his back.

He screamed – not in pain, but anger. A wave of invisible force knocked Drake away and Noemi lost her grip on the katana's hilt. They were thrown back together, Noemi atop Drake, across the ground towards the base of the red and white steps.

Drake would have kept sliding but Noemi hooked her foot between a concrete bollard and a tangle of metal piping and pulled them to an abrupt stop. She cried out. The revolver flew from Drake's hand and struck one of the spider monsters.

'You OK?' he asked, pulling himself out from under her. 'Come on, can't stay here.'

Drake pulled her to her feet and Noemi tested her weight on her foot. She winced but it held.

Another noise rose above the chimes of the spider creatures and Drake looked up to the sky, and marvelled as a dozen Alliance attack helicopters swooped into Times Square, over the pillars of twisted crystal sealing them all inside. On the deck of each helicopter sat two gunmen with long, black-barrelled guns as thick as tree branches – or a crystal limb.

The helicopters hovered over Times Square for a long, pregnant moment, and then opened fire into the crowds of spiders. The rounds from the massive guns churned through the crystal creatures and split them into a mess of tangled limbs spewing glowing ichor.

'Never thought I'd be happy to see an Alliance chopper,' Drake said and nudged Noemi.

The helicopters began swooping in and out of the kill zone, taking turns to strafe the creatures and the crystal pillars with high-calibre fire.

Drake took a deep breath. 'Where did Brand go?'

The Skeleton Man knelt on one knee near the limousine, the sphere of glowing mist from Whitmore's shield behind him growing dull. Whitmore, still clutching Amy, emerged from his shield in time to see Brand grit his teeth and wrench Noemi's blade from his chest with a cry of triumph.

Brand met Drake's gaze only a handful of metres away – and swung the rifle hooked over his shoulder into his hand. Whitmore ran to join Irene and Tristan near the trunk of the limousine as the helicopters lit up Times Square. Takeo had cleared enough of the crystal spiders around the limousine and steps that Irene, Tristan, and Whitmore, with Amy in his arms, could dash around, away from Brand, to stand near Noemi and Drake.

A swarm of flying cockroach creatures hurled themselves at the line of choppers hovering above the battlefield – the pilots never stood a chance. The weight and ferocity of the beasts sent half a dozen of the choppers spinning into the crystal pillars that had birthed the cockroaches. Loud explosions rocked Times Square as fiery husks of crystal and chopper slammed into the ground, taking with them at least a few more of the crystal spiders.

Burning metal and jet fuel joined the mess of hot, acrid scents drifting over New York City.

Brand laughed at the chaos and took a step forward. He raised his gun, pointing the barrel at Noemi, who stood between the two separate groups, and winked at Drake. Drake stepped in front of her and clenched his crystal fist. *This needs to end – I need to speak to Bluebird.*

'Wonder how many bullets it'll take to put you down, Drake?' Brand asked. 'Let's find out.'

'*No!*' Whitmore roared. '*Stand down, Mr. Brand.*'

Brand's finger slipped onto the trigger.

Drake braced himself and cursed. *He's not playing for your team any longer, Whitmore. This is going to hurt.*

Brand's finger twitched again and a hail of hot, deadly metal filled the air.

Irene's heart leapt into her throat; the hairs on the back of her neck stood on end, as the clatter of machine-gunfire broke across Times Square, mixing with the cacophony of sound from the crashing or fleeing attack helicopters and the buzz of crystal wings.

Brand opened fire at the same instant Drake raised his arm – not in front of him, but towards Irene, a determined look on his bloody face. She screamed as Brand's fire spattered across her group of allies – and Whitmore – and swung over Drake, peppering him with dozens of bullets. Takeo pulled Noemi out of the way, behind Irene, who found an impossible shield in front of her, protecting her from the deadly projectiles. Some of the bullets struck the shield and sparked ripples of blue light across its surface.

The rest struck Drake.

Drake's jeans and shirt were torn open, the denim blossoming with bright red spots under the hail of gunfire, and he fell to his knees, thrashing like a puppet on strings.

Irene drew a harsh, ragged breath as the clip ran dry and Brand threw aside his gun. Drake slumped, swaying as if he were about to fall face first into the sidewalk.

And then he stood.

A thousand bright spots of crystal light burst from the dozens of wounds across his body and Drake looked up, a horrific, bloodstained smile on his face, and *hurled* himself at Marcus Brand.

Irene almost didn't see him move, but he left a trail of neon-blue light in his wake and covered the distance between himself and Brand in half a heartbeat.

Drake slammed into Brand and a wave of concussive force echoed outwards, forcing Whitmore, Tristan and Brand to stumble back. Any windows and glass across the square and up the hotel skyscrapers still in one piece shattered in a rain of shards. Irene felt the ground shake behind the shield. She steadied herself as Will Drake shrugged off a clip's worth of bullet wounds as if they were no worse than mosquito bites – and tore into the Skeleton Man.

In the heartbeat after the first of Brand's bullets struck Drake, he found himself once again in his mother's kitchen.

Dead or dying, he had time to think. *Just like when I fell from the chopper with a bullet in my head.*

The creature from under the Rig, the alien wearing his mother's face, didn't even pretend to convince him this was real. Wherever he was, it was happening in some place between seconds – what had she said last time? Something about how consciousness, and coming close to death, opened lines of communication.

'Hello, Bluebird. Brand shot me again,' Drake said. 'A whole bunch of times. Didn't know how else to get in touch with you.'

The creature frowned, splitting the fake human skin of her forehead and revealing the dark crystal underneath. A million blue lights swirled in her skull, a nexus of alien thought.

'You made it to New York,' Drake said. 'Or, your Crystal-X did, anyway. It's choking the city. Weird bugs and insects are attacking people. Make it stop.' The creature said nothing, only looked at him with a curious expression on her face. 'What are you, really?'

'Ancient,' she said. 'Restless. Hungry.' She paused. 'Betrayed.'

The floral blouse and skin Bluebird wore faded away, melted, as did the reality of the kitchen around him. Before Drake stood a creature seven feet tall, thin, shaped in a rough approximation of a human, but with a nest of crystals growing out the back of her head like tree roots. He tried not to think how his crystal arm resembled the arms of the creature. And, as ever, sparks of blue and white ethereal light swam beneath her skin.

The kitchen had been replaced with something horribly familiar. Drake stood on the helipad on the southern platform of the Rig. Only now it was twisted and ruined, wrapped in bands and pillars of crystal from under the water. Of the other platforms he could see very little, just glimpses of the structure through the alien growth. A fierce Arctic wind bit at his face and ears – a wind he had hoped never to feel again.

'Are we . . . really here?' he asked. He glanced at the sky, strewn with thunderstorm clouds, and decided life had grown somewhat strange, over the past few weeks.

When the creature spoke, she still sounded like his mother, but the words echoed in his mind, and made his teeth hurt. 'This is where we may speak. The game has changed, William Drake. Marcus Brand is blinded by his hate for you. This hate . . . is of no use to me.'

'Those sure weren't chocolate kisses he was sending me from the barrel of his rifle. Are you healing me again?'

'He is a blunt tool. One, I believe, beyond sharpening.' The lights in the crystal face formed a pair of pure blue eyes. 'Stop him. Defeat him, William Drake, and I will not revive him again as I have done for you.'

'This is the second time he's killed me. Third time he's shot me. What makes you think I can stop him?' Drake pressed two fingers against his eyelids and fought against just sitting down and giving up. 'Never thought I'd say that. Follow the web, Drake,' he muttered. 'Follow the web.'

'I will not extend your life again,' she said. 'I cannot. Your mind is fractured, drowned in my radiance. And I will need you in the days to come. You must rest . . . learn. And grow strong.'

Drake clenched his fists and took a deep breath. 'I can't bloody sleep, can I? How much time is passing here? If Brand is hurting my friends –'

'Seconds are hours here. Hours can be months.'

Drake took a deep breath and exhaled slowly. He considered, and then nodded. 'OK, I'll keep playing. Fix me up good, no stupid kiss-shaped scars, and I'll put an end to Brand. Already had a plan for that, anyway, before all that crystal nonsense burst from the sewer. You're just getting in my damn way.'

248

The creature tilted her head and Drake swore he could feel a smile on that expressionless, spark-filled face. She reached a long, thin arm of crystal towards him. Drake took a step back and raised his hand.

'One thing – I'll fight Brand, but you leave New York alone. However you brought the crystal here, you take it away. All those creatures, as well. There's too many people living here. You don't get to hurt them.'

'Agreed,' the creature said.

Drake blinked. 'What? Just like that?'

'One city more or less will not make a difference in the war to come. Stop him, and I shall withdraw. Fail, and I will take the city. We have our understanding, William Drake.' The creature pressed her hand against his chest and a blinding white light eclipsed Drake's vision.

Hot fire rushed through his body, a torrent of power, and the world fell away. He blinked and once again stood in Times Square; his body had never left, and light as white as snow bled from the dozens of bullet holes in his chest, legs, and arms.

Only been a second, not even, he thought, glimpsing the horrified faces of his friends. *No time to explain.*

Drake's body flooded with power, with alien light, and he hurled himself into Brand with enough force to smash concrete to dust. He grasped the melted Rig armour fused to Brand's shoulders and threw him across Times Square as if he weighed nothing.

Brand, an ugly snarl on his face turned into surprise, bounced off the trunk of Whitmore's limousine and rolled along the ground. The limousine rocked from the impact and, out of the corner of his eye, Drake saw Whitmore's security forces, those that had survived the monstrous assault, move in, rifles raised. Whitmore waved them away, a dangerous, curious glint in his eyes.

He wanted Drake and Brand to fight.

High above the cockroach monsters had settled on the crystal pillars and the skyscrapers, seemingly to watch Drake and Brand fight, as well. The spiders that were still whole and undamaged did the same, stopping in their tracks. None of them moved, even as the police and security forces continued to fire at them.

She's keeping her end of the deal . . . now I have to keep mine.

Drake *bled* light. Bullets that hadn't passed clean through him *melted* from the heat, while his flesh knitted itself back together. He felt no pain, not even a pinch, but the churning heat in his chest intensified and a wave of dizziness made him sick to his stomach. Over two weeks ago now, just after absorbing the Crystal-X, his body had healed itself. But not like this – he felt nothing, not even a small tingle from the light, as the bullets were forced from his body and the wounds healed.

As Brand started to pick himself up, Michael Tristan appeared on Drake's left.

'Your eyes are blue,' he said. 'Whatever you're about to do, I guess you think it's the right thing.'

'You have them, yes?' Drake asked.

Tristan nodded, as the drone spun around them over their heads in quick circles, recording everything. He dug into the backpack and produced two crystals, one as blue as lightning, the other as red as blood. The same crystals that

Drake and Brand had created back at the train derailment in Newfoundland.

'He did just as you said he would, mate. We can –'

Drake cut Tristan off as Brand regained his feet and howled at the night sky. '*Just be ready!*'

The light had healed Drake swiftly. He didn't know how, but he'd hoped as much, although creeping fatigue pushed through the river of power. Even the light had its limits, given how much he'd been using it, and how much he'd needed to be healed. *I can't rely on this much longer.* The creature had told him as much, too. His mind was drowning, which was just a fancy way of saying he was slipping. Going mad. His crystal arm swam with a whole school of sparks, moving in quick spirals. As Brand clenched his remaining hand into a fist and yellow lightning burst from between his palms, scoring the sidewalk, Drake's arm erupted in blue flame.

The whole limb, from the tips of his dark fingers to the edge of his shoulder, was alight with undulating fire. He felt no heat. The ragged sleeve of his shirt was burnt away.

He met Brand halfway, in the heart of Times Square, but this time the madman was ready for him. Brand didn't budge an inch as Drake slammed into him, going for the guard's throat with his flaming arm. Brand's crackling hand fell on Drake's shoulder and a shockwave of conflicting energy, harsh yellow and electric blue, burst into the air and cracked the sidewalk beneath their feet.

'You meet the boss lady?' Brand asked, as he threw his power against Drake. 'She heal you up again? We've work to do, Drake, you and me. Neither of us can die until that work is done.'

'Actually,' Drake growled, 'she told me you're fired!'

Drake met the attack with force of his own, intensifying the flames running down his arm until the fire was almost too bright to behold. Brand's wasted hand on his normal shoulder, the shoulder untouched by crystal, burnt into his skin, but blue light met the assault there, as well, healing the burns as soon as they appeared.

That arm did feel like it had been set on fire.

Drake gritted his teeth and managed a feral grin. 'That thing, she wants me to kill you.'

'That *thing* is a god, Drake. She chose me, as I burnt in the *Titan*. *She chose me!*'

Drake stumbled back a step and Brand pressed forward. He moved his left hand from Drake's shoulder and gripped his crystal arm. The energy pouring from Brand sizzled against the crystal limb. For the first time, Drake felt something in his mutated arm – an intense heat and pressure, as fierce as if he'd submerged his limb in acid.

'It's bad news,' Drake growled. 'You have to see that!'

'She saved me, and gave me the power to destroy my enemies – to destroy you!'

Drake barked a laugh. 'Then how am I still standing, you bastard?'

Drake lashed at Brand with his free arm, but he couldn't muster more than a fraction of the power rushing through his crystal limb. Still, he punched Brand's ruined face and felt the man's jaw break. Brand did nothing. He twisted his head to an unnatural angle and stared at Drake, stared *through* Drake, his coal-black eyes vacant and lost.

'Can you hear her?' he said with a sigh. 'She's trapped under the Rig, Drake. You were supposed to save her, but you're flawed. We can't free her yet. She hasn't had time to grow, but that time is coming.' Brand shook his head and focused his gaze on Drake – on his arm. 'And you, my little daffodil, you don't deserve this gift!'

With a roar Brand clenched his remaining hand around Drake's crystal limb and a surge of sheer power rushed through his skeletal form. For a moment, Drake saw through his wasted skin, to the power flowing through his veins like blood. For a moment, Brand was as clear as crystal. *He's nothing but the light*, Drake thought. *That's all he is now. No blood, nothing. Just held together by the light.*

And a heartbeat later: *How the hell can I kill that?*

His resolve wavered and Brand exerted all the force at his command against Drake's arm, using the ruined forearm of his handless limb for leverage. From a great distance, Drake heard chimes, and then the shattering of glass on stone. His eyes widened and he screamed '*No!*' as a sharp spider's web of cracks splintered along his crystal arm.

Brand cried out in triumph and Drake reeled as his arm *snapped* about halfway between his elbow and shoulder. The crystal limb broke away from the rest of his body and a fountain of sparks fell like a waterfall from the jagged stump as he hit the ground. The sparks splashed against the sidewalk and ran in streams around his form.

Brand held the rest of the dull, obsidian limb above his head and laughed at the sky, as the pool of liquid light from Drake's arm ran under his feet.

Keep laughing . . . you're standing in gasoline and smoking, buddy. Drake cast a look over his shoulder.

Tristan was there, crouched behind the limousine. Irene was with him. He nodded and threw the backpack across the space between them. Drake, his limb still bleeding light, forced himself up onto his knees with his good arm and caught the pack.

He reached in and retrieved the two colourful crystals.

'Light them up!' Tristan cried. 'It'll work!'

Drake did just that.

He tossed the crystals at Brand's feet, into the pool of light, and thrust his stump of an arm in the same direction. A torrent of power struck the crystals, which were already glowing from the pool of spilt energy.

It took less than three seconds, as Brand tossed Drake's broken arm aside and reached for the prize at his feet. He was too slow.

The crystals sucked in the light and did as they had done the night they were created. A split in the air formed, directly in front of Brand, and he leapt over the crystals as the portal opened, the air falling in on itself behind him as it rent a hole between Times Square . . . and whatever world existed on the other side.

Brand took another step forward, reaching for Drake as he shuffled back on his good arm towards Irene and Tristan. His friends grasped Drake from behind and pulled him to the back of the limousine as the force of the portal opening *dragged* Brand backwards.

Brand snarled and looked over his shoulder. He fought for a step forward, crackling with energy, but the force of the portal's

254

opening was too much. He fell back, arms outstretched, with a furious cry. Silhouetted against the portal, Drake watched Brand fall with a grim satisfaction. As he had seen back in Canada, the portal opened on a world of grey skies and ash-covered ground.

The portal swallowed Marcus Brand whole.

But not before an arc of wicked light, as thick as knotted rope, burst from his remaining palm.

The wild whip of power didn't hit Drake, as he stood and gripped the trunk of the limousine. The whip didn't hit Tristan, or Irene, as they stood beside him. It shot past within spitting distance of Noemi and Takeo, on the other side of the car. The light slithered in the air, moving like a snake, and struck Lucien Whitmore, who stood before his daughter. Whitmore raised his arm, dressed in his finely tailored suit, and the light wrapped around his hand.

Let it go, Drake thought. *You idiot, let it go!*

With a grunt and a flash of white light from behind his sunglasses, Whitmore threw the whip of energy aside – and it jumped to the next nearest person.

To Amy Whitmore.

Her father realised a heartbeat later what he'd done, as the light spun around his daughter's chest and picked her up. The look of horror on his face was the first real emotion Drake had ever seen the president show.

And like a fish caught on a hook, Brand reeled in the line from whatever awful place of ash and crystal spiders the portal led to, and Amy was thrown through the air above the limousine, crying out for help.

Irene lunged for her kicking legs and missed.

Drake threw his only arm forwards, close enough to see the fear in her eyes, and his fingertips grazed the edge of her shoulder as she flew past.

Little Amy disappeared into the portal after Brand.

Lucien Whitmore screamed.

Irene threw her arms around Will and stared at the portal in the air, at the ugly world beyond. Brand stood on the other side, Amy Whitmore in his grip, and pounded against the portal as if a wall of invisible glass, or a magical shield, barred his path back to New York.

He hurled his fist into the portal, as ash swirled around him, and was knocked back.

'It's only one-way,' Tristan said, pushing his glasses up the bridge of his nose. 'He can't get back through!'

'Then neither can Amy . . .' Irene whispered.

Brand made to slam his fist into the portal again, but stopped at the last moment. He looked over his shoulder, at something out of sight, and then turned back to stare at Drake.

He held that stare for a long, awful moment.

Brand grinned and scooped Amy Whitmore up beneath his arm. She was in tears, screaming and thrashing. He disappeared out of sight on the other side of . . . wherever that was.

'Bring her back!' Whitmore roared. He grabbed Drake, tore him from Irene, and slammed him against the limousine. 'Bring her back!'

Drake's broken arm still bled crystal light, glowing drops, onto the street, but it was less now – a trickle where it had been a stream. He looked dazed, to Irene, and sick. *His poor arm.*

'It wants you, Drake,' Whitmore said. The president of the Alliance bunched Drake's collar in his fists and pushed their faces together. 'Can't you feel it? It has called you here. This was meant to happen. Step through the portal.'

'Uh, no.' Drake actually laughed. 'What? No. You do it.'

Whitmore glanced at the portal and shook his head. 'Step through, return my daughter to me, or I will kill your friends,' he said. 'Soldiers! To me! I'll start with the lovely Miss Finlay. I swear, Drake, I will splatter her brains across the sidewalk.'

He means it, Irene thought. She was no good at reading people, not like Will, but every instinct she had was telling her that Whitmore meant to shoot her – to shoot them all.

Drake lips formed a thin line. He was furious, Irene saw, more than he'd ever been. 'Well, the way I see it, Mr. President, she's been sent to a prison of your making. So who better to get her out than me, eh?' He met Irene's gaze and offered her half a smile. 'You know where I need you to be, right?'

Where you need me to . . . 'What?' She stepped forward, reached for him, but the cadre of Alliance goons that had surrounded the limousine made her pause. *Why have the spiders stopped attacking? What happened?* Half a dozen weapons followed her every move. 'Don't you dare! I don't know what –'

'You'll let them all go,' Drake said to Whitmore, and calmly pulled the president's hands from the collar of his shirt and took a step away. 'They walk now, Whitmore. All my friends. Hell, you'll give them a private jet to where they need to go.'

'You'll step through the portal?' Whitmore asked. He took a step away, too, and ran a hand back through his silver hair. 'You'll rescue my daughter?'

'You gonna come with me?' Drake asked.

Whitmore said nothing.

'Didn't think so.' Drake scoffed. 'And of course I'll go after her.'

Irene rushed to his side. 'You can't go in . . . into *that*!' She wrapped her arms around his shoulders. 'You idiot. Look at your arm, look at that place!'

The portal had shrunk a few sizes. Where it had been half a metre taller than Brand, anyone passing through now would have to mind their head. *Amy . . . I'm sorry.*

'You must go!' Whitmore insisted. 'Bring her back and destroy Marcus Brand.'

'Figured out he's not on your side any more, have you?' Irene snapped. 'Will . . . Tristan, talk to him.'

Tristan stood quietly next to Drake and paused before speaking. 'He's got that look in his eye, Irene. The one that got us off the Rig.'

Irene shivered as Drake wrapped his remaining arm around her and gave her a quick hug. He stepped away, towards the portal, and she had to force herself not to pull him back. He pointed a finger at Lucien Whitmore.

'Your word, Whitmore, for what little it's worth, that you'll let them go. On your daughter's life, that you'll honour our agreement.'

Whitmore clenched his fists hard enough to turn his knuckles white. 'You have it,' he whispered. 'Please, please just . . . go. Save her.'

'It's not even a question. I'm bringing her home,' Drake said. 'But you won't hurt or hold my friends. I'll do what you ask, but first Irene leaves with Takeo and Tristan. Noemi, I can't ask you –'

'I stay with William Drake,' she said.

'I'm not leaving you. We travel together!' Irene stamped her foot and drew a line in the air with her hand. 'Will, after everything you can't just disappear.'

He smiled at her – infuriatingly calm and missing an arm. 'Irene,' Drake said. 'I need you to follow the web. Please go with Takeo and Tristan and *follow the web*. Do you understand what I'm saying? I'll see you again soon, I promise.'

And Irene did understand. She understood all too well and knew she might never see William Drake again.

'The creature, Bluebird, promised to withdraw,' Drake told Whitmore, not telling him how he knew that or the bargain he had struck for the city. 'If I stopped Brand. This is close enough, I reckon.'

'The Alliance will protect New York – for as long as we can, to give you time to *do as you're told!*'

Drake nodded and took a deep breath; he punched Tristan lightly on the arm with a wink, and then wandered over to the portal. Silhouetted against the grey world beyond, Drake glanced back over his shoulder at Irene as Noemi joined him.

'Be good,' he said, and leant down to pick up the two glowing crystals. He gave them to Noemi, who placed them in the inner pocket of her burnt cloak. 'Tristan, remember the plan. I . . .' A marvellous grin spread across his face. 'I love you both. Cheeseburgers and milkshakes when I get back, OK?'

Drake laughed, his eyes flashed with cerulean blue light, and he walked backwards through the portal, ducking his head at the last minute. Noemi followed.

Irene moved to stand between Takeo and Tristan, wary of the Alliance guards. Drake's and Noemi's forms shimmered on the other side of the portal, and a light dusting of grey snow – *ash* – fell on their shoulders. He waved at her.

The portal zipped closed with a loud snap and Irene gasped. Will Drake was gone.

Chapter Twenty-Four

Blackberry Jam

Drake emerged from the portal into a world he'd only glimpsed in his dreams. He looked back at Times Square and saw Irene and Tristan as if through a distorted lens. They looked far away, further than they should have. He waved at them as Noemi joined him and, with a sound like paper being torn, the portal snapped closed, two halves of reality crashing back against each other to seal the hole in the air.

Drake rolled his eyes and chuckled. 'Typical. No way to go but forward. We're being herded, Noemi, I'd bet my last pot of jam on that.'

'Herded by what?'

'What, indeed . . .' He thought about the crystal creature, about Bluebird, and shook his head. 'Well, Times Square went better than expected, to be honest. Tristan, you may have gathered, was a double agent. We triple-crossed his pretend double-cross by making Whitmore think it was a single cross, so he could get his hands on those portal crystals in your pocket. We wanted to force Brand through the portal, cut him off here. Better than killing him, you know, because I'm not even sure we can.'

Noemi glared. 'You felt no need to share this plan with us, your allies?'

'Wasn't sure it would work. I didn't expect to lose my arm. And Tristan took a big risk going back to the Alliance. We had the drone stream our "falling out" back to the Alliance headquarters. Used their own surveillance against them. Whitmore had to believe it, had to let Tristan in with all his data and research he'd done on me and my abilities.'

'And I take it this excursion was not a part of your master plan.'

'Well,' Drake said and hated the way his voice wavered. 'No, this wasn't part of the plan. Neither was Whitmore offering me a job with Crystal Force, but it worked in our favour . . . sort of. Whitmore got what he wanted, in a way. Both me and Brand through the portal.'

'I do not believe he intended to lose his daughter in the bargain,' Noemi said. 'The portal crystals have gone dull, their power expended for now. We may not have a way back.'

Drake shrugged and waved at the world around them with his stump of an arm. 'We'll crash a helicopter into that bridge when we come to it. For now, take a look at where we are.'

Towering pillars of twisted crystal marred the landscape, crooked teeth in the jaw of some monstrous beast, under a bruised sky heavy with grey and red thunderstorm clouds. A foul stink of burning metal clung to the air. It hurt to breathe, stung the back of his throat. Some of the pillars, rising in

262

jagged, dusky angles, pierced the clouds and disappeared into the crimson storm.

'Well, this is messed up,' Drake said. He and Noemi stood on a plateau overlooking the warped and twisted crystal world, above a valley of stone ruins and a river of gushing black water speckled with sparks of yellow light. 'Do you see Brand or Amy?'

Noemi held her hand to her nose, her face pale from the stink on the air, and her gloved hand, hiding her crystal fingers, to the hilt of her sword. 'No, I do not. What is this place? You recognise it, don't you?'

Drake shrugged and tapped his forehead, tapped the burn tissue in the shape of a kiss. 'Seen it before, haven't I? In some spooky dreams.'

'This is no place on Earth.'

Drake had thoughts about that but kept them to himself. He had an inkling, a scary instinct, that perhaps this was some place on Earth – just not yet. He took a deep breath, regretted it as the acrid air stung his throat again, and pointed along the valley, upriver, towards a mess of tangled crystal pillars. A spire of crystal as dark as moonless midnight was buried at the heart of that mess, the sharp tip breaching through the lighter veins and crowned with ugly red cloud.

A skyscraper of pure crystal, sharp and ugly even compared to the rest of this place.

'That looks like the Evil Overlord's stronghold of doom to me,' he said. 'If I were Brand and doing the Dark Lord's bidding, that's where I'd head. He doesn't believe Bluebird wants him dead, though. Uh-oh.'

'Sweet mercy,' Noemi breathed. 'Are you not scared, William Drake?'

Drake felt the red fire burning just behind his eyes and in his chest. The anger and hate that would drive him mad, if he slipped. He wanted nothing more than to stop, to eat a dozen pizzas and sleep. 'I'm too pissed off imagining how frightened that little girl must be. So, too late to back out now, Noemi. You go where I go, remember? And I'm going thataway.' He glared into the distance. 'How far is the tower, do you think?'

'It looks like a bramble patch of crystal and rose thorns. It's hard to say, but perhaps a little under two miles.'

'Yeah, I'd say the same.'

Drake stared down at the stump of his crystal arm, still bleeding a small snowfall of white sparks. *Brand will pay for that, too.* He wasn't surprised to see fresh obsidian crystal growing from the bleeding wound. His arm was regrowing. 'You know, it's only been a few weeks for me – all this crystal nonsense – but it feels like years. When did things get so absurd?' He trailed away and sighed. 'You saw me shrug off those bullets in Times Square, right? Like they were nothing. Whatever the Crystal-X is doing to me, whatever she, Bluebird, is doing to me, I don't think it's going to let me stop. What if . . . ?'

'What if you lose your mind?'

Drake nodded. 'Yeah, it's a worry, isn't it? I mean, hell, who could stop me if I lost control? Carl Anderson brought the eastern platform of the Rig crashing down in his madness – and, knowing what I know now, he could still be alive. Alive and mad.'

'The Path of Yūgen will keep you sane,' Noemi said with conviction. 'And more than that, you are a good person.'

'I've hurt people, Noemi. People that didn't deserve hurting.'

'You also just stepped through a mysterious portal and into a dangerous world, chasing a monster that has kidnapped a scared child. You could have fought your way out of Times Square. With Brand gone, the Betrayer would have been unable to stop you. You did not give up your chance to escape because Whitmore threatened your friends, you gave it up because that little girl needs you.' Noemi cupped his cheek and met his gaze. 'And I love you for that.'

Drake found half a smile. 'I'm still worried about all this power I have. It could go so wrong.'

'Our paths have merged for a time, William.' Noemi squeezed his calloused and bloody right hand in hers. She felt warm, sure – strong. 'And I will see you to Japan before long. Once we escape this place with Whitmore's daughter.'

'Escape I can do, I think.' His arm was repairing itself, slowly but surely, the crystal curving into a new elbow. 'I'm gonna find Marcus Brand and beat him with this glowing stump until he breaks, and then I'm opening a door back to . . . to *away* from here. Then we're going for milkshakes and something greasy – pizza, perhaps.'

'Cheeseburgers, you said in Times Square. You always remain remarkably upbeat, Will.'

Drake grinned. 'I'm tired and hungry, and somewhat armless, but I've been waiting for something like this to happen my entire life, Noemi, despite the mad worry. Not going to pretend otherwise. I think every kid sitting in another boring maths or science class daydreams about saving the day. In a way, I've won the lottery.'

'Perhaps, but the cost is far greater than a daydream,' she said. 'Far greater. Shall we? There are tracks in the fall of ash, heading towards that towering crystal monstrosity. I believe, I hope, they were made by Brand.'

Drake hoped and believed, as well.

A rough path of scorched earth, strewn with nothing but flakes of ash, led down from the plateau towards the river. Noemi did not let Drake's hand fall as they set off towards the churning river of black water. After about ten slow minutes of winding through the rubble, he and Noemi found a wider path running alongside the river. Stark, dead trees, the wood long since petrified, stood every ten metres or so, amid the ruins. The water flowing to their left, speckled with yellow light, stank of decay. The path ahead looked rocky but seemed to strain towards the obsidian spire.

'It's all so grey and dead,' Noemi said. She tilted her head. 'I sense no life here.'

'You can . . . sense life?' Drake shrugged. 'Huh. Cool. Another of those talents I'm not supposed to ask about?'

'Precisely. This world is dead. In New York, for example, if I opened my senses I would be blinded by the sheer number of people and living things. Here, only ash moves. I can sense you, and the occasional flicker ahead – perhaps young Amy – but nothing else.'

Drake grunted and something not quite grey caught his eye, buried under dust and loose rock. He skirted around a broken tree and kicked at the rock, clearing the mess away to reveal something familiar – something that confirmed his worst suspicions.

'Well, bugger me.' He needed to sit down, but worried he wouldn't get back up.

'What is it?' Noemi asked.

Drake knelt down instead and pulled a faded red and blue sign, about the width of a hubcap, from under the rubble. It was ruined, scratched and dusty, and would never shine again, but the single word on a blue background, surrounded by a dull red circle, was unmistakable.

'Underground,' Noemi read the sign. 'Underground?'

Drake whistled low and shook his head. 'Yeah. These are all . . . all over London,' he said. 'They mark entrances to the Tube – to the underground subway.'

He let the sign fall from his remaining hand and gave the ruins, mostly old stone and pulverised concrete, another look. He eyed the river beyond, the curve of the land, and what might have been roads and the husks of old bridges, and a building that might have, once upon a time, been a clock tower with an impressive set of bells.

'Will?' Noemi's voice was nothing but a whisper.

'Blimey, I should have seen it sooner . . .' He chuckled, but nothing was funny. 'This was a city, Noemi. This was London.'

From the airport, Takeo drove Irene and Tristan through the city streets in a rented black sedan, and it was only then, after they were certain the Alliance could not be listening in, that they spoke freely of all that happened in New York. Irene listened, hugging her knees close in the back seat, as Tristan explained Drake's plan – a plan that had got him trapped in a strange world, with only Noemi for company.

'He told me pieces, little pieces, when we first got to the city and we were sitting on the steps of the library,' Tristan said. 'Drake knew we wouldn't be able to escape from the Alliance in New York. All the cameras, the networks, and the people looking for us. I told him what he already knew, confirmed we were already caught.' Tristan smiled softly as they headed east across the city. 'So he went into Rig-mode, as if we were trapped in a prison again. He typed out a rough plan on his phone and showed it to me. Basically, the plan was to get the other portal crystal from the Alliance and use it to get rid of Brand. With Brand gone, we had a chance. I don't know how long he planned it or whether the idea just came to him then. But it was good. Good*ish*. And, you know, after the Rig I was willing to trust him.'

'I wonder why he didn't trust me with more of this plan.'

Tristan snorted. 'He didn't trust me with all of it – just pieces. But look how far he's come since we met him on the Rig. Back then, he was going to escape without us, if he could. Now, well, think about where we're going, what he *has* trusted you with, Irene. For the half a year I've known him, there's been nothing more important than this to him. He *knows* we would have gone through the portal with him, but he *trusted* us with this. You've changed him, for the better, I think.'

The look on Tristan's face turned sad and Irene sighed. 'I care for you both,' she said. 'So much. You're the best friends I've ever had. We've all been good for each other. We're better together.' She paused. 'So he wanted Whitmore to think you'd betrayed us so you could get close to him?' Irene chuckled, but clutched her knees hard, worried about

Drake and uncertain about what came next. 'You were like a super spy. A double agent?'

'Something like that. Either way, I was pretty cool. I mean, not "slapping someone with their own severed hand cool", but still pretty cool.' Tristan pushed his glasses up the bridge of his nose. 'And I don't think it was about trust, really, why he didn't tell us more of the plan. He wasn't making it up as he went along, but he was reacting to a lot of things he couldn't control. The plan was fluid, random. He was juggling a hundred flaming knives, blindfolded. But Drake is so clever, Irene. I meant that, when we had to pretend to fall out on the balcony so the Alliance would buy it. They were watching through the drone. Sorry, by the way, about what I said.'

'You are forgiven,' she said seriously, and squeezed his hands. 'He is clever. You were right about that. Clever and so very recklessly dumb.'

'I mean, it's like he never sees a problem he can't face, a wall he can't climb. A trap he can't escape. He did the same thing he did on the Rig with Warden Storm. Instead of trying to outsmart the problem he outsmarted the man – or men, I suppose – creating the problem. Storm didn't see it coming and neither did Whitmore or Brand. They expected something smart, but got clever instead. Drake, he's . . . scary.' He paused. 'Actually, recklessly dumb fits perfectly. Heh.'

Irene hugged Michael Tristan as the car left the main road and wound down a series of alleyways. 'Call him Will, all his friends do.'

'He'll be back, you know,' Tristan said, fiddling with his phone. 'Ah, finally found the network.' He reached into the backpack at his feet and switched on the Alliance drone. 'And when he does get back, the whole world is going to know his name. Not as the terrorist, but as the boy who stood up to the Alliance and what they did on the Rig.'

'Are you sure about this?' Irene whispered. Takeo had spoken little since fleeing New York, but she knew his people in Haven had kept Yūgen a secret for centuries. What they were about to do would blow the lid right off that.

'Will wanted it, Irene,' Tristan said. 'Drag them into the light, he said. Although with a bit more cursing.' He took a deep breath and held up his phone. 'Hit *send* and all the footage the drone recorded, from the train crash to him stepping through the portal in Times Square, will be uploaded to the internet. I missed the dinosaurs at the museum, but I got him falling from the helicopter as Brand shot him. It's incredible footage, and with what happened in Times Square they won't be able to deny it. He saved the city. You want to do the honours?'

'Won't the Alliance pull it down? They own all the social media sites and stuff.'

Tristan shrugged. 'Once it's out there, it's out there forever. People will share this a thousand different ways, through the old Bluetooth networks and in the deep web. In about thirty minutes, Will Drake is going to be the top trending name in the world. The Alliance can throttle the internet, do their worst, but in the end it'll be like trying to hold water in a sieve.'

Irene considered, and then nodded. 'Whitmore will be furious.'

Tristan grinned. 'Good.'

'Just hit *send*?'

'Just hit *send*.'

Irene hesitated, thought of Will and hoped that, wherever he was, that he and Noemi, and Amy, were safe. She couldn't afford to dwell on the fact that he was lost. *I'll see him again. He'll find a way to escape.*

She pushed *send* on the phone and Tristan slipped the device back into his pocket.

'Can't wait to see the fallout,' he said, as the car pulled onto a side street full of tightly packed terraced houses. The road was narrow, bordered with cobblestoned sidewalk and green hedges.

Takeo pulled over and put the car into park. He glanced over his shoulder. 'Two doors down on the left,' he said. 'This is the place.'

'Maybe you should go first,' Tristan said. 'Explain the situation.'

Irene's heart hammered in her chest. A shiver rushed through her, but it was only nerves – good nerves, not *oh-God-this-plane-is-crashing* nerves. *What will I say? How can I explain?*

She got out of the car and pulled her jacket close around her shoulders. The skies were blue and the sun shone down on the little street, but it was a cold day. She brushed her hair back from her face, trying not to think too much about her scar. *We've all got scars, some worse than others. Noemi is right about that.* Two doors down and she walked up a small path in a little garden, no bigger than the cells back on the Rig, and stopped in front of a white door with a brass knocker in the shape of a lion's head.

271

Irene knocked three times, her heart pounding against her chest even harder, and bounced from foot to foot. She heard shuffling from inside, the click of a lock, and the door creaked upon slowly.

A frail woman, pale and sickly, stood in the doorway, leaning hunched over on a single crutch tucked under her arm. She was tiny, barely scraping past five feet, but her smile was warm and her eyes – *Will's eyes* – were brown and kind. Her angular face, sunken from years of illness, was framed by light brown hair and a thin fringe, brushing slim eyebrows.

'Hello,' she said. 'Can I help . . . ?' Her eyes widened.

Irene swallowed and looked down the street to make sure Takeo and Tristan were still there, parked in the black sedan up against the kerb. 'My name is Irene,' she said. 'Irene Finlay. Your son . . . Will. He . . . Will sent me to come and see you, Ms. Drake.'

'Lana,' Lana Drake whispered, a hand clutching her neck. Tears sprang into her eyes. 'Please call me Lana. I saw your picture on the news. They're saying such nasty things about my Will, about what he's done. I don't believe them. My Will would never, but the media people won't stop calling. I would have unplugged the phone, but Will called me a few days ago – were you with him?' She paused to take a breath, tears fighting her excitement. 'But you escaped with him? Are you in trouble?'

'I did escape with him, yes. Ms. Drake . . . Lana, there's a lot we need to talk about. But the Alliance aren't after us any more. Not at the moment, anyway. The important thing is Will wants us to go somewhere safe.' Irene was certain they were still being watched. And given the video they'd just sent out across the web, made more of an enemy of Lucien Whitmore, which was why they had to follow Takeo to Japan – to Haven. *Follow the web.*

'The Alliance came to see me, as well, gave me medicine,' Lana said. 'That stopped yesterday. I worried they had found Will. Is he OK?'

'There's a place we can take you,' Irene said and stepped forward, across her threshold, to grab Lana Drake's arm if it looked like she might fall. 'And I . . . we may be able to help you get well. Something better than the medicine from the Alliance.'

'Is Will there?' she asked, a tear clinging to her eyelash before cutting a slow track down her face.

Irene nodded. 'He's going to meet us there soon. He promised.'

'My Will never breaks his promises.'

'No, no he doesn't. Will you come with us?'

Lana considered and then nodded. She made to stand up straight without her crutch, but wobbled from the strain. Irene offered her arm. 'Can you help me pack a bag, dear, and grab a few jars of the blackberry preserves from the pantry? Has Will ever told you how much he loves blackberry jam?'

Irene laughed. 'Oh yes. He never shuts up about it.'

End of Book Two

Acknowledgements

To Pete Sturdy and Jonathon Bush, two smart guys whose feedback was not only absurdly helpful, but unnecessarily (and yet delightfully) cruel. You did good, lads.

To Tracy Erickson, who I will defeat in medieval combat on the shores of Crater Lake one day soon.

To Drusilla Connor. Thank you for reading the early drafts, Dru.

To Eugenie Furniss, my supportive and brilliant agent!

And to my amazing editor Naomi Colthurst, who not only paved over the many potholes in the road, but steered me on a better path for the story. Thank you, Naomi.

Joe Ducie

British-born Joe currently resides in Perth, Western Australia. Joe attended Edith Cowan University and graduated in 2010 with a degree in Counter Terrorism, Security and Intelligence. Joe has also studied Creative and Professional Writing at Curtin University.

When not writing stories, Joe's work over the past few years has involved border protection, liaisons between domestic and international military forces, private security consulting, living out of a suitcase, and travel to some interesting places dotted around the world. He is primarily a writer of urban fantasy and science fiction aimed at young adults and, when not talking about himself in the third person, enjoys devouring books at an absurdly disgusting rate and ambling over mountains. Preferably at the same time. *The Rig*, Will Drake's first adventure and Joe's first book, was the joint-winner of the 2013 Hot Key Books and Guardian Young Writers Prize. Follow Joe on Twitter: @joeducie

Thank you for choosing a Hot Key book.

If you want to know more about our authors
and what we publish, you can find us online.

You can start at our website

www.hotkeybooks.com

And you can also find us on:

We hope to see you soon!